Wilthaven

BPD File P1983

Wilthaven

By

Oli Jacobs

Copyright Oli Jacobs 2020

ISBN: 9798643283775

For the residents of my own Wilthaven…

Also by Oli Jacobs

Filmic Cuts 1: Sunshine & Lollipops
Filmic Cuts 2: Luchador Monkey Crisis
Filmic Cuts 3: Curse of the Ellipsis...
Filmic Cuts 4: Title Pending
Filmic Cuts 5: Suplex Sounds of the 70s
Filmic Cuts 6: The Lament of the Silver Badger
The Station 17 Chronicles
Kirk Sandblaster: Space Adventurer
Kirk Sandblaster & the Ice Pirates of Llurr
Kirk Sandblaster Plays the Game of Yloria
Kirk Sandblaster Faces TETRAGEDDON
Kirk Sandblaster vs. Montague Santiago
Kirk Sandblaster & Xlaar's World War
Kirk Sandblaster vs. Protocol 9
Bad Sandwich
The Children of Little Thwopping
Strange Days in High Wycombe
Wrapped Up In Nothing

Featured in:

Flash Fear
Subject Verb Object

(Authors note: The following were presented to me by an acquaintance who worked within the BPD, and believed my talents as a writer – they loved Bad Sandwich – would help showcase it to the world. Why they wanted to do this, I don't know. They're strange like that, hence why they're an acquaintance and not a friend. Anyway, I'm rambling. And didn't need to type that. Or this. Shit. Hope you enjoy.)

```
BPD FILE 1983: WILTHAVEN
```

*(Stencil drawing found as part of Operation Dunkelheit - **Petrovic**)*

Contents

- **Intro by Agent Alexis Petrovic**
- **BPD Director's Note**
- **1966-1978**
    - BPD Report – *Prelim Report (Fyfe/1966)*
    - Material - *Mayor's Welcome*
    - Material – *Wilthaven Meeting Minutes (11/10/1967)*
    - BPD Operation Report – **OPERATION TURISTA** (1968)
    - Hq'tar Report #1 – *Early Stage Assumptions* (Fyfe/1969)
    - Material – *Police Report: Various Viscera (18/03/1972)*
    - Material – *Police Report: Strange Noises (14/07/1973)*
    - Material – *Newspaper Article: Tyson Disappearance (21/09/1975)*
    - Material – *Police Report: Lost in the Woods (09/05/1976)*
    - Material – *Book: An Adventure into the Dark Heart of Man's Curiosity* - *The Musings of Charles Crest*
    - Material – *Police Report: Wild Avenue Incident (21/02/1977)*
    - Media Material (Radio) – *Brown's Last Recording*
    - Hq'tar Report #2 – *Takeovers (Fyfe/1978)*

- **1980-1997**
    - BPD Report – *Changeover Report (Marriot/1980)*
    - Material – *Newspaper Article: Mayor Robert Crest (02/01/1970)*
    - Material – *Book: The Children of Little Thwopping*
    - Material – Police Report: Grayson Grocery (30/02/1983)
    - Media Material (TV) – *Crop Report*
    - Hq'tar Report #3 – *Art* (Marriot/1987)
    - Material – *Lake Closed*
    - Material – *Newspaper Article: Weird Weather (09/11/1992)*
    - Hq'tar Report #4 – *Crossover Event* (Marriot/1994)
    - Material – *Tekeli-Li: Live!*
    - Hq'tar Report #5 – *Quinn Interview* (Marriot/1995)
    - Material – *Newspaper Article: Holloway House (14/09/1996)*
    - Media Material (Phone) – *Internet*
    - BPD Operation Report – **OPERATION NUKKUJA** (1997)

- **2000-PRESENT**
    - Director's Note (BPD Director Alpha)
    - Material – *Poster: Lost Dog*
    - BPD Operation Report – **OPERATION DUNKELHEIT** (2001)
    - Material – *The Wilthaven Way*
    - Material – *Newspaper Article: Mayor Massacre (03/03/1975)*
    - Material – *Safety Dance*
    - Material – *The Diary of Chester Laymon*
    - Material – *Wilthaven Church*
    - Media Material (TV) – *Collins/Nitko Interview*
    - Material – *Police Report: Holloway House Escape (14/09/1998)*
    - Material – *Police Report: Radio Break-In (23/08/2000)*
    - Media Material (Radio) – *Avatar Interview with Peter Haven*
    - Material – *Wilthaven Walks*
    - Hq'tar Report #5 – *Bar Patron Interview* (Petrovic/2009)
    - Material – *Business Proposals*
    - Material – *Etching: Crest Family Tree*
    - BPD Operation Report – **OPERATION POROPITI NGARO** (2016)
    - Hq'tar Report #6 – *Conclusion* (Petrovic/2017)

INTRODUCTION BY AGENT ALEXIS PETROVIC

Wilthaven does not exist.

You will find it on no maps, and listed in no historical documents. There are no 'official' papers on the town, no census entries, and nothing in any medium to suggest it is somewhere on this Earth.

And yet, Wilthaven *does* exist. It exists because *we* have the papers. *We* have the reports. *We* have flyers advertising local events, clippings covering news around the area, as well as various tapes, discs, and other assorted storage devices containing multimedia from Wilthaven itself. We have collected these from a variety of sources - charity shops, collectors, abandoned locations. They have been found everywhere from Western Europe, to Central Japan, all the way to being buried in the vast deserts of Africa.

So, with this in mind, we know Wilthaven exists.

Somewhere.

Here at the BPD, we are dedicated to uncovering the things that exist beyond the realm of normality. That is our fundamental goal. Wilthaven is one of those things, but exists in such scope, such variety, that to simply dilute it to one solitary report would be omitting a literal tonne of material that has been recovered over the last 50 years.

It has been passed to me to work on for the last 15, and over that time we have found plenty more material to suggest that not only does Wilthaven exist, but it exists in a world that is quite different from ours. A world that has different countries, different geometry, and a different history to the one we know. Not only that, but it also contains a great deal of what, under BPD parameters, could be construed as Black Level Paranormal circumstances and events.

Does this mean Wilthaven is dangerous? We cannot confirm that at time of writing. All we do know is what we've gathered so far. Hopefully, over the course of this thorough report, you can help ascertain some facts about Wilthaven, and maybe even help us locate it.

Wilthaven doesn't exist. And yet, it does. That is simply the first in the many paradoxes associated with it. But these paradoxes are what we thrive on here at the BPD. Therefore, while this is not a definitive report due to the many inconsistencies and logical fallacies, it is detailed to a level we believe is close to 90%.

Good luck, and remember, keep safe.

- Agent Alexis Petrovic

PLEASE NOTE

All materials herein are logged under their specific title, with the only exception coming with multimedia items and BPD reports. Items have been logged in the order they were discovered, rather than chronologically, to prevent timeline confusion.

As per BPD procedure, a 20-year limit was implemented on Agents dealing with this P-Class. The Agents responsible for P1983 - and this report - are as follows:

1960-1980:   Agent Howard Fyfe
1980-2000:   Agent Brendon Marriot
2000-Present: Agent Alexis Petrovic

I remind you to respect their notes and evidence presented herein, and to direct any questions to them.

Due to the private nature of this file, all information is presented in full with no redactions so as to not impede internal review. Any censorship that is done has been ordered by the BPD Directors for your safety.

Be safe.

- BPD Director Lambda

BPD PRELIMINARY REPORT (07/02/1966)

Gentlemen,

    This is the preliminary report for our most recent discovery, the presence of a town called Wilthaven. As per BPD procedure, this has been given designation **P1983** as deemed by the BPD Directors.

    This P-Class Dimension was uncovered due to the discovery of several historical documents found at a local car boot sale in Bursledon, Hampshire. These were brought to our attention by a civilian who reported the documents to the local library, where one of our Agents worked undercover and gained ownership of the items in question.

    These documents range in both value and scope, but all suggest a place that is outside P0 (our dimension). P1983 has geometry that while similar in some respects to P0, also varies wildly in certain areas. In addition, there are a number of people, places, and events that did not occur in our known history, but are common within P1983. Therefore, as is procedure, we are to class Wilthaven as an Orange Level Dimension due to the inherent unknown dangers within.

    At time of writing, no further evidence of P1983's existence has been located, but now it is known to the BPD a closer investigation will now take place to discover any further materials. Given the materials we currently have on file, we can confirm that this is a localised phenomenon within the United Kingdom, and potentially Western Europe. In keeping with procedure, we have notified our fellow Bureau members across the globe in order to potentially correlate any existing materials, and to raise awareness for any potential materials in existence.

    I, **Agent Horace Fyfe**, will be taking charge of this file from this point, and any further details will be documented by myself until procedure dictates that it will be assigned to another Agent. At present, I can confirm that P1983 does not seem to represent a threat to ourselves or P0, nor any other P-Class, so any risk of a crossover event should be treated as minimal for now. Naturally, should this change, we will adapt accordingly.

    Thank you for your time, and as always, be safe.

    - Agent Horace Fyfe, Bureau for Paranormal Discoveries

MAYOR'S WELCOME

Found addressed to a Mrs Violet Skinner of West Wycombe, Buckinghamshire, this document was duly returned to sender, but ended up lost in the postal network until BPD Agents working within the service discovered it and delivered it to the relevant department on November 1965. After analysis, it was determined to be part of P1983, and the Agent who failed to report this link was assigned Orange Level duty.

The item in question is a simple flyer within a sealed white envelope. Flyer is printed on basic paper, in black and white, and shows only degradation to the image, while the text has remained intact.

Text is presented below in full, with no missing sections.

- Fyfe, Bureau for Paranormal Discoveries

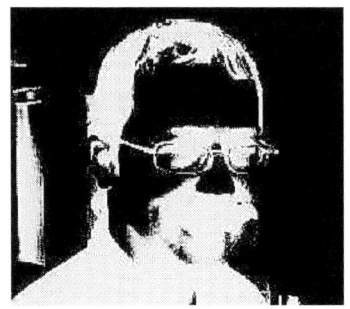

Welcome to Wilthaven!

As our latest resident, it is my utmost pleasure to welcome you to our small town. You will have already noted the many natural wonders that Wilthaven offers, from our vast parklands, to the mountain range that stretches for miles and is quite the challenge for your average hiker!

Not only that, but I am sure you have also noted the friendly and welcoming atmosphere that Wilthaven projects. We are a community town, and like our residents to feel like part of one big, happy family. My first advice to you would be to seek out the Wilthaven Way flyer, which will help you ingratiate yourself not just with the townsfolk, but with Wilthaven itself. Just make sure to stay clear of the damned avatars. Those folk are trouble with a capital T!

Do take a moment to visit the local library, and read up on the rich history of Wilthaven. Materials such as the History of Wilthaven Church, A Wilthaven Bestiary, and of course the exceptional Annotated History of Quentin Crest – and I say that not just because he is my Great-Grandfather!

I hope you have a wonderful time here in Wilthaven, not just for the short term, but also for many years to come. Wilthaven is a town with many layers, making us the most appealing of onions, you could say. Just don't peel too many of them away, or you could end up in tears!

So why not go out, make yourself at home, and discover the Wilthaven Way. Just remember to do so when the sun is in the sky!

Hail Hq'tar!

Mayor John Crest

WILTHAVEN MINUTES (11/10/1967)

The following material was found as part of a filing check at Camden Council. A clerk noticed the difference in paper colouring and font, and reported it to their superior, who is an acting conduit for the Bureau of Paranormal Discoveries.

The material is a set of transcribed Council Minutes taking place within P1983 ("Wilthaven"), featuring a number of senior figures within the P-Class itself. Key names have been added as signifiers for future reports, as well as other important aspects.

Material is presented below, transcribed in full, with no edits.

- Fyfe, Bureau for Paranormal Discoveries

Meeting Minutes for the 11th October 1967

Members Present:

        Mayor John Crest
        Chief Constable Robert Gaines
        James Lloyd (Local Businessman)
        Dr Frederick Hudson

Primary Subjects Discussed:

    Halloween Fiesta
    "Winnies"
    Easy Listening Station

Transcription:

Mayor Crest: Good evening, Gentlemen. Allow me to bring to order the Wilthaven Council Meeting for the 11th October. How are we all?

Lloyd: Apart from a bit of back pain, mustn't grumble.

Dr Hudson: I did tell you to come see me about that…

Lloyd: And I told you that I've seen your prices.

All: (Laughs)

Chief Con. Gaines: Niceties aside, what's on today's agenda?

Mayor Crest: Well if it pleases the room, I'd like to begin with the proposal for a 'Halloween Fiesta' at the local Young Residents Centre.

Dr Hudson: Didn't Summers suggest that?

Lloyd: The teacher, yes. He's always trying to drum up some sort of gathering for the children. Remember the Harvest Festival?

Dr Hudson: One of my busiest nights.

Chief Con. Gaines: I second that.

Mayor Crest: Then you probably know my verdict, but let us entertain the proposal anyway. Mr Summers wants to provide a disco, buffet, and other general party licenses…

Lloyd: Can we just all agree the man's an idiot?

Chief Con. Gaines: That's not all he is.

Lloyd: Care to elaborate?

Chief Con. Gaines: Not on ongoing cases, James, you know that.

Mayor Crest: Yes, well, personally while I am all for events that enrich the community spirit, due to the timing of this event, not to mention the fact it would fall after sundown and produce a lot of noise, I simply can't see it being feasible. Sunset is… what, at the moment?

Dr Hudson: Four Thirty.

Mayor Crest: Exactly. It is, quite simply, not only unsustainable, but ferociously dangerous.

Lloyd:	Why not just let him host it? Let him deal with the consequences by himself?
Chief Con. Gaines:	I've told you before not to bring those sort of suggestions up in Council Meetings, James.
Mayor Crest:	Gentlemen, please let's remain cordial here. Perhaps moving on to a subject of Mr Lloyd's pleasing would better suffice.
Lloyd:	I'd appreciate that, Mayor. Now, I've had a business proposal here from Winston Crane…
Chief Con. Gaines:	The ethnic fellow?
Lloyd:	If you wish to put it that way, yes. He wishes to take over the old lot over on Quinn Street that used to be Pickman's Painting Supplies.
Mayor Crest:	Quite sad what happened there. Miss Pickman was a lovely sort. What business is he proposing?
Lloyd:	Nothing fancy. A restaurant-slash-diner, the kind that were popular a while back.
Mayor Crest:	I don't see any reason why not. Has he gone through the usual procedures?

Dr Hudson:	Tests came back negative. Pupils were fine, bloods were fine. As far as I can tell, he's free of anything to be concerned about.
Chief Con. Gaines:	We had no reports of any family members going missing either, so no contamination there.
Mayor Crest:	Excellent. Well then, I approve of Mr Crane opening his eatery… what was the name?
Lloyd:	"Winnies".
Mayor Crest:	"Winnies", that was it. All members concur?
All:	Aye.
Mayor Crest:	Then it has passed. Mr Lloyd, tell Mr Crane that he can begin opening immediately.
Lloyd:	Very well.
Mayor Crest:	Going back to the subject, any positive diagnosis lately, Doctor?
Chief Con. Gaines:	Shouldn't we leave that to the end?
Mayor Crest:	You're correct. Therefore, next on the agenda… the suggestion for an Easy Listening Radio Station?

Chief Con. Gaines:	Yes. A young man by the name of Derek Brown thinks it would raise morale.
Mayor Crest:	And how does he plan to man this radio station? You know what happened last time.
Chief Con. Gaines:	Himself.
All:	(Silence)
Dr Hudson:	Himself?
Chief Con. Gaines:	So he's been telling people.
Dr Hudson:	Is he mad? Do you want me to test him?
All:	(Laughs)
Lloyd:	I suppose if it was manned it would be easier to keep safe.
Dr Hudson:	Is it necessary though?
Mayor Crest:	Anything to improve morale in Wilthaven is necessary to me. Does he plan to take over the old radio building then?
Chief Con. Gaines:	All the parts are there. We cleaned up everything since the incident last time, so all he'd need would be a good number of

	electricians and builders, and he'd be ready to go.
Mayor Crest:	In that case, I approve of Mr Brown's proposal for an Easy Listening Radio Station. All Members concur?
Chief Con. Gaines:	Aye.
Lloyd:	Aye.
Dr Hudson:	Nay. He's putting himself on a platter.
Mayor Crest:	Noted, Doctor. Well, with a majority vote of 3-1, the proposal is passed. James, are you OK to pass on the good news?
Lloyd:	Of course.
Mayor Crest:	Right then, any other important items?
Dr Hudson:	The disappearances.
Mayor Crest:	Well obviously. Very well, who have we lost this week?
Chief Con. Gaines:	Let me see… George Aaron, Rebecca Crisp, Michael Cundy, Peter Fox, Sarah Fox, Jemima Guest, Horace Knight…
Lloyd:	Not Horace?

Chief Con. Gaines:	I'm afraid so. Patricia Lennon, Dennis McDonald, Ian McDonald, Angela Owen, Benjamin Owen…
Mayor Crest:	The Owen family?
Chief Con. Gaines:	The whole family. Daughter Gemma & father Thomas as well. Happened last Wednesday.
Mayor Crest:	I told them so many times to be careful…
Dr Hudson:	Rumours were that the avatars had an interest in them.
Mayor Crest:	Well we'll get to that in a minute. Please continue, Robert.
Chief Con. Gaines:	Don't worry, not too many left. Silas Prince, Oliver Randall, Marcus Richards, Dennis Smith, Terrance Smith, Vincent Smith, Sandra Thomas, and Francis Umber.
All:	(Silence)
Mayor Crest:	Well, can't dwell on these things. They knew the risks. What about returns? Dr Hudson?
Dr Hudson:	Not too many this week. Conrad Davies, Henry King, Samantha Lewis, John Robinson, Iain Smith, and Georgina Wilkinson. All have been

	looked over for signs of the plague, and all tests came back positive. Pupils not dilating, blood levels tainted, the usual.
Mayor Crest:	Any behaviour we should be wary of?
Chief Con. Gaines:	Samantha worked… works, sorry, as a cleaner at the local stores. Christopher noted she had tampered with some of the locks in his storage rooms, and that the lights are no longer working. I sent some men to have a look over the place but, aside from some signs of avatar activity, none were present.
Mayor Crest:	Small blessings, I suppose. Anything else?
Lloyd:	Tim's dead.
Chief Con. Gaines:	I was getting to that… we think Wendall Harper, one of last week's returns, was successful in luring out Timothy Chapman. His remains were found the other day.
Mayor Crest:	I see. Dare I ask for details?
Chief Con. Gaines:	I'll have Billy send you the report.
Dr Hudson:	I'll warn you, Mayor, you won't like it. Took me a good day or two before I could eat soup again.

Mayor Crest:	I look forward to that, then… Where's Wendall now?
Chief Con. Gaines:	In custody. We're going through the standard procedures for Returners now.
Mayor Crest:	Good. Any other business?
Lloyd:	Oh, yes. Mrs Martin is having a charity bake sale on Sunday.
Mayor Crest:	Oh really! Well that is good news. She does make a fantastic lemon drizzle.
Dr Hudson:	If I could put it on prescription, I'd probably make a lot of money.
All:	(Laughs)
Lloyd:	I know that feeling. Anyway, it starts on Yahweh Crescent at one pm, so I expect to see you all there?
Chief Con. Gaines:	I'll get Marie to make a stew.
Mayor Crest:	Good thinking. In that case, shall we call this a day?
Dr Hudson:	Sounds good to me, I've work coming out of my ears.

Mayor Crest: Quite. Well then, gentlemen, hail Hq'tar.

All: Hail Hq'tar

REPORT: OPERATION TURISTA

OBJECTIVE: PERFORM SURVEILLANCE OF COUPLE REPORTED TO BE FROM P1983

BACKGROUND

The beginnings of Operation Turista came from early reports from BPD Agents based in Southampton, Hampshire, of a young couple operating around the city in a manner deemed stimulating to the interests of the Bureau. These reports began with this entry by Agent Raven, who operated in Southampton under the guise of a local police officer.

- Fyfe, Bureau for Paranormal Discoveries

RAVEN REPORT (13/09/1968)

Incident was brought to my attention when local proprietor Geoffrey Warren, of Warren's Bed & Breakfast, came in to raise concerns about new guests he had received. His main concern was the currency they used to pay for their stay, which I have photographed and included below.

(DIRECTOR'S NOTE (02/01/1995):

Due to new legal agreements between the BPD and the British Government, any replication of bank notes – no matter how anomalous – is to be removed from all reports (past, present, and future). Instead, in the interests of BPD Material Retention, the anomalous image is presented below. On the original note, this image was present instead of the one commonly associated on UK bank notes, that of Queen Elizabeth II. Other imagery that was present on the note that differed from a standard bank note have also been removed due to hazardous reasons.

- BPD Director Omega)

(DIRECTOR'S NOTE (30/07/2001):

Due to a number of complaints, I will add a further note to this report stating that, yes, while it does impede our work, we have to co-operate with Government Officials – especially of Royal Status, despite our own misgivings. Everyone remembers what happened on P8295, after all

- BPD Director Rho)

    Mr Warren also noted a number of other concerns, but outside of Bureau procedures, a formal interview could not be conducted. Instead, I took a series of notes listed below which covered Mr Warren's main points.

- Couple claimed to be from "Wilthaven", known to Bureau officials as P1983
- Couple expressed surprise at the City of Southampton, stating that they'd "never seen it on any maps before"
- Couple expressed heightened concerns about Mr Warren's curfew time of 11PM, stating that they'd "never consider being out so late". While perfectly

natural, Mr Warren noted that their demeanour shifted to a state of fear he hadn't seen since the war
- When presented with their room, couple asked why there were no shutters present
- Couple paid upfront with aforementioned anomalous banknote, with image of Queen replaced by strange figure, as well as other imagery that caused medical issues in those that studied it for too long. Warren states that he accepted the note because it was "sterling", but that the face unnerved him. When he developed symptoms associated with seeing aforementioned imagery, he placed the note in an envelope before bringing it to our attention
- Instead of thanking Mr Warren, couple said "Hail Hq'tar" as a parting comment

Due to the verbal references associated with P1983, I recommend this be sent to Agent Howard Fyfe for further investigation. Will update my reports should more information come to light.

At this point, due to the active nature of the couple – henceforth known as Subject Jack & Subject Jill – it was decided between BPD Directors and myself to launch Operation Turista. Through this Operation, we would monitor Subjects Jack & Jill, record their movements, and see if they can supply us with any further information regarding P1983. The decision was also made not to engage with Subjects, lest we disturb their pattern of behaviour in these early stages. As part of these Observation Reports, Agent Stanley Butcher was assigned to check into Warren's B&B and help perform close surveillance, while Agents Brian Patterson & Lloyd Furner will perform general surveillance.

- Fyfe, Bureau for Paranormal Discoveries

OBSERVATION REPORT #1

9:39AM — Subjects Jack & Jill leave room, enter dining room for breakfast. Mood is pleasant and friendly upon casual greeting. However, instead of the standard 'Good Morning', Subjects greet with 'Hail Hq'tar'.

10:41AM — Jack & Jill leave dining room and head back to their lodgings.

11:04AM — Jack & Jill leave Warren's B&B without addressing myself or any other folk within building. Surveillance switched to outside Agents.

11:32AM — Jack & Jill enter City Centre. Walk through Hoglands Park and settle for a period of 24 minutes on a bench

	within Palmerston Park. Subjects are noted to be looking at a map with confusion, but are otherwise in good spirits.
12:27PM	Jack & Jill, after 31 minutes of wandering around Above Bar Street & High Street, enter café on East Street. We enter and take seat within listening distance, and note that Jack & Jill talk about their surroundings. Strong note is made of how they've 'never heard' of several places and landmarks in Southampton, nor the city itself. Propose that Southampton is a 'new place recently built'. Jack jokes that 'maybe Hq'tar sent us here' and that he would 'ask Mayor Crest'.
13:09PM	Jack & Jill leave café, and spend next 162 minutes walking a circuit down High Street, toward Ocean Village, before circling back to the City Centre via Bernard Street & Queensway.
16:34PM	Whilst viewing an antique shop, Jack looks at watch and immediately becomes slightly agitated. Once Jill notices this, she too enters a state of distress, before Jack attempts to calm her down. Both subjects then make their way back to Warren's B&B at a swift pace.
17:06PM	Jack & Jill enter Warren's B&B and exchange pleasantries with Mr Warren. They leave him with a 'Hail Hq'tar', before going up to their room where they remain for the rest of the evening.

Observation Reports #2-#4 follow a similar pattern, with Jack & Jill's behaviour mirroring that of tourists with a high intrigue over their surroundings. Conversations overheard by Agents Patterson & Furner suggest nothing out of the ordinary, with the only language of interest being the phrase 'Hail Hq'tar' using as an exclamation.

The only item of interest that did arise was after Observation Report #4, when Mr Warren received a letter for posting from Jill, with additional comments praising the security of the B&B. The letter was intercepted by Agent Butcher and is transcribed below, along with the anomalous address.

- Fyfe, Bureau for Paranormal Discoveries

Henrietta West
67 Cornell Lane
Wilthaven
Cromshire
WH1 5∑µ

Dearest Henry

We are writing to you from a lovely, if incredibly badly protected, bed & breakfast in the city of Southampton. Now, before you tell me there isn't such a place, I assure you there is, and both Richard & myself were as surprised as you no doubt are. Allow me to explain…

As you know, we were planning to spend a week in South Exham, but after falling asleep on the train (Richard was supposed to keep us awake!), we awoke to find ourselves arriving in this Southampton place. Thinking there was some error on the signage, we alighted and made our way into the city, looking to find somewhere to rest our heads before sundown came.

Now, I will confess, I subscribe to your theory that the night terrors are located specifically in Wilthaven, but you know what Richard is like. Anyway, after a brief moment of panic, we found this delightful place to stay and paid for 6 nights, although the man in charge became a bit rude upon

Richard providing the fee. He kept muttering something about Milton's face being there instead of 'the Queen'. Most peculiar.

As I say, the place was very poorly secured, with no shutters adorning the windows. Unfortunately, it was too late for us to venture out, even though the owner told us he would be open until at least 11PM! Perish the thought! All that said, though, we had a wonderful nights sleep, the best in I don't know how long.

Southampton itself is very nice. Lots of strange brands and shops here, but I'm assuming they are having some sort of festival, hence the change in the city's name. Richard has calmed down a lot (that's what a good night's sleep will do to a man), and we've spent the last couple of days looking around these curious places, and taking it all in.

You simply must come yourself one day, as it is a fine break from the screams and horribleness we have to endure back home. Still, mustn't grumble, as Mayor Crest says, otherwise we will end up like that poor Cherry boy. Has he returned yet?

Send my love to Simon and the children!

Hail Hq'tar!

Wendy

Final progress was made with Observation Report #5, where Agent Butcher managed to facilitate a communication with Jack & Jill, and spent the day with them under the guise of 'showing them the sights'. While most of the report came back showing the usual mundane activities Jack & Jill had pursued days previous, Agent Butcher was able to ascertain a great deal of information over the course of his interaction with the Subjects, and provided said information in the following interview.

- Fyfe, Bureau for Paranormal Discoveries

Agent Fyfe:	First of all, Agent Butcher, may I just thank you for your efforts in this Operation.
Agent Butcher:	My pleasure, sir. As we say, all for the good of the Bureau.
AF:	And the world itself.
AB:	And the world itself.
AF:	Now, let me start by confirming what we know in the Observation Reports. Most activity by Jack & Jill…

AB:	Who we now know as Richard & Wendy.
AF:	Quite. But, for the purposes of this report, we shall stick to their subject names.
AB:	As you wish.
AF:	Their routine was fairly mundane with minor anomalous elements, would you agree?
AB:	Indeed. Both Rich… sorry, Jack & Jill behaved in a manner befitting most tourists, with only the odd moment of intriguing behaviour, especially regarding sundown.
AF:	Noted. Would you like to start with that particular subject or from the beginning?
AB:	If it pleases you, sir I'll start from the beginning.
AF:	Go on.
AB:	Well as you know, I managed to enter a rapport with Jack & Jill on Day 5. We had exchanged the usual pleasantries – complete with their curious exclamation of 'Hail Hq'tar' – and on this day we finally entered into a conversation. I used this to introduce myself as a visiting local, and gain their trust.

AF: Can you expand on the 'Hail Hq'tar' comment?

AB: Unfortunately, when confronted with this curious greeting, they merely wrote it off as a 'Wilthaven thing'.

AF: Very well. What did you learn about P1983?

AB: A moderate amount. First, it appears to have some sort of Eldritch Geometry. In the same breath, Jack & Jill would talk about its lush woodland, snowy mountains, and vast desert.

AF: All in one location?

AB: If not in close proximity to each other.

AF: Curious. Anything else?

AB: They confirmed that the status of their visit was for leisure. They had planned to go to South Exham, as noted in their letter, and seemed to believe that Southampton was indeed still the same place, just under some sort of guise.

AF: What sort of 'guise'?

AB: They posited a theory that 'Hq'tar' may be behind it, but were coy on explaining further.

AF: Anything else?

AB:	They seemed very pleased with their holiday thus far. Talked of recommending the visit to one Mayor Crest.
AF:	A familiar name. Did you find anything further on him?
AB:	A little. His family are apparently the de-facto leaders of Wilthaven. Jill mentioned that they had been in power, so to speak, for nearly 100 years.
AF:	Interesting. Did they say anything further about Mayor Crest or his history?
AB:	Just that, by all accounts, he was a nice fellow who kept Wilthaven, and I quote, 'safe'.
AF:	I see… What else?
AB:	Unfortunately this was as much as I could ascertain about these subjects, but it was their behaviour around sundown that I found most informative.
AF:	Explain.
AB:	Well, we were still in the City Centre when Jack noted the time and entered in a panic. Naturally, in my guise as a local, I attempted to

	calm him and encourage him to stay out, but he was quite insistent and became aggressive. Jill apologised for his behaviour so I acquiesced and we went back to Warren's B&B. There, over a gift of strong liquor, we sat down and had a conversation about their troubles with the night.
AF:	Alcohol, there's no better truth serum.
AB:	Very much so, and more pleasant to the taste. After a couple of glasses of wine Jack was more forthcoming about their fear of nighttime. He spoke of how, in Wilthaven, people would disappear if they stayed out after dark.
AF:	Disappear?
AB:	Yes. Jill expanded on this by telling me that Hq'tar's 'avatars' would hunt for people out at night, and take said people to Them.
AF:	Them?
AB:	Hq'tar. It seems whoever it is has no assigned gender.
AF:	Curious. Go on.
AB:	While Jack seemed to consider this threat to be nationwide, Jill was not so sure. Either way,

they both agreed that they had not heard any screaming here in Southampton and that maybe they were safer out of Wilthaven.

AF: When you say, 'screaming'?

AB: Yes. Apparently a common occurrence in P1983.

AF: Did they explain why?

AB: When asked, they simply dismissed it as 'one of those things'.

AF: Stiff upper lip culture for you there. Understandable. Anything else?

AB: I suggested if such a threat existed, why not move from P1983? However, both were reluctant to leave their friends and families. In fact, despite the reaction dusk had on them, and the talk of this Hq'tar entity, not to mention the accounts of screaming, they simply regarded it as a facet of everyday life. No different from a heavy storm.

AF: I see. Anything else?

AB: No. Conversation veered onto their departure the next day and an invite to see them in Wilthaven.

AF:	Very well. Excellent work there, Agent Butcher. I'll put in a good word for you to the Directors.
AB:	My pleasure, sir. A Bureau Agent's work is never done.
AF:	Very true. Well then, be safe.
AB:	Be safe, sir.

The next day, despite all attempts to track Jack & Jill, both Subjects checked out of Warren's B&B and made their way to Southampton Central Station. After a moment of confusion regarding their location, they were observed entering an empty carriage at 11:56AM. Agents Patterson & Furner attempted to join them on the carriage, but were prevented from doing so due to the doors remaining closed. Despite the train itself not moving for 3 minutes, all attempts to board were unsuccessful. Upon departure, both Agents noted no other passengers on board, aside from Subjects Jack & Jill, and no apparent staff on hand to confront.

It should be noted that when asked by platform staff about the departing train, no person could confirm that the train had been scheduled, nor where it was due to go. All timetables suggested that no train was due to leave at that time nor ever had been across the whole season.

The last piece of evidence available to Bureau Agents came from Warren's B&B. Agent Butcher intercepted the following written comment in the establishment's guestbook:

> Excellent conditions, despite the minimal security. Would come again when not in festival season. Hail Hq'tar!
>
> Richard & Wendy Bellinger

CONCLUSION

The Operation allowed a small insight into both the behaviours and the mentalities of Subjects originating from P1983. A tangible fear of the night, as well as the common usage of the phrase 'Hail Hq'tar', adds much more knowledge to our already limited files.

All physical evidence, including the anomalous bank note, letter, and guest book signing, have been taken for study by the Bureau Research Team. The names of Milton, Mayor Crest, and especially Hq'tar, have been upgraded as potentially important signifiers in future reports.

Agents Patterson, Furner and Butcher have been put forward for special praise given the performance of their duties, while a Bureau Investigative Team have been assigned to watch Southampton Central Station for any further sightings of the mysterious train that took both Subjects away.

Operation Turista is to be considered a 2* success, and is henceforth closed to all Bureau of Paranormal Discoveries staff outside of Director Status.

- Fyfe, Bureau for Paranormal Discoveries

ELDRITCH REPORT (HENCEFORTH KNOWN AS HQ'TAR REPORT) #1

(14/08/1969)

Gentlemen,

As I'm sure has been brought to your attention, there has been further proof - via materials we have received as part of our continued investigation into P1983 (Wilthaven) - of the presence of an Black Level Eldritch Abomination within the Dimension. While a full theological profile is on-going at this point in time, let me inform you of the basic information we have procured thus far.

Naturally, one of the first instances that aroused our suspicions of an Eldritch was the familiar greeting of "Hail Hq'tar" between denizens hailing from P1983. Much as we would greet each other with a simple "hello" or "goodbye", these subjects would use this particular phrase instead. This ranges from everything including casual encounters, multimedia sign-offs, and the endings of letters and other correspondence. In each of the materials we have acquired, this greeting is used in such common frequency that it was theorised an important significance was associated with it, for its continued usage even when in an environment where it would be alien raised suspicion.

When Operation Turista was implemented, this was when the usage of "Hail Hq'tar" was used by the subjects under surveillance with frequency and natural cadence as to cement it as something of interest to our study of P1983. Despite the confusion from those who received the greeting, the subjects who used it showed no discomfort or embarrassment throughout the surveillance. While we did not garner any further information about this "Hq'tar" from Operation Turista, the conformation of its importance was deemed satisfactory by my team.

This brings me to the final piece of the puzzle that helped us maintain that this "Hq'tar" was an important figure and, more specifically, a possible Eldritch. The Town Meeting minutes we discovered contain a number of instances when Hq'tar is mentioned in terms that fulfil the conditions of Eldritch interference within a reality setting. While Hq'tar's powers and full capabilities have not yet been ascertained, I believe that these documents help us to further our evidence that such a being exists in P1983, and may be responsible for the paranormal and unusual instances that occur there, as alluded to in various other materials.

These are early stage assumptions, gentlemen, and I appreciate that. However, I firmly believe there is more to this "Hq'tar" than we are seeing now. While it may be a long time until we can paint a full picture of this potential Eldritch, it is with great confidence that I believe we will, and therefore find a firmer conclusion to P1983.

Thank you for your time and, as always, be safe.

- Agent Howard Fyfe, Bureau of Paranormal Discoveries

POLICE REPORT – 18/03/1972

After a fallow period regarding P1983 materials, the following Police Report was found within the files of Loddon Valley Police Station on 06/11/1973. Officers there confirmed to BPD Agents that the file itself had not been present during recent checks and, under usage of serum found within P2306, this was found to be true.

Agents have been advised to keep a check on all Police Authorities nationwide in case there are any other reports that have turned up within authority archives.

As always material is produced as found and transcribed in full with no omissions.

- Fyfe, Bureau for Paranormal Discoveries

WILTHAVEN POLICE

INCIDENT REPORT #19091986

REPORT ENTERED: 18-03-1972

REPORTING OFFICER: PC WILLIAM HUGHES

APPROVING OFFICER: CHIEF CONSTABLE ROBERT GAINES

INCIDENT TYPE: FATALITY

LOCATION: EAST CARTER STREET

PERSONS INVOLVED: UNKNOWN

OFFENDERS: UNKNOWN

NARRATIVE: AT 09:38AM ON 18-03-1972, PC TIMOTHY SMITH & PC WARREN EVANS WERE CALLED TO THE LOCATION OF EAST CARTER STREET BY RESIDENT FIONA ARKHAM. MRS ARKHAM BROUGHT TO THE ATTENTION OF THE ATTENDING OFFICERS A COLLECTION OF VARIOUS VISCERA SPREAD OUT ON THE ROAD OF EAST CARTER STREET. UPON CLOSER INSPECTION, VISCERA CONSISTED OF 2 LEFT ARMS (SEPARATED AT SHOULDER), 3 RIGHT ARMS (2 SEPERATED AT SHOULDER, 1 SEPARATED AT ELBOW), 1 TORSO, 1 LEFT LEG (SEPARATED AT KNEE) & 2 RIGHT LEG (SEPARATED AT GROIN). VISCERA WAS IN A FRESH STATE AND SHOWED NO SIGN OF DECAY. MRS ARKHAM REPORTED VISCERA WAS SIGHTED AS SHE OPENED HER SHUTTERS AT 09:14AM. MRS ARKHAM REPORTED NOISES DURING THE NIGHT BUT NOTHING OUT OF THE ORDINARY

AND, DUE TO REGULARITY, IS UNSURE AS TO EXACT TIME OF NOISES. NOISES PUT DOWN TO USUAL ACTION OF "AVATARS" KNOWN TO WILTHAVEN AUTHORITIES.

DR FREDERICK HUDSON HAS CONFIRMED THAT BODY PARTS HAVE BEEN BUTCHERED BEYOND THE POINT OF RECOGNITION, AND WITHOUT ANY HEADS, ANY FURTHER IDENTIFICATION IS SEEN AS "IMPROBABLE".

FURTHER INVESTIGATION AROUND AREA OF EAST CARTER STREET FOUND BLOOD STREAKS LEADING TO NEARBY WOODLAND AREA, BEFORE VANISHING DOWN A WARREN WITH AN ENTRANCE 3FT X 4.5FT WIDE.

NO CLOTHING FOUND ON VISCERA, NOR IDENTIFYING MATERIALS. LOCALS HAVE BEEN QUESTIONED REGARDING ANY RECENT DISAPPEARENCES, BUT DUE TO EXCESSIVE NUMBERS, NO MATCHES HAVE BEEN MADE YET.

THIS REPORT TO BE PASSED ONTO MAYOR CREST FOR FURTHER ACTION.

POLICE REPORT - 14/07/1973

The following material was found as part of archives at the Northern Constabulary in the Orkney Islands, during an investigation prompted by the discovery of files In Loddon Valley Police Station.

While blending in perfectly with a number of other files, the difference in typeface and layout caught the attention of BPD Agents, and thus the file was acquired and submitted for review. Keyword analysis by the Linguistics Division confirmed link to P1983.

As always, material is produced and transcribed in full below with no omissions.

- Fyfe, Bureau of Paranormal Discoveries

WILTHAVEN POLICE

INCIDENT REPORT #12061983

REPORT ENTERED: 14/07/1973

REPORTING OFFICER: PC OWEN COURT

APPROVING OFFICER: CHIEF CONSTABLE ROBERT GAINES

INCIDENT TYPE: DISTURBANCE

LOCATION: LONGBRIDGE AVENUE

PERSONS INVOLVED: SHEILA DUNCAN, MAURICE DUNCAN

OFFENDERS: UNKNOWN

NARRATIVE: AT 21:42PM ON 13/07/1976 PC ALVIN MCELLAND WAS ALERTED TO A CONCERN AT THE PROPERTY OF MARRIED COUPLE SHEILA & MAURICE DUNCAN. DUE TO CURFEW, PC MCELLAND WAS UNABLE TO VISIT THE PROPERTY, AND THUS ADVISED OVER THE TELEPHONE. DURING THIS TIME, PC MCELLAND REPORTED TO HIS CHANGE-OVER OFFICER – PC OWEN COURT – OF WHAT OCCURRED, BEFORE PC COURT WENT TO VISIT THE DUNCANS HIMSELF.
PC MCELLAND REPORTED THAT THE DUNCANS WERE IN A STATE OF GROWING DISTRESS DUE TO A NUMBER OF UNKNOWN SOUNDS EMANATING FROM OUTSIDE THEIR FRONT WINDOW. WITH FULL KNOWLEDGE OF THE CURFEW, THEY DID NOT CONSIDER LOCAL YOUTHS A FACTOR, AND KNEW BETTER TO CONFRONT THE SOURCE OF THE NOISE ITSELF. HOWEVER, DURING THIS TIME, PC MCELLAND ADVISED PC

COURT THAT THE SOUNDS HE HAD HEARD WERE "UNNATURAL" AND "UNLIKE ANYTHING HE'D [EXPLETIVE DELETED] HEARD BEFORE".

UPON VISITING THE DUNCANS, PC COURT WAS ABLE TO GATHER A MORE PRECISE PICTURE OF WHAT OCCURRED. SHEILA DUNCAN ADVISED THAT BETWEEN THE HOURS OF 21:56 AND 22:11 SHE HEARD A NOISE DESCRIBED AS "A CROSS BETWEEN A FOX CRYING AND A BABY LAUGHING". WHEN PRESSED FURTHER, MRS DUNCAN ADVISED THE NOISE PERSISTED WITHOUT PAUSE THROUGHOUT THIS TIMEFRAME AND ONLY CEASED WHEN A NEW DISTURBANCE OCCURRED AT 22:11PM. AT THIS POINT, DUE TO THE MENTAL DISTRESS SUFFERED BY MRS DUNCAN, MAURICE DUNCAN CONTINUED WITH THE NARRATIVE. MR DUNCAN ADVISED PC COURT THAT FROM THEN, A CLEAR VOICE WAS HEARD TALKING "GIBBERISH" IN A VARIETY OF TONES AND PITCH. WHEN PRESSED FURTHER, MR DUNCAN ADVISED THE UNKNOWN PARTY WAS "SCREAMING BLUE [EXPLETIVE DELETED] MURDER". MR DUNCAN ADVISED THAT THE VOICE CARRIED ON ITS DISTURBANCE UNTIL 00:54AM, WHEN IT

SUDDENLY CEASED WITH NO FURTHER DISTURBANCES.

AN INVESTIGATION OF THE PROPERTY TURNED UP NO PHYSICAL EVIDENCE AND ANY ATTEMPT TO GAIN AN EXACT IDEA OF WHAT WAS SAID BY THE UNKNOWN PARTY/PARTIES COULD NOT BE CONFIRMED BY THE DUNCANS. FURTHER INVESTIGATION INTO WHAT PC MCELLAND HEARD CEASED WHEN THE OFFICER WAS FOUND HANGED IN HIS HOME ON EREX ROAD.

ANY FURTHER INVESTIGATION HAS BEEN PASSED TO CHIEF CONSTABLE ROBERT GAINES FOR REVIEW BY THE MAYOR.

NEWSPAPER ARTICLE - 21/09/1975

The following article was found in an edition of a local newspaper (**DIRECTOR'S NOTE: Publication name removed due to legal matters - BPD Director Beta**) *within Newton Stacey, Stockbridge on the 21st September 1975. The edition was received by local resident Martina Wolff and handed over to the staff at the newspaper before undercover BPD Agents were made aware of the anomaly.*

The editorial team have no memory of the story being submitted and admit that when the error was brought to their attention, it only appeared in that one issue. This was clarified by a full-scale recovery of all published copies of that day's edition. In addition, due to various signifiers within the article, it is believed it pre-dates previous materials found, but this cannot be confirmed at this stage.

The BPD Research Team found no other anomalous articles within the rest of the newspaper, nor any replication within other editions.

Text is transcribed in full below, as well as the original accompanying photo in its degraded form.

- Fyfe, Bureau for Paranormal Discoveries

LOCAL GIRL MISSING AFTER SCAVENGER HUNT

There was tragedy at the annual Wilthaven Scavenger Hunt today, when local girl Samantha Tyson (pictured) was discovered to be missing. Tyson, 18, was part of a team of students from Wilthaven Girls Academia, who regularly compete in the Scavenger Hunt festivities. Her disappearance was noted at the customary head-count at the Dunmore Inn, wherein local authorities were notified but unable to do anything due to the town curfew.

Tyson, described by her parents as a curious young girl, was last seen heading into the cornfields by Arc Farm, following a clue on her hunt sheet regarding an item having 'ears all around them'. However, while the rest of her team took note of the impending sundown, Tyson was said to be insistent to stay behind as she felt she was 'quite close' to discovering the item. As it turned out, the clue actually related to a barrel of slaughtered pigs ears at the local butchers.

"Sam never was the kind to give up," Betty Farrow, a friend of Tyson's said. "She was determined to beat the team from Wilthaven Secondary School after they had won last year and been quite rude about it. To be honest, the rest of us found the whole thing to be a bit boring so we didn't really think about her when she decided to keep looking. We just wanted to get indoors."

Once it was established that Tyson was missing, local Chief Constable Lachlan Perry was informed at the local Police Station. However, despite calls from Tyson's teacher – Sally Hemmings – and her parents John & Margaret, Chief Constable Perry was adamant that there was, sadly, nothing he could do. "By the time we were notified, it was already 30 minutes past sunset. The sky was darkening up nicely, and you couldn't pay me to walk out there. After all, you've heard the sounds; if she was still out there, she wouldn't be for long."

While Tyson's parents feel an effort should have been made, there has been an overall agreement that Tyson, unfortunately, failed to heed the town's curfew and, therefore, put herself at risk. Due to the common knowledge about night-time disappearances, there was little sympathy among some of the community, with Mayor Grant Crest also not offering much to Tyson's family in the way of comfort.

"We know the risks, we all know the risks," Mayor Crest told us. "Once the curfew hits, you *do not step outside*. You go indoors, lock up, and settle in for the night. My family hasn't looked after this town for several decades just so you can ignore the rules set in place.

Of course, I feel for Mr & Mrs Tyson for the loss of their daughter, but they *must* – as well as the teachers at all Wilthaven schools – reiterate the importance of why the curfew is in place."

Due to this incident, all future Scavenger Hunts have been cancelled, to be replaced by another community event.

If you have any information about Miss Tyson's current status, especially if she reappears one morning, you must im... (BPD NOTE: Article cuts off due to space restrictions)

POLICE REPORT - 09/05/1976

The following was found as part of the survey performed by BPD Agents after the discovery of previous anomalous police reports. This discovery was made by Agents working undercover within the Hampshire Constabulary, based in Basingstoke.

Elements of the files discovery are worth noting. The file was found under a section labelled MISCELLANIOUS (sic), and after questioning one of the officers at the station, it was confirmed that it had been filed by an unknown individual. Said individual had been subject to a minor investigation utilising a handkerchief that had been misplaced by them, but no further evidence of their existence was found.

As always, the report is transcribed below with no omissions. In addition, I believe some complaints have been raised concerning this aspect. I will advise all dissenting Agents to direct their concerns to the Directors if they feel P1983 isn't getting the appropriate level of clarity and inspection believed to be necessary.

- Fyfe, Bureau for Paranormal Discoveries

WILTHAVEN POLICE

INCIDENT REPORT #20061958

REPORT ENTERED: 09/05/1976

REPORTING OFFICER: PC GORDON WILLIS

APPROVING OFFICER: CHIEF CONSTABLE ROBERT GAINES

INCIDENT TYPE: DISAPPEARENCE

LOCATION: WILTHAVEN WOODS

PERSONS INVOLVED: JOHN KERR

OFFENDERS: UNKNOWN

NARRATIVE: AT 08:53AM ON DATE OF REPORT, A LESLIE KERR OF EAST ECHO STREET CAME TO THE STATION TO REPORT THE DISAPPEARANCE OF HER SON, JOHN. MS KERR ADVISED PC ERIC COLE – THE OFFICER ON DUTY AT THE TIME – THAT JOHN HAD BEEN PLAYING OUTSIDE AT SUNDOWN AND THAT WHEN IT CAME TIME FOR HER TO BRING HIM IN FOR CURFEW, HE HAD GONE MISSING. MS KERR WAS REMINDED OF THE IMPORTANCE OF CURFEW AND MADE QUITE A FUSS OVER HOW MUCH SHE UNDERSTOOD IT, ARGUING THAT SHE WAS NOT "A NEGLECTFUL MOTHER" AND

HAD SIMPLY WANTED TO ALLOW HER SON THE FREEDOM TO PLAY. WHEN QUESTIONED WHY SHE DID NOT BRING THIS TO OUR ATTENTION BEFORE, SHE CLAIMED THAT SHE BELIEVED JOHN WOULD HAVE BEEN PICKED UP BY SOMEONE DUE TO THE CURFEW APPROACHING.

AFTER A PRIMARY SEARCH OF THE AREA SURROUNDING THE KERRS ABODE, NO EVIDENCE WAS FOUND OF JOHN'S STATUS. HOWEVER, AFTER PERFORMING ROUTINE QUESTIONING OF LOCALS, A MR. IAN POTTER NOTIFIED US THAT HE HAD SEEN JOHN BEING LED AWAY BY A YOUNG WOMAN TOWARD THE DIRECTION OF WILTHAVEN WOODS. GIVEN THE NATURE OF THE WOODS, SPECIAL DISPENSATION WAS PROVIDED TO OFFICERS BY BOTH CHIEF CONSTABLE ROBERT GAINES AND MAYOR CREST IN ORDER TO PROVIDE FURTHER SEARCH. ENTERING WILTHAVEN WOODS AT 12:45PM AT THE SOUTH-EAST ENTRANCE, NO EVIDENCE WAS FOUND OF JOHN KERR, NOR OF THE MYSTERIOUS YOUNG WOMAN NOTED BY MR POTTER. HOWEVER, AFTER TREKKING DEEPER INTO THE WOODS AT A RECOMMENDED RADIUS OF 1 MILE, PC FRED MITTON

DISCOVERED A SMALL SCARF IDENTIFIED BY MS KERR AS BELONGING TO HER SON. FURTHER SEARCHES WERE POSTPONED DUE TO AN UNEXPECTED CHANGE IN VISIBILITY WITHIN THE WOODS.

(ADDENDUM)

FURTHER QUESTIONING BY MYSELF (PC GORDON WILLIS) TURNED UP SOME EVIDENCE PERTAINING TO THE YOUNG WOMAN WHO MAY HAVE TAKEN JOHN KERR. THIS IS VIA A MR. SIDNEY LAVENDER, WHO ADVISED HE WAS TAKING "NATURE PHOTOGRAPHY" (SEE REPORT #0612983 FOR MORE DETAILS) AFTER SUNDOWN AND MANAGED TO CATCH THE YOUNG WOMAN IN QUESTION.
THE IMAGE IN QUESTION IS ATTACHED BELOW AND CURRENTLY BEING USED TO GAIN SOME IDEA OF THE IDENTITY OF THE MYSTERY WOMAN. PLEASE NOTE: ANY RESEMBLANCE TO MS KERR IS PURELY COINCIDENTAL, AND MS KERR HAS NO RECORD OF HAVING AN IDENTICAL TWIN.

THE MUSINGS OF CHARLES CREST

On the 13/10/1976, BPD Agents were alerted to an extraordinary find at the local car boot sale in Bursledon, Hampshire. A citizen – self-described as "quite the bookworm" – found the following material during said boot sale and considered the find something of a rarity. After an article in local newspaper, The Daily Echo, Agents Lynch & Prebble paid a visit to said citizen and retrieved the material. Given the fact that materials had been located within the same location, it was ascertained that while it was likely this had been part of the original collection and had been missed, due to the time period between discoveries the notion was passed that the site had become a hub for P1983 ("Wilthaven") abnormalities finding their way into our Dimension. Therefore, an ongoing survey will be taking place utilising undercover BPD Agents.

The book itself is bound in a dark green material not unlike reinforced cardboard, with lettering embossed in a pale gold. The pages are yellow with age, and show evidence of a long history of disrepair. Indeed, some of the chapters herein were either destroyed beyond translation, or ripped out entirely. When under investigation, it was determined that these were done long before the material was found within P0.

Aside from this, the only curiosity of note was a light residue found in the binding of the book itself. Our Chemicals Division has performed a full analysis, but are still yet to gain a firm hold on what the residue consists of. At time of writing, they have found traces of elements resembling Boron, Carbon, Arsenic, Barium, and 3 Unknown Elements. Analysis has been ordered to continue by the Directors.

Due to the size of the material, transcription and reproduction has been performed by the BPD Linguistics Division, with any missing material noted. The material is presented in full WITHOUT footnotes, to provide Agents a full picture of the contents.

Please be aware, due to the length of the material, it may take some time to fully digest. So, if you require further materials in the file, I would recommend you do so now. Otherwise, please continue your study below.

ADDITIONAL NOTE: Some Agents have reported symptoms of biliousness, partial blinding, reality shifts, and anti-existence after reading the below. The Linguistics Division have been made aware and amendments to alleviate these symptoms are ongoing.

- Fyfe, Bureau for Paranormal Discoveries

(**DIRECTOR'S NOTE:**

Maybe that will stop Agents using this as a jolly tale to sit down and read, and instead do some damn work.

- BPD Director Sigma)

An Adventure Into The Dark Heart of Man's Curiosity
or
The Musings of Charles Crest

Chapters

1 – An Introduction
2 – A Proposal
3 – A Royal Partner
4 – An Evening of Preparation
5 – A Beginning of a Journey
6 – A Charred Circle
7 – A Figure in the Night
8 – A Confused Trail
9 – A Band of Evil
10 – A Defeat
11 – A Recovery
12 – A Discovery
13 – A Second Chance
14 – A Dangerous Climb
15 – A Damned Night
16 – A Cave
17 – A Confrontation
18 – A Revelation
19 – A Deal with the Devil
20 – A Weary Return
21 – An End

1 – An Introduction

I fear it is time for me to finally write down in words the full truth to how I became Mayor of the small town of Wilthaven, and how I have come to hold that position for so long, in spite of local grumblings.

For many years now my position here has been under question. Many feel that my appointment was done under duress and that the continuing plagues that befall this poor dwelling is somehow my doing. I can only hope that through this telling of my tale, people of this fair town and beyond will understand what it is I have sacrificed in order to be in this position and what I must continue to sacrifice in order to stay in it and – for lack of a better word – keep it safe.

A preposterous notion, I'm sure you'd agree, especially if you were a resident within Wilthaven itself. The nightly terrors that strike our town, combined with the great losses we still suffer to this day, do not give credence to the idea that we are better off. However, by knowing the alternative, one can come to realise that it is a lesser of two evils. Is it better to divert the train cart yourself so it kills a solitary man, than to leave it be and let it kill dozens? When one talks of the plague in Wilthaven, one usually means the terrors and abominations that are a constant occurrence. Only I suffer the true pain of knowledge.

These petty grievances aside, I should introduce myself to you – the reader – should you not have made my acquaintance. I am Charles Dexter Crest, the only son of Nathaniel & Marjorie Crest. I was born here in Wilthaven, in 1826 and have been a resident ever since. I studied ancient history at Wilthaven University and have had a keen thirst for delving into the world's curios ever since - from the Standing Stones of Pynia, to the Arcane Etchings found in the caves of Tavuna. The stranger the find, the more I yearn to discover more about it.

This curiosity did, in turn, lead me to partake in an interesting youth. As soon as I was free of my parents' firm hand, I took whatever travel I could across Pangaea and sought out adventure in the name of finding something unknown. I wanted the Crest name to be the one that was responsible for imparting something across our fair realm, and would not stop until I found it.

Of course, had I known all along that this discovery would be found closer to home, then perhaps I wouldn't have as many stories to tell. In truth, none of them became as interesting as the one I am about to impart to you.

It was in 1859, when I returned from a trip to Bavaria to find that my hometown had been struck by the most awful malaise. My parents informed me that a great number of fatalities had occurred over the past few months and several small children had gone missing during the nights. Of course, the town's authorities had attempted to act on these crimes, but suffered their own misfortune in doing so. One group, led by one James Witfell, was savaged so badly in the great plains that their only remains were a few shreds of clothing and a parchment that read only one word:

FIENDS

The second group, led by Chester Laymon, had more success, but only if a sole survivor is your barometer of such things. Mr Laymon himself returned from a nighttime search in the woodland, only to be struck by the most severe catatonia and covered in wounds not cut by any man or known beast.

I should note now, however, that Chester Laymon is well known in our society as a great author and chronicler of Wilthaven's more severe curiosities. To know him in this period of convalescence was, indeed, a thankful one, but I should inform those not in the know that the time before then were very dark times for the Laymon family indeed.

      Alas, to the disdain of my peers, these tales did little to dissuade me from returning to Wilthaven. Rather, they filled me with such a fevered excitement that I should look into this matter myself. If only I could go back and talk to this young man full of folly, I wonder if I could convince him otherwise. The curse that weighs upon me is large, but such a weight would be minor given the alternative.

      As I say, my true story began on that day, 30th March 1859. If you'll indulge me further, I shall tell you more about it.

2 – A Proposal

With the knowledge of the perils that had stricken Wilthaven in my absence, I appealed to my peers to feed me more so I could devise a plan of action in order to re-establish a sort of balance to the town. Unfortunately the plague that had taken so many lives thus far was being seen as a pestilence without end, and the incumbent Mayor – Quentin Brown – was less than eager to allow me to venture forth by myself.

In a meeting arranged by my father, Mayor Brown informed me in simple terms that they did not wish any further fatalities to befall Wilthaven, and that it may be best to simply leave the town to rot. Now, given my experiences thus far, to see a thriving and beautiful place such as this turned to ash made my blood run cold, and I thought of how such things can taint not just a town or its people, but the land as a whole. Therefore, with this in mind, I informed Mayor Brown that all I required was one chance at looking into what tormented Wilthaven. Should I fail, then it was my folly, not his nor anyone else's.

Of course, I was a young man with a young man's vigour and arrogance. Despite the warning that every peer gave me – from my father to Mayor Brown himself – I pursued my goal of finding out exactly what had struck Wilthaven so badly. I spent days trying to convince them that I should be allowed a path into the nearby woodlands, and was left impotent as, during the night, I listened to inhuman howls and chanting echoing through the air.

It was a stroke of damned luck that finally changed a few minds. A local councilman by the name of Roderick Wright awoke one day to find not only his daughter missing, but his wife too. Desperate for some sort of resolution to be enacted, he fought tooth and nail against Wilthaven's authorities to go out there and retrieve them. In fact, it was in the middle of a hastily called town meeting to further the idea of leaving Wilthaven behind, that I once again made my plans public, and found the backing of Mr Wright.

From there, the pieces fell quite quickly. Mayor Brown found himself assaulted with a deluge of discord from Wilthaven residents, especially when I outlined my plot further. I would walk into the woodland area nearby, where a great many of the disappearances had taken place, and see if I could find that that had not only taken Mr Wright's family and the lives of so many, but also bring back some evidence that it was not as fearsome as some would claim. My experience hunting in the Gaelic Kongo gave me the experienced strength that would suggest I was more than capable of handling a tough foe, and eventually I found myself in a meeting with the Mayor, where the final plans for my adventure would begin.

I informed Mayor Brown that I would leave within the week, armed with a small cache of firearms and hunting equipment, and enough supplies to last me a full week after that. During this time, I would navigate the woodlands, crafting a rough map of the area and setting up a camp, ready to strike at any foes that dared attack me. While this may have seemed like young gumption to the Mayor, I again recalled my stories of hunting the White Cougar in the Appalachian Plains, and how I came face-to-face one night with the beast, armed only with a Bowie Knife.

Suffice to say, such feats raised the brow of the man stood before me.

No matter how detailed my plan was, and no matter how determined I presented myself, I asserted one caveat - I would not venture out alone. Fully expecting to be assigned a posse of the townsfolk – including Mr Wright – I was instead told no man from Wilthaven would walk with me. Joking that I would be taking the female residents instead, my attempt at humour was shot down as I was told that another interested party had been signalling their intention to unravel the Wilthaven mystery.

And the name, to my surprise, was one I was incredibly familiar with - Lord Milton Gough.

The son of our King, Peter IV.

Once again I look at such decisions and feel a weight hang heavy in my heart.

3 – A Royal Partner

The Gough family had ruled England for the past 110 years, beginning with the coronation of King Francis II in 1742. Their reign began as a result of the contemptuous Four Fields War, in which the incumbent House of Wessex, led by King Henry IX, fell to the Gough's superior forces. It was not the proudest day in our fair land's history and one that many historians look back on with disdain, but blood often stains every country's past, I suppose.

Our current reigning monarch was King Peter IV, who took over from his father, Peter III, in 1822. His son, Lord Milton Gough, was born during the same period as myself – 1827 – and was the youngest of 3 children, including brother Thomas and sister Minnie. While the family maintained a certain regal air - their position of power made evident to all in England - Milton Gough lived up to his rebellious youthful status. From the age of 17, he found himself in a number of scenarios that most would deem 'unseemly', and the papers of the time considered him to be the 'Black Sheep' of the Gough heritage.

In truth, he was merely continuing a trend for those at the lower end of the Gough succession to the throne. His uncle, the infamous Lord Samuel Gough, was known for his love of extravagant parties and lack of concern for matters of the land. Often, he used his regal standing to bypass certain legal charges.

Thankfully, for all concerned with the Royal Family, Milton was drawn away from such nefarious activity in his early 20s, when he developed – like myself – a thirst for adventure. Why, I recall in the early days of my adventures, hearing about him sailing down the Marañón River, and of his escapades in the frightfully dangerous glaciers of the Southern Poles.

In fact, one could say I was rather jealous of Lord Milton Gough; seeing his boundless zest for discovery – one that almost eclipsed my own – and seeing the funds he had to fulfil this eagerness, made me wish heartily that I too could be blessed with the luck and finances of a Royal. Instead, I could only follow in his footsteps and read of his adventures like a small boy.

So you can imagine that to meet the man himself was indeed a nervous joy. After being informed by Mayor Brown of Lord Gough's intentions, it was swiftly arranged for us both to meet and move forward with our own mutual plans to investigate the horror that was terrorising Wilthaven.

I will never forget my trip to the summer home of the Gough family - a dwelling in the lush countryside of Chesston. As soon as the Mayor & I had spoke, a car arrived to transport me to the aforementioned place. Just passing the oaks that flanked the vast grounds, covered in acres of rich green fields, was enough to make me feel even more out of place, but the greeting I received when I arrived at the Royal Stately Home was as welcoming as if meeting old friends.

At first, I conferred with a delegate of the Gough's – Algernon Sterling – who led me around the grounds on a tour of sorts. It was here that I was told of how Lord Gough had heard about the troubles in Wilthaven and had equated it to similar experiences he had encountered in places such as Kush and Eastern Bengal. Sterling informed me that Lord Gough believed that Wilthaven was 'afflicted with spirits etched in ancient folklore', and that by venturing forth into the nearby woodland he would be able to either debunk these ideas or find something that would be most fulfilling to an adventurer's spirit.

I could not disagree, and the more I listened about Lord Gough's theories via Sterling, the more I could not wait to meet the man. As it was, a mere few hours later, over a light dinner that was vastly superior to anything I had ever eaten before, Lord Gough arrived and showcased every aspect of his personality that I had expected. The young man was brash, bold, and loud of voice, and shook my hand with an intensity only a bear could replicate.

I was invited for evening drinks, including a bed for the night, and no sooner was a glass of scotch in my hand than the subject of Wilthaven came up. Again, Lord Gough told me tales of paranormal beliefs from countless villages, and of the violent incidents that took place there. He proffered that it was the 'savagery' of these lands that bred such hostilities; so to hear of similar incidents occurring in the comparative civility of England piqued his interest quite highly.

He asked me of my desire to investigate, and I informed him of my familial connection to the town. This seemed to please him further, making him almost giddy at having a 'local guide' to assist him with his adventure. Of course, I was no mere guide, but one does not speak down to a Royal.

It was decided that we should leave promptly for Wilthaven the next morn, and prepare ourselves for the journey ahead. Lord Gough told me that even though this journey would be a local one, we should not underestimate the elements. Even though I was plied with many a spirit, I shall never forget his words before we settled for bed.

"The world is a treacherous one. A man who walks into the unknown without considering all aspects is a man set on preparing his own funeral."

4 – An Evening of Preparation

So it came to pass that Lord Milton Gough & I travelled back to Wilthaven together, ready to embark on an adventure that would test our very resolve. Lord Gough was excited about the whole thing and had brought along a vast array of equipment and utilities for our travels. Again, while I considered myself a dab hand at the skill of adventure, seeing the sheer volume of materials the Lord had at his disposal conjured up many envious feelings within me. Still, I was pleased that despite his obvious superior benefits, he had chosen to accompany me rather than leave me behind to consider what could have been.

Our journey back to Wilthaven passed without incident and the town itself fell into quite the fever upon our arrival. It seemed that, in spite of all the terrors that had been occurring, the visit of a member of the Royal Family was enough to get the bunting out and have a celebration. While the faces that greeted us were tired and worn to the core of their souls, they still smiled behind wane eyes and eagerly greeted Lord Gough with hearty handshakes and open admiration.

This was all well and good, but we had not arrived to be lauded as saviours, no matter how much the people of Wilthaven wanted to bestow that title upon us. We made our way to speak to Mayor Brown, who informed us that during the previous night a number of young folk had gone missing. Apparently, they had been having a small gathering near the mountain ranges in the East and had still not returned.

At this stage I should note a certain curiosity that began during that moment. I had fond memories of Wilthaven and, despite not staying since my travelling days – instead preferring to rest in the nearby North Kilton – each time I entered the town I realised another strange addition to its landscape. While the forestry was nothing new, there were the aforementioned mountains, topped with snow, guarding over the East. If one ventured North a little, they would come to a vast desert that seemed to stretch for miles without end. But the areas that troubled me most were the ones that appeared when I removed my gaze for a moment; whole streets would suddenly plant themselves behind me, lined with factories and strange flora that I'd never seen before. It seemed to me that Wilthaven had become a patchwork land, made up of several geological oxymorons that sprung out of nowhere.

The worst thing about this, however, was that the people of Wilthaven claimed it had always been that way. The skating of the ice lake was an annual summer – yes, *summer* – event. The palms that burst from the concrete of the industrial region were native. Even now, during my time as Mayor, there are still those who swear blind that they were born under the watchful eye of a cliff-face that didn't exist until after they were brought into this world.

Apologies, but such things do lead to digression. Lord Gough & I discussed our business with Mayor Brown and informed him that we would be setting off the next morn. We were armed – as such a term seemed apt – with full camping equipment, several knives for hunting & our own protection, navigational technology which even I had not seen before - but that came with the benefit of being a Royal - and enough supplies to keep us strong and healthy until the next month.

Of course, Mayor Brown still seemed reluctant for such a venture to go ahead, but thankfully the strong words of Lord Gough put him back in his place, and made sure that our journey would continue without any person in the town impeding us. Even my parents were supportive, especially under the charming spell of Lord Gough. To see their son go from youthful wanderer to an adventuring companion of a Royal filled them with a certain amount of pride, no matter the circumstance.

We both agreed to spend the night in the Beaufort Hotel, and spent the rest of our day checking our equipment for faults and enjoying the hospitality of the Hotel's owner, Jean Beaufort.

It wasn't until the sun set and we were sat in the Hotel's lounge, sipping at the expensive scotch Lord Gough had provided, that we had our first experience with the horrors that had struck Wilthaven. While the lights in the lounge were dim, with only a small number of candles illuminating our chatter, we soon felt a presence close by. Our seats were close to one of the windows, and so it was that our attention was drawn to it after a prolonged whine rang out.

Looking out, we were moved back in fright to see a large, thin being stride before us, crying out into the night. Alongside this abomination walked a half-dozen human-shaped beings draped in cloaks that shielded them within the shadow of the night's fog; if it weren't for our keen eyes, we would have scarcely seen them at all, but their motion was enough to betray their presence.

The whines continued for at least an hour, before strong cries rang out and screams echoed past the stars. Lord Gough was fuelled by an eagerness to help, but was prevented so by Beaufort himself, who had locked the doors and began the operation of placing wooden slats against the windows. It wasn't easy to dissuade the Royal from providing assistance, even as the screams continued to call out, but after being informed that it would not only be his safety at risk, he yielded.

After at least 2 more hours of cacophonous wailing and inhuman shrieks, the air lay still again and our trembling hands imbibed more alcohol. Beaufort joined us at this time, informed us that this was a nightly occurrence and that he believed the cries were either one of two things. Lord Gough rightfully concluded that one was from victims being torn from their homes, to be taken to places unknown, but Beaufort was quick to inform him that these were just the later sounds.

The early cries, he informed us, were not victims at all, but the call of the things we had seen awkwardly walk past us, luring people from their homes.

If it hadn't been for Jean Beaufort, our adventure may never have begun, and my story may never have been told.

5 – A Beginning of a Journey

After our restless night, Lord Milton Gough and myself awoke early on the morning of the 14th June, a day that will live in infamy for me personally. Many townsfolk were in Wilthaven's centre, either to wish us well on our journey, or to simply see us before we were lost forever to the oppressive woodlands we would soon be entering. Lord Gough tried bringing some levity to proceedings, postulating that they were simply all there because of a lack of sleep brought about by the cacophonous din of the previous night. In truth, such humour was needed to ease tensions I had in myself.

While I was never truly afraid of such ventures, the events of the previous night had set trepidation in me that was as fresh as it was unsettling. The woodlands before us took on a new hue, one that had washed out the lush greens of the shrubs, and replaced it with gnarled blacks that squeezed out any light from the sky above. It was less a cluster of forestry that welcomed us, more a tunnel lacking an end.

In spite of my pause before entering, it was the hopeful encouragement of my parents that filled my spirits back to a positive level. They spoke to me of their pride at my life so far, and their hopes that they would see me again, whether it would be days, weeks, or even months.

The mere thought of being trapped for months sent a cold shiver through my heart.

In the end, it was the confidence of Lord Gough that set us off. No matter how many distractions, or how many excuses were conjured, our journey had to begin, and it would not with me standing there, watching the trees twist in a mocking dance. With one slow step, our journey began.

I remember it being curious how swiftly the sound of Wilthaven and its people faded as we hiked through the trees. One moment we were listening to the distinct chatter of doom-laden gossip, the next it shifted into silence, to be replaced by the distant call of birds I could not identify. In truth, I was expecting to listen to an absence of sound, given all the rumour that had filled my ears. So to hear birdsong of any sort was a welcome blessing.

The only other sounds to accompany the beginning of our venture were the chatter of Lord Gough, who spoke of his own exploits and how they compared to our current jaunt, and a low breeze that at the time perplexed me, although I could not fathom why. Looking back I realise that before we entered the forest the weather had been quite still and clement, with the mildest hint of sun echoing above the horizon. Now we were settling into our stride, the woods changed the brightness of the day into a dim gloom, and supplied a wheezing drone of air to play alongside it.

As I say, none of this shook Lord Gough. Surely, he was made of sterner stuff than I, taking in the bitter barks of the trees around us and equating the slow rot of the nature around us to escapades he endured in the Olmeca. He did not see how the terrible plague was affecting the world around us, just that it was something new for him to take in and remember for future tomes.

As much as his words tried to sooth me, I couldn't shake the feeling that something here was wrong; the grass below our feet had turned to a crisp black char that was a parody of a path, and the aforementioned trees were equally thick & containing, and thin & sharp. Quite often I walked with renewed confidence, only to find at the last moment a jagged twig aimed at my eyes. I hadn't seen such aggressive growth since the Amazon, but the nature here didn't just seem corrupted, it seemed alive.

Nevertheless, we continued to walk in a Northeast direction. Why we chose this path I do not recall, but it seemed as natural as one would feel walking down a common path. Whether the woods around us were guiding us toward an unknown fate, I did not consider at the time, although the past has a way of telling us stories that we do not recall in fact. All I know is that Lord Gough was taking the lead, and his own brand of curiosity dragged us deeper and deeper into the wood.

To call it a wood would have been precious. The broken nature of the trees suggested nothing like I'd ever seen before. In fact, the distance we covered surely would have taken us far away from Wilthaven and into the next county. As we sat in a rare clearing, imbibing some of the water we had in our supplies, both Lord Gough & I looked skyward to ascertain some sort of direction, but were denied by a combination of crossed wood and misty cloud. The gloom was not of a nightly nature yet, and would not have been considering the time we had taken thus far, but it was difficult to tell exactly what time it was. In fact, in a showing that his resolve was not as strong as I suspected, Lord Gough noted to me that here in the forest, time itself seemed to be as broken as the environment. There was no night or day, just a constant haze.

I wonder now whether this was by design, or whether it was just our minds playing tricks on us. In fact, the time we sat there, taking in our surroundings, seemed to last between a few minutes and many hours. What used to be Wilthaven Woods was now a strange anomaly, perverted beyond normality and turned into the makings of someone – or something's – design.

When we finally rose to continue I remember looking around and feeling that the trees around us were no longer the ones I saw when we rested. In the time we had remained stationary in our journey, everything around us had moved instead, exacerbating the feeling that we were not alone in our voyage.

6 – A Charred Circle

As we travelled deeper into Wilthaven Woods – or at least what we assumed to be Wilthaven Woods – it soon became apparent that our usual techniques when traversing such terrain were to soon be redundant. While Lord Gough & I believed we were continuing on a Northeasterly trail, when consulting our compasses they gave wildly differing views. For what I believed to be a journey Northeast, Lord Gough assured me was actually the opposite - Southwest.

As I alluded to earlier, any hopes of using the sun's trajectory as a alternative for our direction was distorted by the peculiar environment around us, and the thick foliage that lingered above our heads. Instead, Lord Gough suggested we 'trust our instincts'. For him, this was still a thrill that was sating his hunger for hazardous escapades, a way to shake the cobwebs spun by a bored life of regality; I must confess my own resolve was crumbling the longer we trekked from home.

I struggle to recall how long it was until our first curious encounter, as time was now only a construct we recalled with great hope. Instead, I knew that all around me I could only see trees and no suggestion of civilisation, and even the sounds of strange birdsong had given way to the steady, isolating moan of wind. If it weren't for the presence of Lord Gough alongside me, I would have surely gone mad.

As it was, I found myself equally as excited when he called out to me. In his fever he had taken the lead on our expedition and spun his focus this way and that in the hopes of discovering some sort of peculiarity. In this instance, he had been rewarded, and directed me off the vague path we had been following and through some thick undergrowth that only showed me a cross-stitch of unnatural vines.

Once I cut my way through, I saw the scene that had hooked his attention. There was a clearing before us, which had become rare since our last rest. But instead of some fallen logs to rest our legs, we instead found a large charcoal burn in the ground, most likely several feet in diameter. As Lord Gough studied the ash, I walked around it, amazed with the size and scope of the burnt ground. One would assume that to find a scorched earth of this size would suggest a fire of great proportions, yet the trees surrounding the area were untouched, and as lush as the ones that greeted Lord Gough & I as we first entered Wilthaven Woods.

To take it all in was far too much for my eyes, but Lord Gough was of a more astute vision. He noted to me that while on first glance the grass seemed to be burnt into a perfect circle, there were in fact several areas that we fresher than others. This concerned me; as if it had been freshly torched, it gave further credence to the idea that we were not alone.

Lord Gough assured me, however, that such concerns were foolish. The levels of ash upon the ground looked to be deliberately arranged in some pattern and, in his wild curiosity, he threw his camping equipment to the ground, searched the trees around him, and scaled the first one he deemed easiest to ascend.

I would have tried to convince him otherwise, but his thirst for discovery was unquenchable. The speed in which he climbed the tree was stunning, watching his hand clasp at every available branch, and feeling my heart shiver when his foot would slip from a moss-laden trunk. As much as I beckoned him to give up this folly, he persevered until he was at least 20 feet in the air, and looking down at me with a jaunty smile and vigorous wave of the hand.

Left alone in the clearing, I felt a growing sense of unease. Suddenly, the wind-tainted silence I had come to accept in our journey shifted into something more sinister. Instead of the simple whistle of air floating shrill through the forestry, there was a hint of something more behind it. Occasionally, I thought I could hear a word whispered, ancient syllables spat out of tight lips, pursed together in fury at our invasion of their land. I confess I lost control of my serenity and found myself scouring the oaks flanking us for some sign of a vagrant watching on. Some moments, I felt the hint of something move, sometimes rather unnaturally, but each time my brain would tell me that it was merely a trick of the light.

And then, it hit me. All of a sudden, and without warning, the sound of the wind erupted into whispers that spun dark words into my ear, and prodded at me with proclamations that polluted my soul. I felt myself grow weak as the whispers formed sadistic sentences formed of aspects from my own life. My parents' name was sullied, lost loves were mocked and violently assaulted, and my own wellbeing was torn apart in such linguistic detail, it felt like it was happening physically as well as mentally.

Just as it all became too much, a solitary voice called through. Lord Gough had come down from his mighty perch and arrived to find me collapsed to the floor, soaked in sweat. He helped me up, and as I came to my senses, I saw that his usual bonhomie was lacking somewhat. When I asked if he was well himself, he produced a piece of paper.

Whilst I was hallucinating dark thoughts, Lord Gough had etched together what he could see from above. For what I merely knew as a large circle burnt into the ground, he saw as a much bigger picture. It was the centre of a mysterious symbol, arching off in various directions in wild, black lines. Concentric circles surrounded it, and Lord Gough theorised that they stretched on for miles.

Of course, my Royal colleague immediately answered my next question, as he informed me that he recalled no other burnt lines in our journey, lest we had been walking in circles. Either these markings in the ground had been produced recently, as I feared before, or something far stranger was occurring.

  I know not of how long we stood there in the charred clearing, but it was too long for me. Whilst I heard no more sinful whispers, the feeling of unease remained, and shadows still seemed to move outside my line of sight.

  We moved on, and vowed to keep a closer eye on the path we would take.

7 – A Figure in the Night

Our experiences with the ash circle had left both Lord Gough & I in a state of unease that was hard to shake. I dared not tell him of the strange voices I heard while he looked down from the treetops, but I could tell by his change in nature that our surroundings were beginning to affect him in a way that was clouding his previous optimism.

With that, we continued our journey through Wilthaven Woods in a subdued manner, being careful with our pace and direction for fear we were being led by forces outside of our control. Upon seeing the symbol burnt into the woodland, Lord Gough had been musing on it over and over, to the point of obsession, and even I wondered internally as to how such a thing could have appeared without our knowledge.

Such thoughts were to be put aside, however, as the dim gloom that we trekked under soon began to grow more severe. We had been walking for what seemed like hours in a state of perpetual dusk, but now the light beyond the thick foliage began to wash away in one swift motion. No sooner than we were lit by the vague hints of day, than the sky above turned black. I looked up to try and see if any stars shone out to help aid us in our direction, and must confess that I was unsurprised by the complete lack of anything coming from the night. No stars shone, and no moon hovered above our heads; it was as if a complete abyss had been thrown over us, giving us only a deep void in which to look up to.

However, the other curiosity this brought us was that there was some light emanating from somewhere. For to have a complete shroud of darkness engulf us, would mean our journey through the woods would have been directed through blindness. Yet, we still managed to pass through thick wooden trunks and tangled vines with ease, eventually making our way onto some ground that could provide a meagre level of comfort for the night. I wanted to raise the issue with Lord Gough but again, I felt my tongue fastened down and unwilling to share my concerns.

Instead, I remained silent as my travelling companion set about removing his equipment and setting up for the night. The area we chose to make base wasn't as wide nor inviting as the clearing where the burnt symbol was, yet gave enough space for us to rest. Whether that rest would come, of course, was unknown, but Lord Gough had found the chipper spirits he had temporarily lost before, and began to regale me with stories of his previous adventures while we fastened our tents to the ground.

Still, the unknown light made me quite uncomfortable, and I noted as I slowly prepared my bedding for the night that Lord Gough wasn't as at ease as he made out. His eyes flicked out to the woods around us, and occasionally I would see him look up to the sky, searching for something that wasn't there.

At that moment, I did wonder how truly lost we were.

A fire was soon lit up using a small bundle of sticks and kindling, and we ate the tiny rations we had brought with us. Small chunks of pork mixed with charcoaled potatoes, which while not the feast I imagine a man like Lord Gough was used to, was one that helped ease the rumble that emanated from our stomachs. After eating, the Lord produced a small flask he had hidden about his person, and offered me a nip of some whisky he had acquired while meeting with Lairds up in the Highlands. The spirit was a potent brew, and my head began to spin almost immediately. Once again, I looked to the sky and swore that the thick black would shift before me, betraying shapes where there once was none.

I retired to bed and wished Lord Gough a good night's rest, noting that one was needed if we were to continue on this journey. We gave our respective blessings and, once inside my canvas, I suddenly felt more safe than I had been throughout our trek. I feared that sleep would not come as easily as it normally would, so was pleasantly surprised that upon laying on the woodland's firm ground, I drifted off with ease.

Of course, such fortune was not to last, and it was upon 3 in the morning that I was awoken by a noise. Barely moving from under my blanket, my weary eyes opened and noted a shadow pass the flickering embers of our fire. As my mind was thick with sleep, I put it down to my companion merely getting up to relieve himself, but the whispers that teased toward my ear were not spoken in the tone of the Lord himself.

No, these words were as cursed as the ones I had heard before, and they were not alone. My eyes focussed more sharply, and the figure outside was joined by another, and another. Their forms were human in shape, but seemingly covered in long cloaks that gave them an almost floating appearance. Without intention, I held my breath as quietly as I could, watching as they circled around our fire. They seemed to watch both Lord Gough & I as we lay inside our tents.

At no point did the figures try and enter. I could not tell you how long I watched them hover outside. All I can recall is that as soon as they were there, they were gone again, and I was instead greeted by the sight of Lord Gough standing outside what remained of my tent.

It seemed whoever had paid us a visit, did not want us to have any form of sanctuary, as the canvas that made up our homes for the night had been slashed in places, allowing all manner of foliage and smoke to creep in. Looking upon the destruction our little camp had suffered – the fire being spread with ashes dragged around, and various implements we had secured outside now scattered – we both agreed that another night in Wllthaven Woods would not be advisable at this stage.

We were to return home, if possible, forthwith. Of course, little did we know that such a task was not to be made easily. These strangers knew we were here, and were now making themselves known to us.

8 – A Confused Trail

Following the events of the previous night, the expedition undertaken by Lord Gough & myself was deemed to have reached its natural end. We had seen some quite extraordinary sights in the brief time we had been within the woods, and by suffering the attack of mysterious cloaked figures, it was evident that our presence was not appreciated.

Certainly, Lord Gough was frustrated at having to retreat, having always taken on the terrors of the world head on. He was a proud man, and so to have to return to Wilthaven without a proper resolution to his mission was enough to sting his pride.

No words were exchanged between us, instead our hike home was conducted in slumped silence. The air was tinged with disappointment but we could not risk unsettling something we could not overcome. They say pride comes before a fall, and we were loath to become another victim to whatever poxed Wilthaven.

Our navigation equipment had suddenly become a bane in of itself, as compasses spun in impotent circles and any attempt to guide ourselves using the nature around us was equally as infuriating. A renowned navigator such as Lord Gough could lead himself out of a sack of ink in a tarpit, but right now I watched as he looked up to the skies, then to his equipment, and shook his head.

In this instance, memory would be the best guide toward our destination, but each tree we passed, and each clearing we encountered, was as alien to us as anything else we had seen before. Each step we took seemed to draw us further into an area we had not seen before, despite our belief that we were walking in a straight line opposite to which we had came.

After an hour of fruitless wander, Lord Gough stated that we were well and truly lost.

The Wilthaven Woods are not a labyrinth, this is known by all that live close by, and yet right now we were our very own Theseus, walking a treacherous path to an encounter with a beast waiting patiently for us. We both felt it in our spirits; somewhere between the vast oaks and bushes that thatched natural walls around us, something lurked. Such paranoia was silly without firm proof, of course, but at the time I cannot properly explain to you the fear I felt as I walked onward, even under the cover of a bright, yet gloomy day.

We were two men driven by a need to return to a place of comfort, and yet Wilthaven Woods were not willing to release us any time soon. Whether the mysterious figures during the night had done something to vex our journey, or whether we had befallen some shared folie a deux, I could not tell. Instead, I lumbered forward, void of the knowledge that could take us to safety.

Eventually we could do nothing but give up our efforts and take stock.

Lord Gough admitted immediately that he felt something was amiss. The paths we walked had become more rustic, and the foliage around us was not as lush as it once was. Instead, we seemed to be descending into some sort of decay, a land cursed by some unknown evil.

One we would soon become all too familiar with.

In that moment, all we felt we could do was wait. Like all good explorers, when your path becomes unclear and perplexing, you must see what occurs and formulate a new plan of action. Consideration was given to climbing another tree and seeing what was around us, but the branches no longer looked safe, and the addition of a terrible injury upon either of our persons would not do at all.

Lord Gough tried to lighten the mood by regaling me with some of his stories, specifically when he tracked solo across the similar rural wastelands of Sibir. He informed me that, despite the threat of ravenous wolves and predatory natives, he had found welcoming civilisation after a prolonged jaunt of several weeks.

This, with supplies only deemed to last him a week.

While absolutely terrifying me with the thought of being trapped in these woods for weeks, the fact that Lord Gough was already planning an extended trip did assure me. If anyone was able to help us both survive this environment, it would be a man of his calibre, and I felt sure that soon enough, we would be home to enjoy a roaring fire, and a good cup of tea.

I watched as he went about rationing our supplies and was transfixed by the detailed fingerwork he indulged in. It was like watching a surgeon at work, and impressed me more than any other man had before. However, before I could become too captivated, I felt that creeping horror crawl across my skin. I didn't wish to assume we were being watched, but a man knows when eyes are directed toward him.

Casually, without wanting to distract Lord Gough, I took heed of our surroundings, and did my best to ascertain some presence. I was left looking at empty lands, but the way the mist began to gather told me that some form of darkness was close. The light of the day was not the comfort it once was, and the more I looked, the more I saw fog thicken around our position.

When Lord Gough noticed this, his response was instant. We should move, and with haste.

And so, we picked up our packs and threw ourselves forward in an effort to escape. Using that word may seem extreme, but there was something in our souls that told us that if we didn't act fast, we would no longer have the chance to. The day continued to perish before our very eyes, and as a starless sky appeared above us once more, we knew our lives were in danger.

Our pace fast, and our eyes straining through the lighter parts of the fog, we attempted to get to somewhere that would offer some form of relief.

Instead, we found something we had been looking for, but wished we would never find.

9 – A Band of Evil

(*BPD NOTE: CHAPTER MISSING*)

10 – A Defeat

How we escaped, I shall never know. But we did, albeit without the wounds one would gain from such an encounter, both physical and psychological.

I was lucky. The only mark I had on me was a light gash across my cheek, which while quite bloody, was merely superficial. The mental scars were much deeper, and I confess that even now a lot of what we encountered is lost to my protective mind.

Lord Milton Gough was far worse off. In our retreat, I had to dispose of much of our equipment in order to secure him to my back and keep him alive. Fools rush in, but despite this fact Lord Gough was no fool. He was a hero and had acted as such.

Alas, this meant that he had paid the price. Heavily.

Bones were broken, blood flowed freely, and when he briefly had moments of lucidity, all he could do was scream. I am not too much of a man to confess that I wept often as I carried the Lord to safety, having to listen as he lamented the fact that he was now a broken shell rather than a human being. Looking back now, I wonder to myself if he would have been better off dead, or at least left there in Wilthaven Woods.

The result would have been the same, after all.

How long I carried him to sanctuary is a memory too far. All I can recall is the speed and determination that drove me forward. Mothers will lift boulders to save their children, and I feel I was being filled with the same sort of spirit to ensure the welfare of both our persons. Whereas before the woods had been thick and ominous – no doubt a trick induced by the Cultists – now paths were clearer and more linear.

I briefly recall that once I saw a hint of civilisation, I cried to the Heavens in thanks.

When we reached it, I collapsed in a heap and kissed the ground.

The people of Wilthaven, despite their fears over what lurked in those dark woods, were not without their charity and bravery in assisting two adventurers who had overstepped their mark. They picked us up, took us to the nearest place of medicine, and attempted to heal our wounds. Many nights passed before either of us were close to a state of recovery, and as I say, I was the one lucky enough to pull through.

The morning I saw the sun rise out of my window was one I shall not forget. The blessings of light from a God who dealt in life, not death, filled me with hope and helped heal any wounds carved into my spirit. I asked the presence of a preacher, and was given the chance for confession, despite no sins staining myself. But having merely touched something so dark, so awful, was enough for me to want to be cleansed by the Almighty.

Lord Gough had no such recovery. For those first few weeks, all I knew of his condition was what visitors allowed me to know. They informed me that he was still in an unconscious state, that he had said nothing except twisted mumblings in his catatonia. His physical wounds healed, slowly at first, but the mental ones would leave scars long after these days. I wanted to get up, go to my comrade and wish him well, but alas…

I had nightmares, I can tell you this. Vivid visions that I was still in those woods, still lost in an eternal darkness that would not abate. No matter how long I walked, nor how long I waited, no light rose from the horizon, and no trees parted to give me a clear path. Not only that, but evil figures lurked close by, whispering cruel words that hurt to hear. They teased and tricked me, taunting me with disgusting statements regarding Milton, my family, and myself.

And then I would find Lord Milton Gough, but it would not be the man I travelled with. His eyes would be black, and his face would be etched with a perverted smile that birthed rotten teeth and even more foul words. He would taunt me before begging me to join him on the other side, despite my knowledge that he was still alive. But such things mattered not; he was cursed, and wished me to be cursed alongside with him.

Invariably, when I woke from these dreams, I would be screaming as loud as Milton did when I dragged him to safety. Sometimes I would be placated quickly, but other times my lament would last well into the afternoon. Friends would come by, and I would shiver in their presence. My mother and father would try and calm me, but be met with fear and loathing. Even the preacher, when providing me with absolution, would be laughed away at the knowledge that dug deep into my psyche.

Each time, according to those that cared for me, I would utter the same phrase over and over again. I would later learn that Lord Gough would say the same, but instead of being fearful, he would sing the words, almost revel in them.

Either way, they were words that made good people sick. Made them realise that no matter what strength they summoned, it may not be enough.

"Hq'tar lives," I would cry out. "Hq'tar lives!"

11 – A Recovery

As the weeks evolved into months, my convalescence reached a stage where I could go out during the day with the aid of a trusted friend or family member. While the plague that had stricken Wilthaven had calmed since Lord Milton Gough & I had returned, recently events had grown more peculiar, and an air of danger lingered.

I get ahead of myself here, of course. This is due to the faults that an old man's memory is prone to. As I began to say, my rehabilitation was slow, but productive. I had developed a fear of the outside from our jaunt into Wilthaven Woods, and confrontation with Hq'tar and It's Cultists. But through the strength of my peers, I managed to slowly appreciate the outside world again, and regain my zest for what secrets it held.

This, in spite of seeing a dark underbelly that shook me to my core, and added nausea to my appetite.

Our intervention within those woods had paid forward, however, with a brief cessation of abnormal horrors that previously had stricken Wilthaven. The nights were more quiet, and the mornings birthed forth bright hope, rather than the remnants of brutality.

One curious notation was the maudlin nature of those that had fallen under the Cultists spell within Wilthaven itself. Of course, we were aware that some had become - what we called - Avatars for their evil, but since Lord Gough & I had faced fear itself, they had become more solemn, more sluggish. It was as if a part of their own spirit had been broken and, who knows, maybe they had been saved.

A foolish thought in retrospect.

With this in mind, I made the effort to see Milton during his own rest. Many details regarding his health had been kept from me, and doctors were keen to distance me even now from seeing my comrade-in-arms. Still, I persevered; demanding that separating us would do no good at all.

Once I saw him, I thought to myself how I should have taken heed of the advice of my fellows.

Lord Gough was not a well man, not anymore. His appearance was gaunt and broken, as his eyes sank under black circles, and his skin hung off his body like a sheet. His bushy locks and facial hair now were wild and ragged, forming a nest around his face that hid any form of expression. Not that Milton could express himself either way; he remained in a comatose state, and even when I offered him a soft greeting, his eyes barely flickered.

But part of him was conscious. In the short time I sat with him – under watch from the medical staff doting on him twenty-four hours a day – I heard him talk in breathy murmurs. Only on occasion could I hear his words, but I still could not understand them, for they fell into a word salad that even now I cannot recall.

One thing was for sure, however, in that one word he kept announcing was the same that tortured my memories:

"Hq'tar."

There was nothing more to be done by seeing Lord Gough, other than plunge my already fragile mood even further into a dark abyss. No, I had to leave him be at that point, and pray that good health would swiftly come back to him.

My own nightmares continued and I grew frustrated at the damage I had endured in that rotten episode within Wilthaven Woods. My mind, although trying to attain some sense of control, still was wracked with venomous veins that crept into even the happiest thoughts. At times, I would come round in a stupor, and see my carers and family stand over me in bloody cloaks, with eyes void of any life. The temptation to indulge in opiates was strong, but I feared that my constitution would fail me and I would become a drug fiend like many before.

No, I would battle the mental scars in my own way - through strength, courage, and a hardened resolve.

This, I believe now, was what saved me at the time.

It was not easy, but soon enough I was becoming more relaxed around folk, even cracking the odd joke. Eventually, my doctor took me for a beverage at the nearby public house – what we now know as the Paterson Arms. Just being in that form of revelry, with no evils prodding at my mind and no corrupted visions clouding me, meant that my recovery was more firm, rather than fleeting.

If only I could say the same about Milton. It seemed the more I recovered, the more he faltered.

A vicious curse indeed.

In fact, on the day I left my care and felt fit and healthy enough to make my own way, I decided upon something. At the time, people called me foolish. My parents wept at the idea that I proposed to them, and many people told me that the wisest thing I could do now was go back home and leave Wilthaven forever.

But their words had no effect on me. I looked at what had befallen Milton, and knew that to save him, I had to do something quite drastic.

I had to walk into the valley of the damned once more, and strike hard at the heart of these accursed excuses for human beings.

If Hq'tar would haunt me, then I would haunt it back.

12 – A Discovery

A wise man would tell you that to embark on another journey to face fear itself was nothing more than utter insanity; a suicide mission, which would serve no one bar your own foolish pride.

A wiser man would tell you to do your research before doing so.

It was with this idea in mind that I made my way to the Wilthaven Library, and prepared myself for an intense session of reading. I would scour over old tomes and various clippings in order to get a better sense of the mould that stained the underbelly of Wilthaven, and use this knowledge to track back to the woods and confront that wretched band of Cultists.

The only negative to this endeavour was the utter isolation I brought upon myself. Every person in the town saw my mission as nothing more than the purest lunacy, and when it became obvious that I would not listen to any man or woman who would try to divert me away from such an adventure, only then was I left to my own devices. Even my parents, who long worried that this was another dangerous side effect of my previous encounter, decided to let me do what I had to, rather than sway me.

Wilthaven Library was not the powerhouse of knowledge that it is now, and in fact rather than a few of the classics, I found nothing that would grant me any further knowledge of the town and its history. The gentleman who ran the service – Elijah Carter – was not the most helpful of individuals, having grown suspicious of my motives and even, at one stage, accusing me of being in league with the very fiends I vowed to confront.

I was not to be deterred. Dismissing Carter's concerns, I plunged deep into what little I could find. Various newspaper cuttings chronicling the decades of terror that Wilthaven had endured, from the obvious missing individuals and curious cries at night, to more graphic horrors such as mutilated cattle and buildings being assaulted by unknown forces.

Each time, these matters were downplayed and blamed on mundane matters such as foxes or strong winds. I ask you, dear reader, whether you would believe these days that a mere fox could slaughter a cow in such a manner that it no longer resembled a cow at all?

Back then it appeared the impossible was more easily accepted than the improbable.

I managed to strike luck when one day, Carter, already tired of my insistence, granted me access to the sub-basement of the library itself. Down there I was to find the information that would change my whole adventure.

The sub-basement was an imposing place in itself. It was lined by cold walls of old stone, very much unlike the welcoming embrace of the storage basement above it. Here was a place that men should not tread, and if they had to, they should tread lightly. The masonry suggested it was built hundreds of years previously, and the items held there had not been touched for almost as long.

The only light I was provided was a simple lantern, which only lit a few feet in this oppressive environment. I will confess that fear wrapped around me like a cloak, but my determination to bring some sort of solace to Wilthaven - and my comrade Lord Milton Gough - was enough to ensure that I pushed on. My mind would play tricks on me, suggesting cloaked figures waiting in the shadows alongside me, whispering their cruel words in my ear, but I resisted and continued forth.

Once I managed to open old crates bound by rusted chains, I lost all sense of time and place. The books inside were certainly old;

their spines creaked as they were opened for the first time in decades. Inside, archaic writing shared space with images that were as violent as they were terrifying. Figures surroundings pyres of flames, while monstrous entities stood tall over them. I was getting an insight into a history of the land long since hidden, buried so deep that no person would even dare to invoke it again.

Alas, it seemed such ideologies had risen once more, and had brought a doom to Wilthaven.

The tomes spoke of Old Gods, being from a period before time as we knew it, and who saw in humanity nothing worthwhile except for servitude. The men who wrote these works, and who were depicted in the crude visions detailed in the pages, were devoted to these beings out of space, and to their continued hold upon our land.

The more I delved into these works, the more often I saw a word that shook my bones.

"Hq'tar."

Such a God was not alone. By it, were named what I can only name as 'things'. Things such as Alkah, Volgart, and monikers written in characters alien to my eyes, depicted in drawings as gigantic, unreal beings with dimensions that were utterly impossible.

While these names were all of great intrigue to me, there was only one that mattered at that moment. The more I read about the Old God known as Hq'tar, the more I understood the behaviour of the Cultists from before; their manner, their use of tongue, all made sense when equated to the writings in these ancient works.

I couldn't help but feel that with these books, the people of Wilthaven would not just no longer fear the night, but also have the knowledge to strike back at such abominations. But it was the words of Elijah Carter that set me straight. For not everyone was a man of action like I was, and most would be more pleased to have such evil placed aside in a dormant state, than to face head on and tackle.

At the time, I saw this as weakness. A condition born of sheer terror, which could only be cured by proactive means.

However, in one's youth, one does not fully understand the sheer scope of horror that exists beyond the very mind of mortal men such as us. We see the world in simple fractions, dimensions born of three easy-to-understand ways. To have anything beyond that, would be to harm the range of our minds.

I cared not about such things then, but I was soon to learn that by facing beings of immense nature, I was exposing myself to something far bigger than I could ever understand.

That was a different time. I long for that again.

13 – A Second Chance

(*BPD NOTE: CHAPTER MISSING*)

14 – A Dangerous Climb

Upon reaching the mountain, the sheer scale of what awaited me struck me dumb. For from a distance, the ascent looked nothing more than a severe hillock, something one would hike up during an evening stroll. But now I stood at its base, I saw that it towered tens of thousands of feet high. It seemed like an impossible task was now laid before me, but my determination was too strong to give up at that stage.

After all, the journey to get here was vile enough to encourage me to go further. How I had survived, I cannot recall, but what I know now was at that moment, turning back was no longer an option.

Therefore, with my heart and soul sufficiently steeled, I prepared to scale the natural abomination before me.

In remembrance, I seem to recall that the first stage of my ascent was alarmingly easy. Obviously, at the time, I was more focussed on performing my climb, but now I see that a path had been laid for me to ease me toward my final destination. Thin trails, no more than a few feet in width, seemed to be carved into the side of the rock, and any ledges I needed to grab were thick and firmly implanted.

Of course, I had not prepared for such a task, and so should I have reached a point where even the keenest mountaineer would stumble, I would be stuck. However, the range seemed to yield to me, allowing me to swiftly move up without too much of an issue.

Alas, I would make the mistake of any amateur climber by looking down to see how far I had scaled so far. I was amazed to find myself looking down at hundreds of feet of mist. The ground below vanished under thick cloud, providing a bright void that would be my fate should I grab the wrong ledge, or place my foot upon a loose rock.

The mist itself was no surprise, as it had guided me to the mountain. Within its swirls were disguising terrible things, making sure I knew that I was entering a world that would violate me as soon as it would welcome. The vapour became more and more thick as I climbed, making it feel as I was wading through a decaying ink. However, my vision was not as impeded as I expected, although I still could only see a few feet in front of me. The further I ascended, the more I became shrouded in this perpetual gloom, one that ate sunlight and birthed only darkness.

I was so soaked with adrenaline that I could not stop if I wanted to. Besides, the mountain afforded me no place to rest, no small ledge to sit and take stock. The paths had shrunk in size, and I found myself clinging to the rock like a spider. At the time, my mind entered a state of sheer focus that to consider anything else except my ascent was to invite madness into my heart. All I could consider was reaching this infernal summit, confronting the evil that plagued this land, my home, and surviving that journey.

However, the latter was incredibly optional. Should I die, I would hope that I would do so for a cause, and not in vain. I had seen what Hq'tar did to those unfortunate to receive such a fate through Milton, and knew that death would be a sweeter release than whatever curse would be inflicted upon me.

Dear reader, I wonder now when looking back at that climb, whether death *would* have been a preferable option. In this chronicle, I don't wish to interrupt the tale of my past with current reflections, but it is hard not to wonder if I have been, indeed, cursed anyway. I shall come to the circumstances of my current predicament shortly, but I do wonder how, if I had fallen from that peak, or undertaken any other form of punishment, whether I would be absolved from this eternal struggle?

Or, perhaps, I was always destined to adopt this mantle. The ease in which I climbed the mountain, despite having no experience in such matters, tells me now that maybe the path was provided for me. Maybe, Hq'tar's Cultists wanted me to meet them, confront them, and ultimately defeat them. Maybe I was the last cog in their infernal machine, and my continued life keeps that damned thing going.

These are but the considerations of an old man who has seen too much. Their importance is lost in time, and all one can do is consider the present. Whilst doing so, I also hope to inform you all of my past in the hopes that not only will you understand why I do what I do now, but also that you will accept the sacrifices I have made. And learn not to make the same mistakes I did.

For my mistakes were made in pride, my errors born of folly of spirit. I did not consciously do any wrong, nor perform illicit activities that would see me locked away for the rest of my days. My crimes are not written in the law as we know it, but in old tomes that rest in sub-basements of libraries, long forgotten and covered in inches of dust.

As I climbed that mountain, all I thought of was my goal, my ultimate destination. I thought of my parents, my family, and all of my loved ones. I thought of the people of Wilthaven – as I do *every* day now – and how I can save them from the terrors that plague them.

Most of all, I thought of Lord Gough. Milton. I thought of how I failed him, how I'd held his hand as he succumbed to his own spiritual corruption. How, while I did not anoint him with the mark of evil, I did nothing to stop it.

I am not a guilty man in the traditional sense, nor do I pray for salvation. I carry a weight that can never be lifted, for it can never truly be understood.

If I knew all this back when I scaled that mount, I would have let go of my grip and fell back like an angel cast from Heaven; into the tar-like mists, to be eventually blessed with a crushing landing that would hopefully gain me entry into a life better than this.

    Better than our own living Hell.

15 – A Damned Night

To inform you that time became an illusion during that climb is an obvious statement. From the mountains sheer presence, to the warped nature of its rock, everything about it was wrong. Why would time itself be any different? I knew what I was dealing with did not care for the simple physics of life, and so surely it would play with the environment as much as it played with me.

I cannot tell you how long I climbed, only that when I did reach some sort of summit, there was not a drop of light in the sky to greet me. Why, I was not even sure that I *had* reached the peak of this mysterious range, instead just praising the fact that I was on land that lay horizontal rather than vertical.

When I first got there, exhaustion set in almost immediately. I collapsed to the ground and felt cold winds embrace me, settling over me like a blanket made of death. I could have remained on that ground, letting the conditions around me take me into another life. But as I have already said, I was fuelled by a greater thing than my own mind, and soon found myself up and preparing to make camp.

The tent I had brought with me wasn't some deluxe affair, but just enough to give me meagre shelter while I gathered my energy and took in some much needed sustenance. The wind here was bitter and unrelenting, tearing at what exposed skin I provided it with violent intent. The simple act of raising a tent became an hour-long struggle, as I gripped the ground and held firm against the worsening weather.

Eventually a break allowed me to pitch up and collapse inside. Suddenly, all that adrenaline, all that determination slipped away and left a shell of a man, one who had pushed himself far beyond the limits he had and drained as much life as he had left.

Once again, failure was not an option in my mind. As tired as I was, I would not let these wretched souls defeat me. I had come to confront them, and was damned if I would fall now.

I consumed my supplies with the hunger of a street urchin, and took stock as greedily too. I still could not fathom that I had scaled such a huge incline and yet, looking out my tent, I saw no further peaks. Of course, the sky had turned a rich onyx now, and the mists continued to swirl in Stygian tendrils. Preachers would tell you that Heaven is in the skies, and Hell exists below our feet, but I was seeing now with my own eyes that there was no Heaven here. No salvation or loving God sat high above in these heights, replaced instead by a horror that was as implacable as it was evil.

I cannot think of how long I had been awake, and cannot say whether I did indeed fall asleep on that cursed summit. The sights I recall, as well as many other senses I experienced, blend into the absurd and unusual, but by no means seem alien or dreamlike. They were as real as this town and its residents are, just with a warped sense of reality. Of what is right, and what is wrong.

When the mists lifted, occasionally I would be greeted with the sight of what lay upon this mighty summit. It seemed to stretch for miles around, and in spite of my mind telling me I was camped close to the edge, I was instead placed in the middle of a mighty expanse. There were no landmarks here, no signifiers of civilisation or any form of life. Just a deep, black emptiness, that seemed to go on forever.

It was designed to unnerve me, I have no doubt, but by that point I was firm of soul enough not to let illusions trick me. This was obviously sensed by what dark spirits danced on these lands, as the emptiness warped and became more wretched the longer I looked.

Skies became ground, and walls curved before me. Even now, I struggle to comprehend how the land around me twisted itself inside and out. It became wrong, perverting itself in dimensions and directions that simply could not be. And I was trapped in the middle of it, unsure if I was still on the summit, floating in the air, or falling to those dark mists that I considered diving into.

Even my physical body began to betray me, with my eyes watching my hands turn inside themselves, and my legs melting into old stone. The rock from before was natural, but this was far from it. Etched with markings of a lost civilisation, and made of a colour that was not of this Earth. It confused my eyes, before removing them and making me watch my own self be as corrupted as the land around me was. My body was moulded and mixed in all sorts of unusual positions, and I was made to hear my heart beat and cease, and my blood flow loudly and freely through the atmosphere.

The best way I could describe it to you, dear reader, is that I was dissected in a way that man cannot comprehend. I was alive, tortured almost; slaughtered in a way designed to break that one part of me that remained firm.

My own mind.

As I said at the beginning of this chapter, time had no place here. My physical state was played with for so long it could have been an eternity, but never at any stage did I cry tears, nor burst into maddened laughter.

That was what saved me. That was what blessed me with a grey morn, where light was only permitted the slightest of existence.

Hq'tar and It's Cultists had tried to break me, and failed.

Now, they invited me into their homes.

16 – A Cave

I could not tell you when I first noted the appearance of the cave. One moment I was in the depths of a vast, endless vista, the next I was staring into the dark maw of an entrance. The mountain around me was now hidden behind dense smoke, and the only path that was clear led to that cave.

Events continued to transpire that led me in a direction not of my choosing. My journey was to be a linear one, which would accept no change of course nor independent thought. Of course, at the time, I was too broken of mind and beaten of spirit to think of such things, instead just blindly leading myself toward a pre-destined fate.

From the outside, the cave offered no sense of how deep it lay, nor what dangers it possessed. Instead, its entrance simply stood as a black circle carved into the rock; a shape burned beyond this world, offering nothing except absorption of whatever stepped toward it.

My memory is hazy, but I would be shocked if I had not prepared for such a scenario. Some form of lighting apparatus would have been about my person, and yet I stood there with only the clothes on my back to aid me. My tent had been lost in the dense dark smoke, and anything within was no more.

All that was left was I.

And the cave.

What choice did I have?

I didn't step inside; I was swallowed whole, slowly digested by a unyielding darkness that wouldn't stop, would never stop. My feet took slow steps, but my own self did not propel me, instead a force beyond anything I had ever known took control. Only once did I turn to look back, and that was all I needed; there was nothing to see in front of me, and now there was nothing to show where I had been.

I was trapped in an eternal abyss, with only my own thoughts for company.

Madness would have come easily, that is simple enough to deduce now, but instead I focussed on my footsteps. Instead of falling and weeping into this existential tar, I kept walking, and walking, in the vain hopes of reaching something.

When I did, there was little relief.

The light hit my eyes almost instantaneously. Whereas I had begun to adopt the darkness as my natural sight, when the fires struck me I fell to the floor, clutching my face with blindness. Once I did manage to look through painful eyes, I saw a vast labyrinth ahead of me.

If this was the inside of this mysterious mountain, then it must have been completely hollow. Hundreds of burning torches lined walls that stretched so far, one's mind could not fully see how long it extended for. There were not even any more mists to hide them, instead I was to see everything that this land expressed, and if I could not place it in my mind, then I would dismiss it for fear of giving in to insanity.

Paths spiralled from the ledges high above, to pits that descended far below me. Some even went from wall to wall, suggesting gravity that was quite impossible to the naked eye. There were ledges that reached out so far, they became less footholds and more plinths for a whole tribe to live upon.

And then, there were what looked like homes. Deep holes within the orange-tinged rock, where more light glowed from within, and shadows moved fast and frequently. I never saw another being while I stood there, taking the scene in, but I always got a sense that there was *something* there.

I had no need to grab a torch, as the whole place glowed with light. Instead, I gradually followed one path that guided me downwards, past alcoves and makeshift windows that hid deep secrets within.

You can imagine my shock that, when I once again took stock of where I was, I found myself on a horizontal plain that was utterly impossible. I nearly felt myself fall, before realising that almost nothing had changed, except my own perspective. If I was to survive in this curious environment, then I had to have my mind accept its geometry.

How long I walked in this land is unknown, but every time I stopped to take it in, the landscape changed. Entire cities seemed to blossom from the walls, and in the distance I swore I could hear water flowing freely, yet saw no falls nor streams.

Then, of course, came the whispers.

They spoke a language I had never heard, but they were words clearly directed at me. They drifted past my ears, echoing in little holes where the shadows would continue to flicker. At one point, in a moment of lost sanity, I chased after one, desperate to come into contact with another being, no matter how evil.

All I found were shades of mocking laughter.

Slowly, I came to believe that this was my coffin, my final resting place. I was in an incomplete puzzle, another broken part that did not fit, and yet slotted in perfectly. I regret to say that this was the point whereupon I gave up and sat down. A nearby ledge offered me a way out, a chance to take my life, and…

Well, I took it.

Of course, dear reader, you are reading my tale now. I can assure you I am not a ghost, nor an undead being born of some dark ritual. I am as alive as a newborn baby is when it is brought into this world. My heart beats, my blood flows free in my veins, and my thoughts continue to develop.

So how did I survive such a fall?

Simple. I did not fall.

I leapt off the side, and landed on what I assumed was the cliff face.

Here, naturally, it was just another floor.

It took everything I had to retain my sanity. Luckily, my journey was beginning to reach its conclusion.

17 – A Confrontation

It transpires to me now that my whole ordeal - from leaving Wilthaven alone, to traversing the wretched woods, even to scaling the mountain and investigating its vast mazes - was one big exercise in breaking my spirit and my mind. I had been lead on a journey that was not of my own design, that I already knew, but now I see why. It was to shatter my pre-existing beliefs, my own soul, and leave it open for the damned to form as it wanted.

As I laid on that ground, fresh from an attempt to end my life, I wept. I realised that as strong as I had thought I was, in the end I was only human; just another man, trying to face the great beyond that obeys no master. The very same otherness that appealed to the beings now before me.

Had they been watching my attempts to navigate their kingdom? Enjoying my curious torture as some form of entertainment? I don't believe so, as that would suggest some form of emotive pleasure from these excuses for humanity. They were not men who basked in the joy of a good newspaper, or day's walk – these were men who begged for forbidden knowledge, and indulged in the impossibilities of the natural order.

And now, they wished me to join their cabal. To renounce everything I had ever known, and embrace absurdity.

I was never to do such a thing.

The figures, clad in cloaks of a dark, but unknown colour, stood before me for a long time, waiting for me to rise up and kneel before them. I knelt, for I could do nothing else, but I would not *kneel*. I stood up on my feet, gathered what little energy I had, and waited for them to talk.

They said nothing, instead just waiting.

I would not give them that pleasure.

If this world was as unreal as it seemed, then there was no impediment to my escape. If the Cultists – and by extension, Hq'tar – wanted me alive, then they would spare me on any path I dared take. Immediately, instead of facing the Cultists who had arrived to guide me, I jumped off another ledge, and found myself descending on another staircase carved from the strange stone that made up this land.

To tell you of my various escapades here would involve a belief in dimensions beyond the three we already know of. Even the hardened men of science, who I have since consulted before trying to write this chapter, have admitted that what I propose is simply not possible by the laws of the universe. Of course, from my experience, I know it to not only exist, but be true enough to exist within. And yet, to explain outside of what I have done before, is beyond my old mind.

Instead, I tell you of the consequences of my escape. The small group of Cultists I had risen before – numbering three if memory serves – remained in their position, now miles above me. However, from the alcoves and mysterious dwellings etched into the walls, more appeared. They did not attempt to handle me in any way, but stood quite firmly in my way. If I were to get past them, I would have to choose another path and make my way there.

Only on occasion did I find that the physical laws of this land did not help me. I would take a leap of faith off one ledge, only to find that the ground I was aiming for was no longer lateral to me, and I was instead falling onto a completely different area. My bones would crack, and my skin would rupture into welts and heavy bruising, but I suffered no injury that would impede my progress.

And all the while, the Cultists would not do anything except watch. There was no attack, nor any attempt to stop me. In fact, this once again seemed like a game to them, with their positioning making me move in a direction they required.

Throughout, I believed I was falling down, heading to the very pits of this maze. So it was to my surprise that, during one long fall, I found myself looking down on this vast internal city, stood in an antechamber that opened up for miles around. Here, the lights glowed not thanks to flaming torches, but the curious properties of the alien stone that made it. From that edge, I watched the Cultists all disappear into the stone, turning back into the mocking shadows of before.

For a moment I was alone, and considered jumping back down into the tangled architecture below.

And I would have, had I not turned around.

That may sound silly, but I found myself distracted by something I could not see. The chamber I stood in gave visibility all around, but I was quite alone, that I was certain about. That did not mean that the sounds and echoes that bounced off its walls did not unsettle me, despite not being able to identify where they had come from.

When I finally adjusted my focus back to escape, I found the stone city no longer at my feet, but at a distance in one of the chambers walls.

A wall, I should add, that I never saw before.

By now, my mind had fought off the lure of madness and instead adopted a pragmatic rationality. I stood there, frustrated rather than bewildered, and shouted curses into the air around me. I damned the Cultists and their infernal God, and vowed to have my revenge. I stood in the hall of evil, and filled my heart with a fire I never knew I had. I dared them to come to me, and confront me as I had decided to confront them.

They did, arriving out of the ether. I ran to one and went to strike him, only to see his shroud fall to the ground as my fist met cloth. I turned to another, and instead of fighting, I tried to remove his hood to see what lurked underneath the shadow that protected his identity.

Again, their physical body left them, and gave me only material to hold in my hands.

This was to be a battle that could not be decided by actions or violence, but words and proposals. With that, I stopped trying to exchange blows, and instead waited to see what they would do next.

The group around me parted, and allowed me passage deeper into the chamber.

18 – A Revelation

The Cultists of Hq'tar had greeted me not with the kind of evil that you would read about in occult horror novels, but a sense of respect that I did not anticipate. While there was no offer of tea & biscuits, there was no attempt to harm me, nor anything that would suggest I was in immediate danger; quite a different affair than our encounter before, which saw the mental destruction of my comrade, Lord Milton Gough.

No, this time, I was led across their chamber to a series of complex tunnels. Soon enough, I found myself part of a long line, moving slowly through this area toward an unknown destination. Each step I took, I noted how enclosed I now was – a vast difference from where I'd come from. The stone remained a glowing element I was unfamiliar with, and the Cultists continued to be silent.

No, that's a lie. They were not silent; they instead whispered a deep chant spoken in an unknown tongue. I tried to make out the words, but my memory has since blocked it out. All I can recall is the more I tried to understand it, the more my head began to hurt. A deep pain stabbing in my lobes, unafraid to make me cower in agony.

Still, I gritted my teeth, and continued to follow. Time was again an illusion, and I can only postulate on how far we marched. The tunnels became tighter, and I felt the strain in my neck as I tried to crouch through.

For the Cultists, they remained the same height as they had always been. Their physical form long since lost to some damned Old God.

I was in a daze when we finally arrived in another room. I call it a room, of course, but only in the sense that it had walls and a floor. Much like the antechamber I found myself in before, its length seemed to be infinite, and when I looked up, I saw that instead of a ceiling stretching on into forever, there was darkness.

I don't want to say it was a sky, as it was no sky I had ever seen. It was empty, dead, blessing those that looked at it with nothing but an eternal void. My mind tried to place it in some context, but instead I just kept looking, kept trying to believe that it was just the shadow of a far off roof.

It was then that I heard the first true words since leaving Wilthaven.

Before me, another group of Cultists walked. Instead of being in the improbable colour of those that had guided me, these were dressed in a more traditional form. A deep crimson lined the black of their cloaks, with their faces briefly visible under their hoods.

Their leader at first lamented at my suffering so far, before warning me that I should not have come. He informed me that I was dealing in matters that did not concern me, and that I should have left after our first encounter together. In reply, I told this figure that I was determined to find out what was going on, and whether the things I saw alongside Lord Gough were, indeed, true.

They say knowledge equals power, and maybe that was what I craved then; the same power that these Cultists had, that enabled them to walk with reinforced spirit, and act with impunity.

Not only that, but a power that binds them to their damned deity, Hq'tar.

No longer did I crave revenge on behalf of Milton, or the countless others in Wilthaven who had suffered. Instead, I wanted answers, clues to solve this obscene mystery. I wanted to bargain, to implore that they stop the plague upon this English town, and instead take their evil elsewhere – to another land, or another dimension.

I did not know what I asked. I just wanted to solve this puzzle.

I just wanted it to end.

The Cultist before me empathised, and once again showed no ill will toward my presence. He informed me, however, that by being here, I was no longer possessor of my own destiny. By daring to come confront them – the Followers of Hq'tar – I had inadvertently applied to become one of them.

I told them this would not happen. This would never happen.

They told me I had no choice.

I was forced upon one knee, and watched as the more human Cultists embarked on a ritual that made me sick to watch. Flames roared from places they should not, and swirls of colours out of time appeared before me in perverted dimensions. The show was like a firework display gone wrong - a mess of hues and shapes that man has no need of knowing. I tried looking away, but found my eyes locked onto the scene.

Then, the noise. The infernal noise. I had heard it only once before, when we had first encountered the Cultists in Wilthaven Woods. When we had seen darkness become reality, and witnessed the impossible step into our world.

When Lord Milton Gough & I had watched Hq'tar attempt to enter our realm.

Now, there was no longer two hardened explorers ready to stop this damned ritual. There was to be no sacrifice, and no temporary resolution.

There just was, and forever would be.

When it reached its crescendo, the winds that had roared out of infinity and the light that burst violently from the air assaulted my senses. The Cultists around me began to break down, too weak to fully absorb their master's form. Here, I had the chance to escape, to stop witnessing Hell appear on Earth. To prevent myself from seeing that our world is just a joke, a painting on an existence too shocking to know.

I had that chance.
I did not take it.
I wish I had.

19 – A Deal with the Devil

(*BPD NOTE: CHAPTER MISSING*)

20 – A Return

I had survived.

I had looked into the face of evil, and had left with my life. Not only that, but I had been gifted my sanity, my own mind. A mind not ravaged by the impossible, nor corrupted by the intensity of eternity.

Not only was I alive, I remained my own man.

However, I was a man forever tainted. A man forever stained by evil.

I did not have Hq'tar's mark. I had something far worse, a weight placed upon my shoulders that not only would I have to carry, but also every generation after me would endure; a weight of responsibility that no man should ever have to face.

I was to be humanity's saviour, and most would never know about it.

Only the people of Wilthaven.

They found me on the morning of February 10th. Nobody dared speak of the time I had been away, only to note that the passage of time had not been kind to me. I impressed myself by reacting with brevity and wit, easing the nerves of those around me. Once again, I was placed in intense care, despite no obvious wounds.

No, my body was battered, but not broken. Instead, it was my soul that had been forever scarred, blighted by an injury that no other would ever have to see.

My parents looked after me during this time. They made sure I was cared for, and that my every need was seen to. They held me during the nightmares, and reassured me during my delusions. But over time even those faded away, and left me in something resembling peace.

The people of Wilthaven were equally as thankful. I received a great number of gifts that, in truth, I did not deserve. Mayor Brown lauded me as a hero, a figurehead for our town who should be immortalised in stone in the market square.

Little did he know what legacy I would soon adopt in Wilthaven.

Over time, I went from my bed, to the various rooms of my parental home, to the streets of Wilthaven itself. Once more, the noises in the night vanished, and Wilthaven experienced a relative peace they had thought impossible. No, in their mind, I had given this to them, and they made sure I knew how much they appreciated.

But I do not wish to tell you of how loved I was then. Such things would be bragging of a disrespectful level. After all, you know my position now, and I know how resentful you are of it. To know that your ancestors, your elders, revered me almost as much as those Cultists worshipped Hq'tar, would turn your stomach. After all, I'm not a God to you – neither do I claim to be.

No. To you, I'm a dictator.

I am anything but.

In fact, let me tell you of how my return wasn't all joy.

One matter I was keen to know of, was the condition of my beloved comrade, Lord Milton Gough. While I had been away, attempting to defeat the unsurpassable, I had hoped that he had recovered, would join me for a drink, and that we would live happily together.

Instead, I was greeted with dark news.

Lord Milton Gough, as you all know, is dead. Or, he is as good as dead. His life ended when we first encountered the Followers of Hq'tar in Wilthaven Woods. Since then, his condition deteriorated to a point where he was no longer the same man I had met all those years prior. Like many of the avatars of Hq'tar, he had become a shell, a parody of the man he once was.

He was accursed, and banished to a place I dared not step.

And yet, I could not end my journey, my mission, there.

My parents informed me that a Royal Funeral had taken place, and that for all intents and purposes, Lord Milton Gough was deceased. However, this was due to the Gough family seeing what became of their heir, and knowing what I know now, that Milton is better off dead in comparison to whatever he is now.

I found him in an area of Wilthaven you won't find on any map. It is a place where day is cloaked in cloud, and the night is home to many terrors. It is an area that, over time, has mixed with our land like a vile Venn diagram. I will not tell you where it is, and for that you will thank me.

When I saw Milton there, I could see he was no more. He was no longer the brave adventurer, nor the man I shared so much with in such a short space of time.

He was an abortion, an abomination that should not be. The words he spoke were stained with corruption, the looks he gave resembling a mask out of this time. He did not smile; he stretched his lips. Neither did he walk, more shimmered in the dark.

And his eyes... his eyes did not look at you. They just hovered in an eternal abyss, lost and white with emptiness.

While he mocked me for my hopes that he would remain well, I realised that the weight of what I was to endure wasn't just limited to Wilthaven itself. It extended to every man, woman and child that dared live here, dared to call this town home.

The people told me I had saved them.

Milton – or at least, what was now Milton – told me the truth.

Wilthaven would never be saved. It would just be protected.

For now.

21 – An End

The motto of our town is clear:

WHILE THERE IS A CREST, THERE WILL BE SALVATION

Some have challenged that; others have claimed it is wrong and a lie.

No one has ever succeeded in either venture.

Once I informed Mayor Brown of my intentions, he scoffed. While he was grateful for my assistance, he was the democratically appointed Mayor. He would step down for nobody, not even a man who had saved his town.

He died two days after the beasts came.

From then, I was mayor. I remain mayor now, and will do until it is passed on to my children. And my children's children, and so on until perhaps the end of time.

For, when we no longer rule over Wilthaven, that will surely come.

Many cursed me for when the beasts came, but now many of you are aware of how to co-exist with them, and that their presence was due to Mayor Brown's selfish actions – which, of course, we do not blame him for.

We follow the rules of Wilthaven, the very ones that I have laid out for you. We do not tempt the night, and we do not go to places we should not. Those that do, are orchestrators of their own fate. No parent can weep to me about their lost child, no person can lament their lost love. People make their choices here in Wilthaven, and these choices have consequence.

The Avatars walk among us, yes, and we have to accept that as well. These… beings, I suppose, are indeed still the people we once knew. They are still our brothers, our mothers; they are still our sons and our daughters. But underneath, they no longer hold the feelings and passions we once passed to them. They act for Hq'tar, and we must make peace with that.

There is no deal you can give, no offer that you can provide, that will change that.

The only trade is one-sided. The only agreement results in your own end.

We will protect outsiders as best we can from our unique situation, but we are not their guardians. Wilthaven is selfish, yes, but it is for our own safety. We need to live, for in death, we no longer have power. We no longer have spirit that can stretch far beyond our little town.

Again, we must respect the rules of the agreement, whether we like it or not.

I know that many of you have rebelled against this ideology. By the same token, many of you have seen where such rebellion leads. You have lost so much, and gained so little, and by releasing this tome, I hope you see the true nature of what we do. You see that this town isn't just cursed, it is blighted. It is held hostage not by me, but by forces beyond our control.

But you must see the other side of this coin. You must understand that there still is hope, just in a different place than one would like. We continue to live because we follow these rules. We continue to be because of the mercy of the very God who would harm us. We remain, because it allows us.

That is why we do what we do.

This is why we follow the rules.

And this is why there will always be a Crest as mayor.

I don't expect you to understand. Neither, do I expect you to accept. People are their own, and are equally blessed and cursed with free will, a gift you believe was given to you by the Catholic God. But make no mistake, the will you have comes not from a deity from Christianity, but from something far beyond this simple plain of existence.

Hq'tar lets us live.

Hq'tar lets us prosper.

And Hq'tar punishes us should we not obey the rules.

This time will never end. This time is not limited to a number of years or decades. This time is infinite. Hq'tar is infinite. Its rule is absolute. Its will is implacable. You obey, you do not question.

With that said, and everything that is written in this book, I hope you take heed. I hope you continue to live your life, not challenge it. I hope that you continue to make Wilthaven the wonderful town it is, and help it continue to grow. That you bring in industry. That you bring in beauty. That you give birth to beautiful children and that they continue the traditions of our fair township.

For if we do not, it isn't just our small part of England that is under threat.

It is everything.

Everything.

Hail Hq'tar.

POLICE REPORT - 21/02/1977

As opposed to the Police Reports we had discovered prior – from various authorities across the United Kingdom – this report was sent directly to us for my attention. The envelope had no return address, and as far as our Security Division can attest to, there is no known person to have delivered it.

After scanning for potentially harmful, anomalous materials, the file was deemed safe to open and revealed the following Report. No other materials were found inside, despite being referred to in the text, and no further message was provided to give rhyme or reason to its delivery.

I have discussed this with the Directors, and we believe that this may be the first in a direct communication from beings within P1983. Further investigation will go into seeing about making future discoveries, but for now we must be extra vigilant for any further activity concerning P1983 and "Wilthaven".

As always – with the exception of the aforementioned additional materials – the text of the Report has been transcribed in full, with no omissions.

- Fyfe, Bureau for Paranormal Discoveries

WILTHAVEN POLICE

INCIDENT REPORT #21091983

REPORT ENTERED: 21-02-1977

REPORTING OFFICER: CHIEF CONSTABLE ROBERT GAINES

APPROVING OFFICER: MAYOR GRANT CREST

INCIDENT TYPE: GREVIOUS BODILY HARM/ATTEMPTED MURDER

LOCATION: MAYOR'S WALK

PERSONS INVOLVED: SIMON GRACE, CHARLOTTE HARRIS, LOUISA CREST, PC HENRY BRIGHT, PC THOMAS CUTTER

OFFENDERS: KENNETH HYATT

NARRATIVE: ON THE EVENING OF 20/02/1977, I – CHIEF CONSTABLE ROBERT GAINES – WAS INTERRUPTED DURING MY EVENING MEAL TO REPORTS OF AN INCIDENT TAKING PLACE IN WILD AVENUE CLOSE TO MAYOR'S WALK. NORMALLY, SUCH INCIDENTS ARE LEFT TO MY CAPABLE OFFICERS, BUT DUE TO THE PROXIMITY TOWARD MAYOR'S WALK AND THE

SEVERITY OF THE INCIDENT, IT WAS IMPERITIVE I ATTEND.

AT 17:41PM, I ARRIVED AT THE CORNER OF WILD AVENUE & RENFIELD CLOSE – HALF A MILE FROM MAYOR'S WALK – WHERE I BORE WITNESS TO THE HAVOC THAT OCCURRED BEFOREHAND (SEE ATTACHED PHOTOS). IT WAS THERE I WAS CONSULTED BY PC THOMAS CUTTER ABOUT WHAT HAD PREVIOUSLY OCCURRED.

AS THE FINAL MINUTES WERE DRAWING IN BEFORE CURFEW, PC CUTTER AND HIS FELLOW OFFICER, PC HENRY BRIGHT, NOTED AN UNUSUAL EVENT OCCURING IN REGARDS TO THE WEATHER. THE SUN WAS FAR FROM SETTING, AND A CLEMENT ATMOSPHERE BROKE THROUGH THE USUAL DULL FEBRUARY WEATHER. FROM THERE, THEY MADE NOTE OF THE MOVEMENT OF THE SUN, AND WERE CONTINUING TO DO SO WHEN THEY HEARD A LOUD SCREAM.

ARRIVING FROM THE CORNER OF CARRION LANE & WILD AVENUE, WAS A YOUNG WOMAN IN GREAT DISTRESS – LATER NAMED AS CHARLOTTE HARRIS. MISS HARRIS DREW TO THE ATTENTION OF THE ATTENDING OFFICERS THE CONDITION OF HER PARTNER – SIMON GRACE (FOR FURTHER INFORMATION ON

WHAT MISS HARRIS SAW, PLEASE CONSULT HER WITNESS STATEMENT ATTACHED TO THIS FILE). MR GRACE EMERGED FROM THE CORNER OF CARRION LANE & WILD AVENUE IN A STATE BEST DESCRIBED AS "WOUNDED" (SEE ATTACHED MORTUARY FILE FOR MORE INFORMATION REGARDING MR GRACE'S WOUNDS). FROM BEHIND MR GRACE, CAME WHAT WOULD BE KNOWN AS THE PERPETRATOR OF THE WHOLE INCIDENT – KENNETH HYATT.

MR HYATT WAS KNOWN TO WILTHAVEN POLICE AS A RECENT "RETURNER" AND BY EXTENSION "AVATAR". MUCH LIKE ALL PREVIOUS RETURNERS, HE WAS KEPT UNDER STRICT SURVEILLANCE FOR A PERIOD OF INSPECTION. HOWEVER, DUE TO REASONS STILL UNDER INVESTIGATION, IT APPEARED HE BROKE FREE FROM HIS HANDLERS, AND WAS NOW ENGAGED IN A FIT OF VIOLENCE QUITE IMPROBABLE FOR A MAN OF 83. FROM PC CUTTER'S REPORT, MR HYATT CONTINUED HIS FATAL ASSAULT ON MR GRACE, AND BEGAN TO RUN DOWN WILD AVENUE WITH A SPEED THOUGHT UNLIKELY FOR A MAN HIS AGE.

IT WAS AT THIS POINT THAT PC CUTTER CONTACTED ME, AND BEGAN TO ENGAGE

– ALONG WITH PC BRIGHT – IN STOPPING THE OFFENDER.

UNFORTUNATELY, BETWEEN THE TIME OF CONTACT, AND MYSELF ARRIVING AT WILD AVENUE, PC BRIGHT HAD BEEN HEAVILY WOUNDED AND NEEDED MEDICAL SUPERVISION. PC CUTTER INFORMED ME THAT THEY HAD DONE THEIR BEST TO SLOW DOWN MR HYATT, BUT THAT – IN THE WORDS OF PC CUTTER – HE "POSSESSED A STRENGTH QUITE UNLIKE WHAT WE WERE EXPECTING". THAT SAID, BOTH OFFICERS HAD PERFORMED VALIANTLY, AND MANAGED TO BREAK MR HYATT'S LEGS BELOW THE KNEE, RENDING HIM TOWARD A CRAWLING STATE. (FOR MORE INFORMATION, PLEASE CONSULT INTERVIEW WITH PC BRIGHT ATTACHED) AFTER BEING BRIEFED BY PC CUTTER, I WAS LED TO WHERE MR HYATT CURRENTLY WAS. HE WAS NOW CRAWLING ALONG MAYOR'S WALK, HEADING TOWARD THE CREST ESTATE. HIS PACE NO LONGER SUGGESTED A THREAT, AND I MADE MY WAY OVER TO THE OFFENDER AND BEGAN QUESTIONING HIM ON THE SCENE (FOR FULL TRANSCRIPT, PLEASE CONSULT ATTACHED FILE).

ONCE MR HYATT WAS UNDER ARREST AND HIS GOAL – TO KIDNAP LOUISA CREST – WAS THWARTED, SUNDOWN CAME AND IMMEDIATE EVACUATION WAS PERFORMED BY WILTHAVEN POLICE. AS OF TIME OF THIS REPORT, NO FATALITIES HAVE BEEN CONFIRMED, HOWEVER THERE HAS BEEN 3 DISAPPEARENCES AND 12 ATTACKS.

I HAVE ARRANGED MEETING WITH MAYOR CREST IN ORDER TO DISCUSS FURTHER HOW TO PROCEED WITH THIS MATTER. HAIL HQ'TAR.

RADIO REPORT #1

The following was discovered during a routine surveillance on Numbers Station by the BPD Audio Frequencies Division on 05/10/1977. The transmission was on a looped repeat that lasted from discovery of the recording, until 17/12/1977 when the final transcription was recorded and the frequency was lost.

Frequency was on shortwave 4122kHz. Monitoring has continued since contact was lost, but with no further reports. Transmission is transcribed in full below, with no omissions.

- Fyfe, Bureau for Paranormal Discoveries

"This is an emergency recording from Wilthaven Local Radio, stationed at 45 Joshi Street. My name is Derek Brown, and I'm the host... the idiot... of Wilthaven Easy Listening. I have been trapped inside this building since the 6th September, with little food and drink. They won't let me out. They refuse to let me out. They're using the shadows and...
(Pause. Light scratching is heard in background)
"And they want me. They want to take me. They heard the show and... and they know. They're using the shadows...
(Subject breaks down into sustained weeping for 14 seconds)
"I just wanted to bring something to the people here. I just wanted to help them through the night, man. We all hear it, every damn night. The wailing, the screaming... the scratching. Every night, at our doors, the

scratching. I thought playing some nice music would put peoples minds at ease but... but I didn't expect this. I didn't want this.

(Scratching continues in background for 4 seconds)

"Sometimes, I hear voices. Like, friends from school, who vanished weeks, even years, ago. They're out there, and they want me to join them. I've tried to record them but... but they know. They know when I try. They're tuned in – my most loyal listeners!

(Subject laughs hysterically for 18 seconds, first in a low volume, then a loud cackling)

"I tried to leave a week ago, but the corridors of the building... they were in the shadows. They hide in the shadows, where there's no light. And then, they broke the lights. Smashed them into shards. Now they can wait as long as they like. Until I run out and... and I don't know, man. I don't bloody know.

(Scratching continues in background for 8 seconds)

"If you hear this, please send help. Please. I know you can all hear this. I know you thought I was an idiot for even trying this, but it had to help. It had to! I got some nice comments about it, some nice people calling in. They liked it, everyone liked it! I just... I don't know. I don't know where it went wrong. God, I just want to go home, to my own bed and my own family. I mean, I'm just a kid. I'm just a kid. I'm just a kid...

(Subject goes silent for 24 seconds, while scratching continues at intermittent points in background)

"I messed up. Please help."

(Loud CLICK heard, before transmission repeats itself.)

17/12/1977 TRANSCRIPT

(Indistinct muttering heard in background. Footsteps heard walking on wet surface, getting louder)

"Is this still on?

(Unknown voice in background, possibly female. Despite all attempts to clean audio, voice still inaudible)

"You're not kidding. Might as well turn it off for now. Mayor got anyone else in mind?

(Unknown voice says something inaudible in background)

"Ha! That'll be interest…"

(Loud CLICK as transmission ends and is permanently lost)

HQ'TAR REPORT #2

(17/08/1978)

Gentlemen,

If you'll forgive the brazenness of my writing, but our efforts into discovering more about P1983 have stalled to a great degree over the last year, possible as a result of Operation Turista. While firm evidence is lacking, it has been posited between Agents working on P1983 - myself included - that the surveillance of Subjects Jack & Jill caused a rift in P1983 materials from which we may never recover.

The reason we have decided upon this rift? Hq'tar Itself.

Before, we began theorising that the reason why materials related to Wilthaven (P1983) were appearing were due to a potential Eldritch crossover event. These events, as we know from the incident regarding P42, see an Eldritch God attempt to enter our P-Class Dimension through people or materials from their P-Class. Now, I will confess, that these materials have been more proactive than the various reports and recordings we have acquired from P1983, but let us not drop our guard simply due to the apparent innocuousness of these materials.

With that in mind, it must be posited that by taking an active role in investigating more about P1983, especially during Operation Turista, we have set off a chain of events that has seen the entity known as Hq'tar more reluctant to try and enter our Dimension. With this in mind, we must consider the fact that, maybe, P1983's file should be closed and rendered 'SAFE'.

However, that is not to say there isn't much more to learn. We have still received materials, albeit in delayed form, and have learnt much from them. The key fact that Agents and myself have learnt from P1983 is the common practice of 'disappearances' within P1983. In one of our brainstorming sessions, based on the evidence we have, we concluded that Hq'tar is behind these vanishings. Given our experience with Eldritch Gods, it is safe to assume that Hq'tar is potentially using the residents of Wilthaven as avatars for It's own evil needs. Now, while these needs have not presented themselves in full yet, we can conclude that the vanishings are not a passive act, meaning there is some reason behind them. We can also conclude that this activity takes place after dark, given the disdain shown by many P1983 Subjects regarding the night hours.

In addition, the evidence we have to show their potential 'return', points toward demonic possession or Eldritch, Avatar-like behaviour. It should be noted that at no point was it evident that Subjects Jack & Jill were Eldritch Avatars, and so we should still consider Operation Turista a reliable success in terms of information.

In conclusion, gentlemen, it is my opinion that P1983 represents no further risk toward our

Dimension – P0. Materials have slowed down in frequency and findings, and anything that has been found can be safely classed as 'mundane'. The information we gathered from Operation Turista was exceptional, and potentially averted any risk shown by this Hq'tar.

    Thank you for your time, and as always, be safe.

                    - Agent Howard Fyfe, Bureau for Paranormal Discoveries

BPD CHANGEOVER REPORT (01/01/1980)

SUBJECT: P1983 aka WILTHAVEN

Fellow Agents,

    With all due respect to my predecessor, he is wrong. Agent Fyfe believed that P1983 did not represent a risk to our Dimension. He believed that the materials passed over were not dangerous, and would not affect P0 in any shape or form.

    I beg to differ.

    P1983 – Wilthaven – is like any other P-Class we have encountered. It is an Anomaly Dimension ruled over by an Eldritch Abomination, responsible for high levels of death, kidnapping, brainwashing and various anomalous activities that we all know of. To simply dismiss it as 'mundane' is to put not only the BPD in danger, but also the whole world as we know it.

    Why do I hold such a firm view on this? Look at the evidence we have gathered so far – Police Reports detailing graphic mutilation of persons unknown. A fear of the dark bordering on psychosis, as witnessed in Operation Turista. Kidnappings that are so frequent, and so violent, that they are mentioned in force in the town meeting minutes, and are regarded with such apathy that it breeds a sense of familiarity and, dare I say it, ignorance.

To the BPD Directors, I say this: Do we want the possibility of an Eldritch God - with powers that could lead to a Rasputin Scenario - to gain a foothold in our Dimension? We have already witnessed several materials inserted with ease from P1983 to P0, including Subjects Jack & Jill from Operation Turista. Who is to say that any of the creatures that are mentioned – or even possessed avatars – could not come to our Dimension and begin the process to end our existence as we know it?

I thank you for assigning me to this P-Class, and know that my strong personality and determination will bring about results that will gain us a firmer understanding of P1983, as well as ways we can combat it should the opportunity arise.

P1983 is not a Safe P-Class. P1983 is a P-Class ruled by an Eldritch God by the name of Hq'tar, one we have little information on as of this moment. In the 20 years I will be heading this file, I will make sure that we are more prepared and, more importantly, respectful of the risk that comes with Wilthaven & Hq'tar.

Be safe.

— Agent Brendan Marriot, BPD

NEWSPAPER ARTICLE – 02/01/1970

As per my suspicions, a sweep within the BPD Global Network found a wealth of materials that we can now link to P1983. While some of these materials are still being processed – having been either damaged in discovery or wrongly filed under a different P-Class – some are freshly available for our documentation.

The following is a newspaper article that appeared in Die Afrikaanse Herald – a now defunct newspaper based in South Africa. Due to the lack of BPD officials during the time, this article was placed as a 'curio' in a local library in Durban Municipal Library, before being found by BPD officials on the 8th February 1980.

The article appeared in a small circulation of Die Afrikaanse Herald – approx. 50 copies – before the error was realised and the edition was reprinted. As far as we know, this is the only surviving copy. Due to this discovery, efforts have been increased to try and find P-Class information on a global scale, including hopeful co-operation with our Soviet comrades with the Комитет Аномальные Сущности.

- Agent Brendan Marriot, BPD

FRESH CREST FOR WILTHAVEN

Celebrations were held today as the newest Mayor of Wilthaven was crowned in the town centre. Robert Crest, 30, followed in the footsteps of his father John by accepting the mantle of Mayor in a ceremony that saw him questioned on his identity and the town of Wilthaven itself. After a jovial few minutes of confirmation, a declaration was made by chosen Town Crier, Geoffrey Williams, and Robert Crest (Pictured) was sworn in by the town committee.

"Obviously it is a huge honour to follow in my Father's footsteps and become Mayor of Wilthaven," Robert said. "It is an important role that transcends the minutiae of small town life, and is one that carries a weight of responsibility that we all know of and respect."

Before becoming Mayor, Robert worked as a clerk at the Wilthaven Bank, whilst also devoting his time to a number of local causes such as the Wilthaven Woodland Society and The Lost Mothers Initiative, which he helped set up with his father, John.

"Robert knows the risks that come with being in such a position," John Crest was quoted as saying. "He himself has seen the troubles that affect this small town. It is with great confidence that I step down and pass the role to him, as I have seen his strength in character and inner fortitude grow over the years."

After serving for the past 20 years, John Crest decided it was time to put the safety of Wilthaven in younger hands, and sure enough Mayor Robert has promised not only to continue the measures that the Crest family have put in place, but also implement some of his own.

"As well as the local bake sales and school sports days, safety is my primary concern," he said. "We've all seen the grooves in our walls, and I can assure you that they will not only be fixed, but also fortified to a degree that will mean not only will we feel safer, but there will be less loss during the evenings."

Townsfolk welcome the new appointment, pointing out the intelligence that Mayor Robert possesses, as well as his in-depth knowledge and personal loss caused by the local troubles.

"I look forward to seeing what he will do, as I know it can only be good," resident

Nicholas Davies said. "Not to say a bad word about John, but it's a perfect time for him to move on and let the new generation take the reigns. Hail Hq'tar."

"THE CHILDREN OF LITTLE THWOPPING"

Item was found in Saskatoon Public Library by Canadian BPD Division – Les Mounties - and reported to the UK BPD Division on the 16th March 1980. Book had apparently been in circulation for 14 years after being donated by unknown parties in 1966. Agent Will of Les Mounties is investigating further into the anonymous donor, but due to minimal leads, follow-up is deemed improbable.

Book is titled The Children of Little Thwopping *and is credited to Howard Williams. So far, BPD officials have not been able to trace any evidence of a Howard Williams, nor the book or any other titles in various bibliographic databases. The book has a publication copyright dating 23rd March, 1952 and is noted to have been published by Wilthaven Press. Given what we know about Wilthaven – aka P1983 – we can safely assume that such a publishing house does not exist.*

The book itself tells a story about a small town (Little Thwopping) that finds itself at the mercy of mutated children born of the female residents. It is written as a horror comedy, and should be noted that some of the troublesome beliefs of the era – that of homophobia, racism, sexism and domestic violence – are presented in a tone that is to be determined as either satirical, or befitting of the time.

Below we have presented the passages of the book that we recommend deserve highest attention. These passages have been chosen due to their closeness in form to previous knowledge regarding P1983, and also for any other hints there may be about aspects of P1983 that we do not yet know.

Agents interested in the full text can place a request with Agent Revilo of the BPD Archives Division.

- Agent Brendan Marriot, BPD

(**DIRECTOR'S NOTE**:

Due to actions that will be made clear later on in this file, the contents of this report have been censored after much consideration by us, the BPD Directors. This is due to the fact that by including such a volume of the original text, we have opened up a maelstrom of epic proportions that threaten the lives of far too many Agents, as well as innocents.

Chronicled symptoms that have occurred due to prolonged exposure to THE CHILDREN OF LITTLE THWOPPING include:

- Nausea
- Migraines
- Heart Palpitations
- Violent Tendencies
- Erratic Gastric Expulsions
- Non-Existence
- Excessive Haemorrhaging
- Constipation
- Spontaneous Arachnid Propulsion
- Instant Biological Duplication
- Joint Pain
- Loss of Colour
- Transdimensional Ruptures
- Unknown
- Blackouts
- Angular Violation
- Infinite Vomiting
- Urinary Variation
- Fever
- Paradoxical Anti-Existence
- Artistic Rash
- Pelvic Erosion
- Unstoppable Sexuality
- Runny Nose

Due to the prevalence of the aforementioned symptoms, the original contents of this particular file have been removed. Please note, that the book itself is still located within BPD files as stated below, but we advise all Agents to avoid indulging in the tome. Studies are ongoing as to whether the story can be read on a chapter-by-chapter basis, and when results are conclusive, this will be updated accordingly.

Finally, reports that the book is readily available through online stockists is undetermined. Investigations will continue.

— Director Gamma)

Overall, while there are many flights of fancy within this tome, there is much — as we've seen in the select passages — to suggest that Hq'tar is a force to be reckoned with. As I said in my primary report, I believe Agent Fyfe was too flippant in his classifying of P1983 as 'safe', and while much of the material found in The Children of Little Thwopping *is played for laughs, the use of Hq'tar as a character and descriptive use of his familiars suggest enough for us to consider the Eldritch as a threat.*

Then again, it could all just be played for laughs. Some materials have suggested that the residents of Wilthaven don't see Hq'tar as a huge threat. Either way, I believe this tome to be important and to be read by all Agents operating on P1983.

— *Agent Brendon Marriot, BPD*

(DIRECTOR'S NOTE:

  If that recommendation is because you're a fan of the book, not because of its importance to P1983, I'll make sure you're placed on fieldwork in the most hostile P-Classes I can find.

- Director Epsilon)

POLICE REPORT – 30/02/1983

This material was brought to my attention by Agent Evers, who identified the collection of P1983 Police Reports as key research materials that have been previously highlighted as of particular interest within this file. However, after much consideration, I have decided that only specific reports need to be digitized into the P1983 Database, and any showing irrelevance are to be boxed by the Archives Division for potential research later down the line.

This particular piece was discovered as part of a cache located in Pune, India, and identified by an undercover Agent working as part of the Indian Police Service on 17th June 1994. Dating between the years 1952 and 1991, the cache contained over 100 Reports headlined with "Wilthaven Police". Again, I have only included the single file below as evidence of the cache, and the rest have been archived.

Upon in-depth questioning, Indian Police noted that they had been collecting these files across the country for the last four decades. When questioned why they had not made their presence public information, senior officers were unable to answer. They have since been re-assigned and replaced by undercover Agents under my guidance.

Thank you to Agent Evers for transcribing the material below.

— *Agent Brendon Marriot, BPD*

WILTHAVEN POLICE

INCIDENT REPORT #53171982

REPORT ENTERED: 30-02-1983

REPORTING OFFICER: WPC SANDRA HAYLES

APPROVING OFFICER: CHIEF CONSTABLE SAMUEL WAYNE

INCIDENT TYPE ARMED ROBBERY

LOCATION: NETTLESWORTH COURT

PERSONS INVOLVED: YANCY LINTON, RICHARD GRAYSON

OFFENDERS: MARK AMES, IVAN OWENS, UNKNOWN

NARRATIVE: ON 29/2/1983, OFFICERS WERE ALERTED TO AN ARMED ROBBERY IN PROGRESS AT GRAYSON GROCERY ON NETTLESWORTH COURT. DUE TO THE TIME APPROACHING CURFEW HOUR – 18:32PM – OFFICERS WPC SANDRA HAYLES & PC GREGORY ALLEN WERE ARMED WITH NON-LETHAL SUPPRESSION

EQUIPMENT AND ADVISED THAT, SHOULD THE UNFORTUNATE HAPPEN, TO REMAIN AT LOCATION OF THE INCIDENT UNTIL SUNRISE.

UPON REACHING GRAYSON GROCERY, WPC HAYLES & PC ALLEN WERE MET WITH GUNFIRE FROM WITHIN THE BUILDING. THROUGH CAREFUL NEGOTIATION, BOTH OFFICERS MANAGED TO GAIN ACCESS TO THE BUILDING AT 19:03PM. THERE, THEY BORE WITNESS TO THE PRESENCE OF YANCY LINTON AND STORE OWNER, RICHARD GRAYSON, UNDER CAPTURE BY 3 INDIVIDUALS.

2 OF THE INDIVIDUALS WERE IDENTIFIED BY WPC HAYLES AS MARK AMES, 20, AND IVAN OWENS, 22. HOWEVER, THE THIRD ASSAILENT COULD NOT BE PROPERLY IDENTIFIED, AND REMAINS UNKNOWN AS OF THIS REPORT.

PC ALLEN ATTEMPTED NEGOTIATIONS WITH THE OFFENDERS, WHO THROUGH MR AMES ADVISED THE REASON FOR THEIR CURRENT SITUATION WAS THROUGH SUGGESTION BY THE UNKNOWN THIRD PARTY, WHO WAS NOT REFERRED TO BY NAME. ALL ATTEMPTS TO SPEAK TO THIRD PARTY WERE UNSUCCESSFUL.

AT 19:28PM, AS CURFEW CAME TO AN END, WPC HAYLES & PC ALLEN WITNESSED THE THIRD PARTY MOVE AWAY FROM WHERE MR AMES & MR OWENS WERE HOLDING MR LINTON & MR GRAYSON, AND STUMBLED AROUND THE AISLES. THE THIRD PARTY WAS REPORTED AS IN PAIN, AND SCREAMING FOR "PILLS". DUE TO HIS ERRATIC BEHAVIOUR, MR AMES & MR OWENS CEASED THEIR HOLDING OF MR LINTON & MR GRAYSON, ALLOWING WPC HAYLES TO ARREST THEM.

PC ALLEN WENT TOWARD THE THIRD PARTY, NOW ROUGHLY DRAGGING THE CONTENTS OF MEDICAL SUPPLIES IN THE STORE TO THE GROUND, BEFORE WITNESSING THE ASSAILANT GRAB HIS HEAD BY THE TEMPLES, SCREAM, AND COLLAPSE TO THE FLOOR. PR ALLEN REPORTED THAT BLOOD BEGAN TO EXCESSIVELY HAEMORRHAGE FROM THE THIRD PARTY'S FACIAL ORIFICES, BEFORE THE SUSPECT REMAINED STILL AND WAS PRONOUNCED DECEASED.

UPON FURTHER QUESTIONING, MR AMES ADMITTED THAT HE AND MR OWENS HAD MET THE THIRD PARTY AT THE NEARBY PUBLIC HOUSE – THE GENIE'S WISH – AND BEEN OFFERED A LARGE SUM OF MONEY TO HELP THEM STAGE THE

ROBBERY IN QUESTION. WHEN CONFRONTED WITH WHY THE UNKNOWN ASSAILANT REQUIRED SUCH ACTION, MR AMES ADVISED OFFICERS THAT "HE KEPT SAYING HE WASN'T MEANT TO BE HERE". DETAILS OF THE FILE HAVE BEEN PASSED ONTO CHIEF CONSTABLE SAMUEL WAYNE, AND THE OFFICE OF MAYOR GRANT CREST.

TV REPORT #1

The following transcribed footage was broadcast on China Central Television during a news broadcast on 19/04/1986. BPD Agents stationed in Beijing managed to notice the rogue transmission, and secured a VHS of the footage from local broadcasters. Due to the racial profile of the figures within the footage, it was not linked to China Central Television and thus no further interrogation was required.

BPD Technical Division attempted to track the signal using data from the recording, but came up with nothing. It is my opinion we need to step up our efforts within this division, or transfer those within to other departments due to lack of expertise in these matters. Proposal has been submitted to Directors forthwith.

(DIRECTOR'S NOTE:

Proposal denied. Our Technical Division is more than up to the task of tracking a signal. Remember, most anomalous signals leave no trace due to Eldritch interference we are still researching. Please do not bother the Directors with minor matters again.

- BPD Director Beta)

Footage transcribed in full below.

— Agent Brendon Marriot, BPD

STATIC FOR 3 SECONDS

FADE IN: MS of UNKNOWN MALE – Caucasian, mid-to-late 40s - in suit sitting behind desk emblazoned with a yellow & green logo saying "WLN". He is looking into the camera with a serious expression while holding some paper in both hands. In the top left corner of the screen is a small box digitally added, with a humanoid figure with glowing red eyes and its hands stretching out toward the camera within.

UNKNOWN MALE: … several hours later, the situation was placed under control and the Avatars were placed in holding. And now, on a lighter note, here's Susan Kain with this weeks Crop Report.

CUT TO: MS of SUSAN KAIN– Asian, late 20s – standing left of screen wearing a red dress. She smiles and looks off camera right, standing in front of a blue background.

SUSAN KAIN: Thanks, Steve (BPD NOTE: UNKNOWN MALE will henceforth be known as STEVE). Well, things are looking rosy in the fields of Wilthaven, with Crop-Holders reporting a steady growth across the board.

CUT TO:	LS of acres of wheat slowly shifting in the wind against a blue sky.
SK:	In the Western Fields alone, wheat and corn have produced a further 78% more than last year, and fruit such as strawberries and falconberries are growing in much larger quantities than anticipated.
CUT TO:	MS of SK, still left of camera while the blue background behind her changes to Stock Footage of people working on the fields, picking fruit from plants. Some of these fruits resemble known produce such as blueberries and, curiously, full-grown melons. However, other fruits do not resemble known fruits, including a berry that is beige in colour and covered in sharp, twitching thorns.
SK:	Of course, this doesn't mean that those overseeing operations have been slack. The annual sacrifice lottery was run at Gozer Farm, with several Wilthaven residents being drawn, including Derek Kale.
	Background changes to that of a MCU of DEREK KALE– identified by a graphic label on the bottom of the screen. KALE is a Caucasian Male in his late 30s. Next to him is an UNKNOWN FEMALE – Caucasian, mid-to-late

	30s – looking upset and holding onto his arm. KALE remains stoic.
SK:	Derek, a local wordsmith for the Wilthaven Local News, had this to say about his selection.
CUT TO:	MCU of DEREK KALE, along with UNKNOWN FEMALE.
DEREK KALE:	Obviously I'm upset that I've been chosen this year but, well, that's just part of the draw, I suppose. After all, we all knew what we signed up for, and you can't exactly argue with that. It's like Terms & Conditions – if you don't read them, then that's your problem.
CUT TO:	SK standing left of centre, in front of a picture (BPD NOTE: cropped and added below. Some elements have been changed due to no known physical dimension within P0) identified by a graphic banner as MAYOR GRANT CREST.

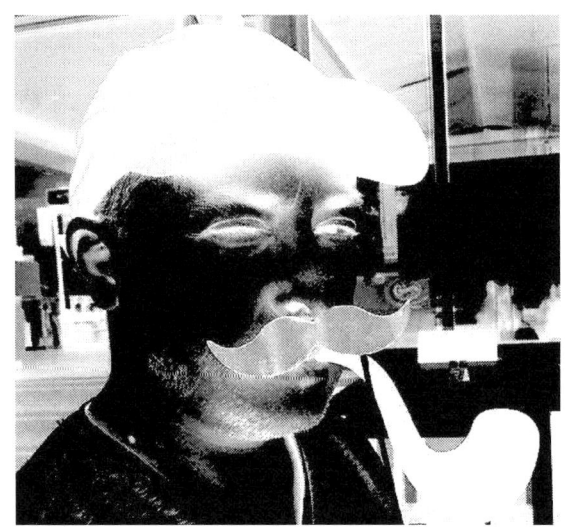

SK:	Mayor Grant Crest paid tribute to every Wilthaven resident chosen in this years lottery, and vowed to their family that the compensation will be fruitful thanks to recent events. He also stated that this year's Sacrificial Cage was the best he'd seen, and praised the children of Wilthaven Junior School for their creation.
	Background changes to a pale blue again.
SK:	So with that said, Steve, it looks like another successful year for Wilthaven. Hail Hq'tar!
CUT TO:	Steve sat behind his desk, looking off camera left. He smiles, nods, and turns to look at the camera.

STEVE:	Hail Hq'tar indeed! Hopefully next year won't be my turn.
CUT TO:	SK standing left of screen, in front of a blue background. She is not smiling or laughing, instead staring off camera right. This shot lasts in silence for 4 seconds.
CUT TO:	Steve is sitting behind his desk, smiling and staring into the camera, both hands holding the paper on his desk. He remains silent for 5 seconds, while his hands slowly start trembling. After an additional 3 seconds, his head begins to lurch back and his mouth opens, producing a low guttural noise.

STATIC FOR 8 SECONDS

END OF TRANSMISSION

HQ'TAR REPORT #3

(03/08/1987)

My fellow Agents,

    One question that has been put to me since taking over this investigation – and, indeed, since the very start under the previous Agent – is why visual materials are few and far between. After all, while our selection of written materials is legion, we are finding ourselves suffering when it comes to pieces of P1983 ("Wilthaven") that we can see with our own eyes.

    The reasons behind this are very simple, and very frustrating.

    You will have noticed, in the few visual items we do have – photographs, posters, etchings – that they are either transcribed or discoloured in such a way that they are almost unusable and difficult to view. This is due not to the complacency of our Technical Division, but a strange corruption that they cannot shake.

    It is not to say that we haven't received artwork and other such materials from P1983 over the course of this investigation. One such piece – titled The Maiden's Lament – showcased a rich view of early Wilthaven, perhaps dating back to the days of Charles Crest. In this painting, we see a young woman seemingly weeping over the fallen body of her husband, while townsfolk stand and watch in the background. The scenery in this portrait is a veritable mix of foliage, vistas, and things that – at the time – we were investigating further due to their own curiosities.

However, when it came to placing this material within this file, the corruption occurred. While I do believe the words of our Technical Division - and am sure they are as competent as the Director informs me - it doesn't excuse the fact that during the photographic replication, the material was damaged beyond any use.

A full investigation by my men saw that Agent Rodden – a senior member of our Technical Division – was tasked with chronicling the artwork, and was present when it was destroyed. His state of agitation and nerves led to him being taken off, but mentions of figures looking at him from within the piece itself cannot be corroborated, due to the fire that took place afterwards

(UPDATE: As I write this report, it has been fed back to me that Agent Rodden has now been tasked with Green Level work. Fitting, perhaps.)

Any material that is located has either been destroyed, or has been corrupted in a fashion that it is now useless. Deep slashes in the original paintings remove key features, and even photographs outside the ones we have are damaged beyond use. As I say, while frustrating, it does not deter the aim and goals of myself and the BPD, and should any materials survive these unfortunate incidents, then we will place them within this file.

Until then, we ask you to remain safe.

- Agent Brendon Marriot, BPD

LAKE CLOSED

Discovered as part of a routine inspection of local businesses in Hyde, Great Manchester on 01/08/1988, the following transcribed leaflet was distributed to a number of buildings on Market Street. While under interrogation, occupants of these buildings denied seeing any person delivering them. BPD Agents are currently scanning local CCTV in order to locate any persons of interest.

Leaflet has been transcribed in full below.

- Agent Brendon Marriot, BPD

NOTE TO ALL TOWNSFOLK OF WILTHAVEN

Due to unforeseen circumstances, Lake Wilthaven will be closed until further notice. This is due to the following incidents:

- Lost luggage
- Tidal storms
- Avatar disturbances
- Miscellaneous polluting
- Poison algae
- Lost children
- Undead entities residing on lakebed
- Waste disposal
- A 11-foot creature of unknown origins
- Dry banks
- Low safety staff

A reminder to all residents that Lake Wilthaven is a FAMILY ATTRACTION, and not to perform undue or unacceptable behaviour in or around its land. This includes the Kraken Shore and The Exorcised Caves.

FAILURE TO HEED THIS WARNING WILL RESULT IN DEATH.

YOU HAVE BEEN WARNED

(Distributed on behalf of Mayor Crest. Any questions please call your local Head Resident)

UPDATE: For the first time in a long time, the BPD Technological Division has provided dividends in their analysis. Please find attached a screenshot taken from CCTV that Agents believe is the perpetrator in question.

- Agent Brendon Marriot, BPD

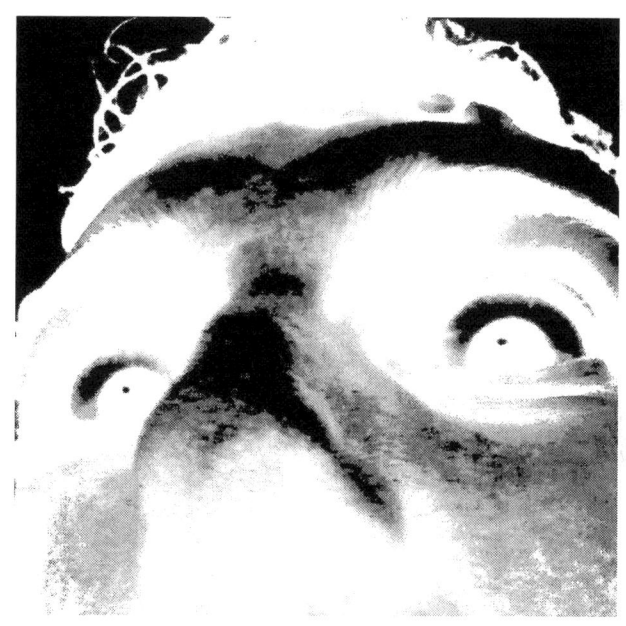

NEWSPAPER ARTICLE - 09/11/1992

The following material was sent to the BPD via an unknown source, and appears to be a cutting from an unknown newspaper. Due to the content within, we have determined it to be linked to P1983.

I have spoken to the Directors about the relevancy of such an item, and they have reminded me that all material linked to P1983 must be chronicled and placed within the file, no matter how trivial the subject may be.

Rather than be sent to our Archives Division, material has been transcribed and presented below. The identity of the person(s) who sent the material to us has yet to be determined, as envelope contains no return address.

- Agent Brendon Marriot, BPD

(DIRECTOR'S NOTE:

While a mere envelope may not seem important, can we please have it sent to our Analytics Division to analyse the postage stamp for any further evidence toward P1983. I realise this may seem to the Agent as "trivial", but all material is to be treated of equal importance.

- BPD Director Psi)

STRANGE STORMS HIT WILTHAVEN

The local weatherfolk couldn't make it up, as Wilthaven saw the end of an autumn like nothing ever before.

While most amateur meteorologists called for a clement and largely standard November for Wilthaven, the past week has seen storms quite unlike anything that has ever occurred before. From tsunamis bursting from the thick forestry of Wilthaven Woods, to a cascade of rotting flesh falling from the sky, it has been nothing short of a month of madness.

Let's take a look at the events that have unfolded so far, with comments by resident weatherman, Uriah Fenton.

NOVEMBER 1st

Rather than the light drizzle residents expected, Wilthaven found itself under the intense pressure of a sudden heat wave. Not only that, but the crushing heat appeared to hit in specific spots around the town, and varied in time length and consistency.

Grendal Street resident Maria Lentil said it best when she told reporters: "I was absolutely amazed by it all really. One minute I was putting on my mac and getting myself ready for a lashing of light rain, the next it was 44 degrees! The plastic of my coat nearly melted. I was going to buy us some hot potatoes, but it was just too much.

I ran home, got changed in my best summer wear – a frilly little thing and some shorts – and stepped outside only to see the sun disappear behind a small cloud, and to be hit with chilling raindrops. I didn't know right from left, I tell you!"

And that was just the start of November's random weather events. Mr Fenton had this to say:

"Obviously, heat waves can happen at the best of times. That's why we call them heatwaves. There was nothing unusual here save for why a woman would try to buy hot potatoes at this time of year."

NOVEMBER 2nd

This is when things really heated up, but quite differently from the prior day. The usual forecast called for some light drizzle, but mostly dry and grim. What residents near Wilthaven Woods got was something quite different.

"There was a bit of sun, so I thought I'd walk the dog," Charlie Smith told us, "when suddenly I walked my usual route on the outskirts of Wilthaven Woods, and heard an awful noise.

Naturally, I put it down to the Avatars who mosey about round those parts, but when I turned to face where the noise was coming from, I saw waves as high as 20 feet, rushing through the trees."

Luckily, Mr Smith managed to find some cover in a nearby bomb shelter before being hit by the enormous tidal wave, but some weren't so lucky. Wilthaven Police reported 12 casualties, 4 of which were unaffected residents.

In response, Mr Fenton said:

"Look, I understand that you don't expect giant waves of water bursting out of the middle of a forest, especially when there is no known mass of water within. But that is the key thing, we don't *know* if there is a large mass of water within the woods. I mean, you can't say that a random torrent of burning water came out of nowhere, can you?"

While true, the woodland tsunamis continued to hit Wilthaven for the next 2 days.

NOVEMBER 5th

Luckily, things returned to relative normality on the 5th, when instead of a cloudy day, Wilthaven residents were treated to a light snowfall instead. Due to the lack of any wet grounding or heated surfaces – surprising given recent atmospheric afflictions – the snow lay heavy and provided Wilthaven residents with an early Xmas present.

Mother of 68 Sian Cvexka told us: "It was beautiful, a real winter wonderland. My little Dennis stayed out nearly all day, and was sad when the curfew was announced. Still, even those lanky beasts seemed to enjoy a good rummage in the snow. Hail Hq'tar!"

According to Mr Fenton:

"We expected snow. To say we didn't is to sully the whole name of the Wilthaven Meteorological Society. I mean, if you don't expect snow in November, you're a moron."

NOVEMBER 6th

Unfortunately, it is difficult to say exactly what the weather was like on this day, as Wilthaven was plunged into a darkness so thick, you could barely see an inch outside your window.

Due to this on-going night, Mayor Crest advised all residents to remain indoors and not let anything draw them outside. Speaking on the phone to reporters stationed at their residence, he said:

"We've dealt with blackouts before. Obviously not to this scale, but it isn't unusual. Like every time prior to this one, I remind Wilthaven residents that everything is under control, and there is no need to panic. Hail Hq'tar."

Despite this, Mr Fenton had this to say:

"It is true that we've had days of purest night, but never to this scale. I believe it was equated to something I call Fenton Black, which is a type of black that is more black than we've ever known before. A black so black, that you wouldn't think anything was there."

At this stage, Mayor Crest denounced the Wilthaven Meteorological Society, and advised all residents to listen to the Official Mayor Notification on the forthcoming weather.

NOVEMBER 7th

Which was wise, as the 7th brought the worst weather yet.

As the darkness ceased and Wilthaven residents were blessed with the sight of a sunny day again, most went out and enjoyed it after being cooped up indoors all yesterday. Children played in the parks, couples courted within the meadows, and it seemed like the strange November had come to a close.

Then, Mr Fenton himself was hit by a wet lump later identified as a kidney.

"I tell you now, this was no ordinary rain. That kidney was as fresh as I am in front of you. By God, there was still blood all around it! I had to have two baths to get the stains off my skin."

In fact, it was more than a sloppy surgery that hit Wilthaven. Once curfew ended on the morning of the 9th (and at time of press),

Wilthaven Police said there were enough body parts to make up 17 cadavers. However, any identifying features were not present in the gruesome downpour.

"Right now we are reminding residents not to be alarmed, and report any digits, viscera, or assorted cuts to their local on-duty policeman," Chief Constable Samuel Wayne said. "We want to paint a picture of exactly why we had everything from intestines to empty scrotums falling from the sky, but at this moment all I can recommend is that when cleaning your homes from this bloody mess, gather any significant parts, and do not consume."

When asked if this weather phenomenon would continue, Mr Fenton could only stammer the following answer:

"Seeing as the Mayor has cut our resources suddenly, and advised us to 'take a break', I can't tell you anything. Who knows? Maybe Hq'tar has decided to have a little game with us. He always does! Remember 3 years ago when everyone had twins? Not even giving birth to them, they just appeared! I had to convince my wife I was me for weeks. And even then, I wasn't sure she was her! It's madness, nothing short of madness!"

At time of press, Mayor Crest advised us that Mr Fenton's position was under review.

HQ'TAR REPORT #4

(27/04/1994)

My Fellow Agents,

    Since we began work investigating P1983 – or Wilthaven as you may know it – one common denominator that always perplexed us was the fact of how these people & items came into our dimension. As you know, most attempts to track these have resulted in failure, with the incident relating to Agent Parker a particularly regrettable event.

    But we are not here to talk about that today. If you need any further information, read the file.

    Instead, we've had the Science Division look into possible ways that P1983 finds itself in our world – P0. Until now, we have been at a loss, and so it is with great delight that I can report a breakthrough.

    As you know, so far the most success we've had with crossover events concerning P1983 is through phone lines. Now, even those have been both random and unexplained in how the connection occurs, but by working with the Technical Division, our Agents in the Science Division believe they have found a vague solution.

    Now, just let me preface this by saying this is not a *definitive* resolution. It is merely a postulation that can, hopefully, set us along the right path. As is the BPD way, any small reveal in the greater picture is better than none at all, so let us treat this with the success it is.

Agent Jarrett - of our Science Division - found that during these moments where we received either phone, radio, or even televisual transmissions, there was a brief anomaly in the quantum field around the area. While research into quantum physics is still being tinkered with, they were able to spot the anomaly and hope that it will provide a basis for future investigations.

In layman's terms, think of it like when you lose a pen. Now I know, receiving people & items from another P-Class is a bit different than misplacing your favourite bit of stationary, but bear with me here. We've all been in that situation where a pen has fallen down the side of our desk and, no matter how much we look, we can't find it again. Quite simply, the pen has disappeared, and that's that.

Much like all P-Class instances before, we think that there is a temporal disruption that results in something from P1983 – be it a person, item, or signal – coming through to P0. Now while in the past most P-Class rifts stay open long enough for us to investigate, these tend to be temporary, and most of all, deliberate.

Yes, this is where P1983 differs from most of the P-Class' we've had before. Whereas some have simply been temporal disruptions, or a mutual Science Team attempting contact, this one seems to be a little of both. Somebody – or rather something

– is placing items in our world, and those of you that have properly studied this case know exactly what the source of this may be.

The entity known as Hq'tar.

At this stage, we don't know the 'why', but the Science Division believe they know the 'how'. Through investigations into the temporal anomalies, they have found that the quantum field has been manually disrupted in a way they class as 'non-scientific'. This means that no tools have been used to open the rift, and no chemical, physical, or quantum disruption has caused the opening. No, it has been opened by other means.

Paranormal means.

Of course, this means that the Occult Division have been called in, and as usual with those folk, they're both captivated by what we've recovered and infuriated that we haven't involved them fully beforehand. Already, they've found curious elemental traces on the documents we've handed them, and are looking forward to being involved in future Operations. In fact, in these early stages, they believe that Hq'tar is a more powerful Elder God than we imagined, and potentially not as benign as we thought.

Therefore, it is in the interests of the BPD to consider raising the threat level of P1983 in the possibility of a crossover event. Before we thought that Wilthaven was just a passive intrusion into P0, but if these events are done manually, especially by an Elder God, then we must be prepared for a more aggressive instance. Potentially, we could be facing a Red Level Event.

Until then, we shall keep investigating, and ask you to remain safe.

- Agent Brendon Marriot, BPD

TEKELI-Li: LIVE!

Material was found in the basement of The Thirsty Barlord public house based in Hartlepool, County Durham as part of a large cache of old promotional music posters listed for sale on the 18/9/1994. The proprietor – Winston Kingsman – offered no knowledge of the band, or of their performance on the date provided.

Research by the relevant departments has yielded no knowledge of the band, its members, or the songs mentioned on the poster. Given the mention of Hq'tar in the material, though, we can correlate this to P1983.

Details of the poster have been transcribed below, along with visual material that was able to be salvaged without decay.

- Agent Brendon Marriot, BPD

GET READY TO ROCK WITH…

TEKELI-LI!

Featuring hits like:

Fool For Thought
Hq'Tar Blues
I Sacrificed My Love (For a Ham Sandwich)
My Inverted Heart
Ain't No Curfew (Hold Me Down)

So join SID MORROW, LANNY DuVALL, and, in his first gig, ANTON VAN BROWN, as TEKELI-LI get ready to rock:

THE LASHING SIREN
30/02/1992

GET ON DOWN, OR DIE TRYING!

HQ'TAR REPORT #5

(01/12/1995)

Given recent Hq'tar activity, it was decided by myself - with permission from the BPD Directors - to see if we could gather more information on the Elder God known as Hq'tar. Therefore, we decided to use the resources available to us, and interview Alan Quinn, a human subject we recovered from P5326. As you know, Quinn has a vast knowledge of Elder Gods given his experiences in P5326, and so was deemed a valuable resource in attaining more information on Hq'tar.

Of course, Quinn is quite mentally deranged, so the process wasn't as easy as we hoped. Still, here in full, is a transcription of the interview with him. As you'll see, while most information was irrelevant, we did acquire some facts that I believe will help us deal with Hq'tar in any future conflicts.

- Agent Brendon Marriot, BPD

AGENT MARRIOT: Alan, how are you today?

ALAN QUINN:	The night moon is waxing tonight. You know what that means?
AM:	Yeah, yeah. Volgart will rise.
AQ:	VOLGART WILL RISE! HAVE YOU PREPARED? HAVE YOU?
AM:	We have.
AQ:	Oh. Good. Because Volgart…
AM:	Is rising, we know. Anyway, we want to ask you some questions about another Elder God.
AQ:	Tyrius the Anarchic? Bol? (Gasps) Surely not Araxitees?
AM:	(Pause) No. None of those. Do you know of one named Hq'tar?
AQ:	Hq'tar? Hq'tar the almighty? Hq'tar the mischievous? Do you speak of the one who basks in chaos? Who plays with the elements of nature itself?
AM:	You tell me.
AQ:	Oh, Hq'tar is a special breed of God. He cares not for you simple mortals. He toys with you,

	like a cat with a felled mouse. He paws at humans, like a cat…
AM:	We get it. Cats, mice, birds. Tell us what you know about him… if it is a him?
AQ:	He is mighty…
AM:	You mentioned that. How is he mighty?
AQ:	He towers above all, his black cloak hovering above an everlasting void, with only his pure, purple eyes beaming out from under his hood. And from that cloak, he will reach out with an arm long and bent at various elbows…
AM:	So he has one arm with multiple joints?
AQ:	What? Yes! And on that arm is a hand, long and spindly, the skin taut on thin bone.
AM:	Do the fingers have multiple joints?
AQ:	(Pause) Err… yes. Yes! The fingers are long too, bending at unnatural angles…
AM:	(To other Agent) Are you getting this?
AQ:	And using this arm, he moves mortals like chess pieces, until he has them at his ultimate goal.

AM: What's his ultimate goal?

AQ: It is his ultimate goal! His grand design! His master plan!

AM: Which is?

AQ: (Pause) Which is why he plays with people! Which is why he uses us as pawns, taking us from our homes in the darkness and bringing us back as avatars for his own destruction.

AM: We already know that from the files.

AQ: Oh. Well… he comes! He comes! HE COMES, HE COMES…

AM: Don't make us tranq you, Quinn.

AQ: Sorry, sorry. Do you want to hear about Cthulhu?

AM: What? We've got miles of docs on Cthulhu. We're interested in Hq'tar for now.

AQ: HE COMES!

AM: OK I think we've got enough here, knock him out.

AQ: No wait! Did I tell you about Jeff? He has…

INTERVIEW ENDS

NEWSPAPER ARTICLE - 14/09/1996

Agents based in Huancayo, Peru discovered the following material whilst reading an edition of El Comercio. Due to the difference in language, the article stood out and was reported instantly to liaisons within South America.

Transcribed in full below, with no omissions. Any questions should be directed to myself directly, and no other Agents working on P1983.

- Agent Brendon Marriot, BPD

HOLLOWAY HOUSE HARD TO HAWK

Wilthaven resident, and aspiring property tycoon, Stanley Faraday responded to claims that Holloway House – a building under his ownership – was not what it seemed. The 3-storey detached home, based on Arkana Road, was the subject of a number of complaints by residents and local real estate agents.

Mr Faraday - who bought the property back in 1989 – maintains that the claims are falsehoods designed to besmirch his character in the growing housing market within Wilthaven, but lead estate agent Connie Laird disputes this, saying that Holloway House is, "not right".

The reports found by reporters dictate that the property has more than 3 storeys – with one estate agent claiming that they climbed the staircase to a point where they could see, "the whole of Wilthaven and beyond" from a window – and has a number of extensions not listed on the blueprints. These extensions range from a marble kitchen that could potentially house hundreds of diners, to a pit that Miss Laird said, "stank of something horrific".

"Quite frankly, Mr Faraday has not been 100% honest with us when it comes to the building," Miss Laird told us. "It has a geometry that is vastly different than the exterior suggests, and I fear that one day I will lose an agent there. And a prospective buyer."

When asked his rebuttal, Mr Faraday went on one of his trademark rants to reporters:

"They're trying to do me wrong! There's nothing wrong with that house, and I'll prove it. I'll give £1000 to anyone who will stay the night there. OK? Will you? Or you? What's the matter with you all? The house is a perfectly fine, 4 bedroom house with patio garden and various utilities."

When Mr Faraday was reminded that the property was listed with only 3 bedrooms, he refused any further questions. However, Mayor Crest has been notified of his vitriolic complaint, and vowed to look into the matter forthwith.

"I understand the concerns of Miss Laird and the Wilthaven Housing Committee," the Mayor said, "and will get my finest men and women to look over the building. And yes, they will be equipped with the finest gear we have for deep exploration. We don't want another incident like we did at Harriet's Hole."

When this reporter investigated Holloway House for himself, he saw nothing peculiar about the abode. However, when local residents were questioned further, they advised they heard various screams from within the building. Furthermore, it was reported that various shadows of unknown shape were witnessed passing windows.

Mr Faraday refused any further comment.

PHONE RECORDS – 18/09/1997

This phone conversation was recorded after it was brought to the BPD's attention of a resident's phone line in Wappenham, Northamptonshire picking up 'unusual conversations'. It was determined that a cross-contamination anomaly had occurred, and BPD Agents monitored the phone line. Unfortunately, after this phone call was recorded, the line went dead and no further anomalous phone calls were made.

The transcription below is complete, with no information left out by the BPD Audio Division.

- Agent Brendon Marriot, BPD

(DIRECTOR'S NOTE:

Due to the handling of this material, it has been raised to the BPD Directors that Agent Marriot's conduct has been less than respectful toward other Divisions. The Directors are aware of this, and are continuing to monitor Agent Marriot. This being said, please bear in mind that Agent Marriot was chosen by the BPD Directors, and we have faith in his handling of P1983 thus far.

- BPD Director Sigma)

The following was recorded at 8:39PM, on the 18th September 1997. Individuals involved were determined to be Subject A – Mayor Leonard Crest – and Subject B – Samuel Watson.

MLC: Hello?

SW: Lenny? It's me, Sammy.

MLC: Hello Sam, how are you?

SW: Well, you know, all boarded up for the night.

MLC: Good, good.

SW: I'm just calling because… well…

MLC: Yes?

SW: We've been getting a lot more requests about this whole 'internet' thing.

MLC: (Sighs) Sam, I told you, we don't need this, 'internet'.

SW: I know…

MLC: If they want information, go to the library! What's wrong with a book these days?

SW: It's just… they're saying that it offers more than a library.

MLC: More than a library? I bet they haven't even been to the library.

SW: (Laughs) You're not wrong there.

MLC: Look, I appreciate that they've probably been told it by pen friends or whatever – which, by the way, I told you was a bad idea – but it is simply not feasible, or even safe. You remember the mine?

SW: Who doesn't?

MLC: Do you want that again? Worst field trip you ever had, if memory serves.

SW: It was nice that so many of the families understood.

MLC: Yes it was, but can you imagine them understanding when we try and put a load of wires under the ground, and it all kicks off again?

SW: I suppose so, but they are seeing it as…

MLC: As what?

SW: Well, they're doing history at the moment, and equating this to…

MLC: To who? What?

SW: The Pangean Alliance.

MLC: Wh…? The Pangean Alliance?!

SW: I know, but you know kids…

MLC: Bloody cheek!

SW: Listen, they hear things, and they do things, and…

MLC: Don't they know we do this to keep them safe? To keep them alive?

SW: Well, yes…

MLC: Are you even teaching them local history?

SW: Leonard, they know about local history. Everyone knows about local history.

MLC: If they did, they'd know that digging up holes isn't the best thing to do in Wilthaven. Not to mention giving a whole new portal for… you know… we barely manage to control the phone lines.

SW: Listen, I'll speak to them, speak to the parents, but we're on a losing battle here I think.

MLC: (Sighs) I think you're right.

SW: Progress unfortunately.

MLC: Unfortunately.

SW: Still there is good news.

MLC: Which is?

SW: Someone came back.

MLC: Really? Why did I not hear about this?

SW: It was only an hour or so ago, word's spreading through the town.

MLC: And it hasn't spread to the mayor?

SW: (Laughs)

MLC: Who?

SW: George Bennett.

MLC: Bennett? Are you serious?

SW: Yep.

MLC: (Pause) Bennett?

SW: That's what they're saying. Turned up outside the hotel just before dusk.

MLC: (Pause) Bennett?

SW: (Laughs) I kno…

MLC: Why Bennett of all people? Man was a moron!

SW: Yes, but I suppose…

MLC: Why not Archer? Or Freya Thomas? She was a lovely girl, so good with the kids.

SW: You can't question these things I gue…

MLC: No. You mostly definitely can't. But Bennett? That boy came out wrong when he was born, let alone after he went missing.

SW: Maybe Hq'tar isn't…

MLC: Don't you say that. We never say that. You know what happens.

SW: True.

MLC: Bennett… what's he doing?

SW: Working back at the hotel. Jenny says he keeps trying to open the shutters, but isn't doing much damage.

MLC: I'll be surprised if he even knows how to open a packet of crisps, let alone a shutter.

SW: (Laughs)

MLC: Bennett…

SW: I know.

MLC: Anything else? How's the wife?

SW: We're just settling down for the night, moans have started up outside.

MLC: (Pause) Yes, I think I can hear them from here. Well, keep safe anyway. We'll have lunch soon.

SW: Or come round? Guest room is nicely and plumped up with fresh bedding, and Harriet desperately wants to try this new stew recipe she's got.

MLC: Sounds nice, although Fen is on a diet.

SW: Really?!

MLC: I know… anyway, sleep well, Sam.

SW: You too, Lenny. Hail Hq'tar.

MLC: Hail Hq'tar.

REPORT: OPERATION NUKKUJA

OBJECTIVE: PERFORM SURVEILLANCE OF INDIVIDUAL REPORTED TO ORIGINATE FROM P1983

BACKGROUND

Operation Nukkuja began when BPD Agents based in New Tremaine, AR gained intel regarding a potential anomalous figure seen around the town. Upon further investigation, this figure was quickly established as originating from P1983 (aka Wilthaven) due to evidence recovered from Agent Coombs.

- Agent Brendon Marriot, BPD

(DIRECTOR'S NOTE:

Unfortunately, due to how this Operation ended, Agent Marriot was reprimanded and demoted to Black Level Field Duty. The following materials are presented in their uncensored format for research purposes.

Please Note: This was nothing short of a disaster for the Bureau. Learn from this, and let us hope that nothing like this happens again.

- BPD Director Zeta)

COOMBS INTERVIEW (16/01/97)

Agent Coombs is one of the primary BPD Agents based in New Tremaine, AR. He is one of the first to make contact with New Tremaine authorities, and has been conducting minor level research into the P1983 Individual (Henceforth known as 'Herb')

Agent Marriot is conducting the interview.

Agent Marriot:	So, Agent Coombs, start at the beginning.
Agent Coombs:	Usual procedure. A local transient pulled in by the local authorities says stuff that doesn't make sense, and our guy on the inside sends it our way.
AM:	Nice. Details?
AC:	The transient, known as Herb, spoke of, 'not belonging here,' and, 'needing to go back'. At first, authorities thought he was just a nut - the usual brand of crazy that they seem to deal with here in New Tremaine.
AM:	What changed?

AC: Agent Thomas, our man based in New Tremaine. He heard Herb talk, and put the pieces together. That's when he called me.

AM: We'll pull up the reports. Got any history on "Herb"?

AC: Informal interviews with New Tremaine officers tell us he appeared sometime last year. Came off the train confused and disorientated. From there, he fell in with the wrong crowd.

AM: You're saying he just appeared out of thin air?

AC: Isn't that standard procedure for P-Class individuals?

AM: Ha. Touché. Anyway, so he appears in New Tremaine, and gets involved with the local homeless.

AC: Pretty much. Obviously, not having anywhere to stay, and his cash being reminiscent with currency seized during Operation Turista, meant that he spent his first few nights on the street.

AM: Says who.

AC:	Says New Tremaine authorities. They had a couple of run-ins with him. But then came his new best friends.
AM:	Fellow transients?
AC:	Bingo. Group known as the New Tremaine Drinking Society. Lowlifes who spend their days drinking, doing drugs, and getting cash by any means necessary.
AM:	Beautiful. Which I'm guessing brings us to our current situation.
AC:	Indeed it does. Herb was in custody a few times, but never really spoke. Now, seems he can't shut up.
AM:	Any more details on what he's saying that would suggest a link to P1983?
AC:	Aside from asking to go home and the funny money?
AM:	You know I need more to work with before we push ahead with this.
AC:	Fair deal. Hq'tar may have been mentioned.
AM:	May? That's a pretty big "may".

AC: That's all I can give you right now, sir.

AM: Very well. We'll have a crew sent to you. Keep up surveillance, and send any documentation you can acquire.

Along with Agent Coombs, BPD Recon Team D7 were assigned to act in an assistive role. While talk of sending in a Grounding Agent was discussed, due to the low level threat at the time, it was deemed an unnecessary use of exceptional resources.

Acquisition of materials was slow at first, but eventually Agents managed to secure a few items of interest. These have been presented below, with some edits made for brevity.

- Agent Brendon Marriot, BPD

(**DIRECTOR'S NOTE**:
We can confirm that Recon Team D7 were assigned and approved to Operation Nukkuja on Agent Marriot's request. However, as known by all within the BPD, Recon Team's are usually not sent in an "assistive" role, and instead are used for more proactive matters surrounding potential aggressive engagement. In addition, the BPD Directors can confirm that there was NO request for a Grounding Agent, nor was there approval for material editing - which we believe was performed by Agent Marriot himself and not a member of the BPD Linguistics

Division. These are just some of the early indicators that Agent Marriot had begun to work beyond his authority.

- BPD Director Zeta)

POLICE REPORT (24/01/97)

Report Entry: Detainee – known locally as Herb – was arrested at the New Tremaine bus station begging the driver to 'take him home'. Upon being told he would not be allowed on board due to a combination of lack of ticket, lack of funds, and intoxication, detainee became belligerent and aggressive in behaviour. Detainee was assisted by other local offender James Cotton, who ran when police turned up on the scene.

Upon arrival, detainee was uncooperative with officers. Detainee kept begging them to help him 'get home', and began screaming and cursing when told to calm down. When cuffs were produced, detainee became hysterical and pleaded with officers not to arrest him. When asked to come quietly, detainee attempted to run, without success.

Once in custody, detainee continued his erratic behaviour, talking of how he 'did not belong here' and was being 'punished by Hq'tar for some reason'. When questioned on these statements, detainee just laughed.

Since sobering up, detainee has become less hysterical and instead is showing signs of severe depression. A police psychiatrist was provided in order to provide some help for detainee, but he was unwilling to answer any questions.

Detainee warned of future behaviour, and released without incident.

POLICE INTERVIEW (27/01/97)

Officer Curtis:	This is Officer Floyd Curtis, interview date the 27th of January, 1997. Suspect is named Herbert, or Herb as he prefers to be called. Suspect refused to provide a surname.
	Now, Herb, do you know why you're here?
Herb:	No.
OC:	You're here because you caused another disturbance.

H:	I don't mean that.
OC:	OK… what do you mean?
H:	I don't know why I'm here.
OC:	I told you, because Mrs Grimes at New Tremaine Homeless Shelter said you had become aggressive toward other residents.
H:	No. No… I don't mean that.
OC:	Come on, Herb. Stop playing games now.
H:	I'm not supposed to be here.
OC:	(Sighs) OK, Herb, listen to me. You've been ranting and raving for the last two months now about how you 'don't belong'. What does that mean, exactly?
H:	I'm not… I'm not from here.
OC:	Well I know you're not local, that's for sure. Accent is a bit of a giveaway. Where are you from?
H:	Sorry?

OC:	Where. Are. You. From?
H:	(Pause) Wilthaven.
OC:	England, right?
	For the record, suspect is nodding.
H:	Sorry, should I speak?
OC:	That would be helpful.
H:	Sorry.
OC:	Hmm. Now, let's talk about what happened.
H:	Doesn't matter.
OC:	That's for me to decide, Herb. You nearly injured somebody.
H:	Doesn't matter.
OC:	Well I think it does.
	For the record, suspect is smiling.
H:	Was I supposed to say that?

OC:	Quit horsing around, Herb. What's going on here? Why doesn't it matter that you beat a guy up?
H:	Because He will provide.
OC:	Who? James? Your dealer?
H:	No. Not... James? Is he here?
OC:	Forget about James. Who will 'provide', and what will they provide? Legal aid? Because buddy...
H:	I am smiling.
OC:	Jesus...
H:	Oh no. Not him. Hq'tar.
OC:	This again... who is Hq'tar?
H:	The one true God.
OC:	Is that right?
H:	He's punishing me. He's sent me here, banished me from the town. I'm shaking my head.
OC:	I can do tha...

H:	Hq'tar hates me. He thinks… I don't know. He's purged me from my home, my family.
OC:	Listen, Herb, calm down. First things first, we've got to get you…
H:	It doesn't matter. Nothing matters. I don't belong here. I belong at home. I belong in Wilthaven.
OC:	Herb, where is Wilthaven? We can make a call, see if you can get hold of your family.
H:	No.
OC:	Why not? Because Hq'tar says so?
H:	Because Wilthaven doesn't exist. Not here.
OC:	For God's sake… are you kidding me?
H:	I checked.
OC:	I've had enough. Back in the tank for you until you sober up, pal.
H:	I'm lost.

OC:	You've lost something alright.
H:	I'm crying.

END TAPE

On the 30th January, 1997, Agent Coombs & Agent Lane of BPD Recon Team D7 managed to bring in James Cotton, a known associate of P1983 Subject Herb, under the guise of assisting him. Cotton co-operated thanks to bribery of various intoxicants & other assorted narcotics.

- Agent Brendon Marriot, BPD

(DIRECTOR'S NOTE:

Agents are forbidden from coercing people utilising items of value, especially those of a dangerous nature such as narcotics. This goes double for narcotics acquired from other P-Class Dimensions, which were used in this instance.

- BPD Director Zeta)

COTTON INTERVIEW (30/01/97)

Agent Coombs:	Mr Cotton, thank you for joining us.

James Cotton:	And thank you for your little… "hamper". Heh.
AC:	Pleasure. Remember, with full cooperation we can make sure you have even more… treats, shall we say.
JC:	Then, buddy, you got me as long as you want me!
AC:	Excellent, that's what we like to hear. Now, we want to ask you about Herb.
JC:	(Pause) What about him?
AC:	What's he like?
JC:	(Pause) He's alright.
AC:	Alright?
JC:	Yeah, alright.
AC:	Mr Cotton, you assured us of your full cooperation.
JC:	Uh-huh.
AC:	This doesn't sound that full.

JC:	What you want me to say? That Herb is a terrorist? A spook? I know what you guys look for. You want to make him into a Manchurian Candidate?
AC:	You misunderstand me, Mr Cotton…
JC:	Because I know what you Black Ops people are like.
Agent Lane:	We're not Black Ops.
JC:	Sure you are. You wear dark suits. Say you're government but ain't got no ID. Plus, you pick me up and take me to some… some factory somewhere to interrogate me.
AC:	Mr Cotton, you're mistaken. We have no desire to interrogate you. Consider the gifts we have provided.
JC:	Yeah… yeah… bribes. Lures. Who knows what you've injected into this?
AL:	You want to try one?
JC:	Why don't you try one?
AC:	This is getting us nowhere fast. Listen, we would like to know more about Herb. What do you know?

JC:	Why?
AC:	(Pause) We're... concerned for his safety.
JC:	He's safe. He's with me.
AC:	Very true... but... we hear he's been acting erratic. Strange.
JC:	Says who?
AL:	Says us.
JC:	And who are you?
AC:	We told you, we're here to help Herb. Help you.
JC:	(Pause) You're spooks. Ghosts. The men behind the men...
AL:	Oh we're worse than that...
JC:	See! Threats! Torture! It always comes back to that!
AC:	We don't want to torture you...
JC:	But you will...

AC:	Listen to me. What do you know about Herb? Where he's from? Why he's so upset?
AL:	And answer the damn question, or we'll be the last friends you ever have.
JC:	(Pause) He says someone is coming for him.
AC:	Who? Who is coming for him?
JC:	(Pause) If I didn't know any better, it would be you.
AL:	We're not getting anything from this waster.
JC:	What you gonna do now? Kill me? Bury me in some unmarked grave?
AC:	Mr Cotton, you've read too many conspiracy theories. Now, if you have nothing else to tell us, you're free to go.
JC:	I got nothing to say, except stay away from Herb. He's alright. He's cool. He's just a little blitzed, y'know? We're all a bit blitzed here. But I got his medicine. I can help him. I got his medicine right here, thanks to you guys.

INTERVIEW ENDS

This final interview is what prompts us to take further action. It was decided that P1983 Subject Herb was under extreme threat by being under the care of James Cotton, and was at risk to himself through the New Tremaine Police Department.

Therefore, it is decided to use BPD Recon Team D7 to extract Herb from Mr Cotton's dwelling. This action would benefit the BPD twofold:

- It would determine the safety of a P-Class Individual
- It would allow us one-to-one access to a P-Class Individual for further questioning, in order to gain intel on P1983

While BPD Directors would not fully sign off on these actions, it was determined by myself that any inaction would result in negative consequences. Therefore, it is decided amongst myself, Agent Coombs and Agent Lane of BPD Recon Team D7 to enact Sub-Operation Kumalbit.

- *Agent Brendon Marriot, BPD*

(DIRECTOR'S NOTE:

At this stage, we must interrupt the Operation Report with some material of our own.

The following is a series of correspondence between Agent Marriot and BPD Director Theta. Theta provided full disclosure to the BPD Directors throughout, and should not shoulder responsibility for the Agent's actions.

- BPD Director Zeta)

MARRIOT-DIRECTOR CORRESPONDENCE (04/02/97)

TO: DIRECTOR THETA
FROM: AGENT BRENDON MARRIOT

    MESSAGE: PERMISSION TO PERFORM SUB-OPERATION IN ACQUIRING P-CLASS MATERIAL.

TO: AGENT BRENDON MARRIOT
FROM: DIRECTOR THETA

    MESSAGE: PLEASE CONFIRM P-CLASS MATERIAL

TO: DIRECTOR THETA
FROM: AGENT BRENDON MARRIOT

MESSAGE: P-CLASS MATERIAL IS INDIVIDUAL KNOWN AS 'HERB'. CURRENTLY BASED IN NEW TREMAINE, AR. UNDER NEGATIVE CARE OF TRANSIENT INDIVIDUAL. URGENCY IS PARAMOUNT IN THIS MATTER. PERMISSION TO PERFORM SUB-OPERATION

TO: AGENT BRENDON MARRIOT
FROM: DIRECTOR THETA

MESSAGE: WHAT PROOF OF NEGATIVE CARE DO YOU HAVE. PERMISSION DENIED UNTIL FULL DETAILS ARE CONFIRMED.

TO: DIRECTOR THETA
FROM: AGENT BRENDON MARRIOT

MESSAGE: INDIVIDUAL IS KNOWN DRUG ADDICT. P-CLASS ALSO UNDER THREAT FROM LOCAL POLICE DEPARTMENT. SUB-OPERATION DESIGNED TO BOTH GATHER INTEL AND PROVIDE SAFETY FOR P-CLASS INDIVIDUAL. AGAIN, URGENCY IS PARAMOUNT. PERMISSION NEEDED ASAP.

TO: AGENT BRENDON MARRIOT
FROM: DIRECTOR THETA

    MESSAGE: AGENT, DO REMEMBER YOUR POSITION IN THIS MATTER. SUB-OPERATIONS, ESPECIALLY EXTRACTION OPERATIONS SUCH AS THE ONE YOU ARE PROPOSING, HAVE POTENTIAL DANGERS TO THEM. ADD TO THE FACT YOU HAVE DESCRIBED THE CARER IN DANGEROUS TERMS IN PREVIOUS MESSAGES, THE DIRECTORS CANNOT CONDONE SUCH ACTION AT THIS TIME. PERMISSION DENIED.

TO: DIRECTOR THETA
FROM: AGENT BRENDON MARRIOT

    MESSAGE: SIR, WITH ALL DUE RESPECT, WE NEED THIS MAN. HE COULD PROVIDE US WITH INTEL NOT GATHERED IN ALL THE YEARS P1983 HAS BEEN IN BPD FILES. WE RECOGNISE THE DANGERS IN AN EXTRACTION, BUT AM CONFIDENT AGENT LANE OF BPD RECON TEAM D7 CAN NEGATE SUCH DANGERS. ONCE AGAIN, THIS IS A HIGH URGENCY SITUATION. WE NEED PERMISSION TO ENGAGE.

```
TO:   AGENT BRENDON MARRIOT
FROM: DIRECTOR THETA

      MESSAGE:    PERMISSION DENIED.



TO:   DIRECTOR THETA
FROM: AGENT BRENDON MARRIOT

      MESSAGE:    SIR, THIS IS AN URGENT SITUATION.
                  SUBJECT IS AT RISK. SUBJECT NEEDS
                  EXTRACTION. ANY DANGERS ARE
                  NEGATED BY BPD RECON TEAM D7.
                  PLEASE GRANT PERMISSION.



TO:   AGENT BRENDON MARRIOT
FROM: DIRECTOR THETA

      MESSAGE:    PERMISSION DENIED.



TO:   DIRECTOR THETA
FROM: AGENT BRENDON MARRIOT

      MESSAGE:    WITH ALL DUE RESPECT, WE NEED TO
                  PERFORM THIS EXTRACTION. IF NOT,
                  CASUALTIES COULD OCCUR THUS LOSING
```

US VALUABLE DATA. FINAL REQUEST
FOR PERMISSION.

TO: AGENT BRENDON MARRIOT
FROM: DIRECTOR THETA

MESSAGE: THIS IS THE LAST TIME I SHALL
            MESSAGE YOU, AGENT MARRIOT. AFTER
            CONSULTING WITH THE BPD DIRECTORS,
            AND TAKING ON BOARD ALL FACTORS,
            WE BELIEVE SUCH SUB-OPERATION
            WOULD ONLY RESULT IN DAMAGE NOT
            ONLY TO P-CLASS INDIVIDUAL, BUT
            ALSO CIVILIANS, BPD AGENTS, AND
            THE BPD ITSELF. IF THIS INDIVIDUAL
            IS AS IMPORTANT AS YOU BELIEVE,
            THERE ARE PASSIVE MEASURES IN
            PLACE TO EXTRACT HIM. PERMISSION
            DENIED, AND ORDERS GIVEN FOR YOU
            TO RETURN TO BPD OFFICES AND ALLOW
            AGENT COOMBS TO TAKE OVER
            OPERATION NUKKUJA.

BPD DISCIPLINARY INTERVIEW – AGENT BRENDON MARRIOT (11/02/97)

Interviewer

Grounding Agent October Tuesday

Subject

The aftermath of illegal Sub-Operation Kumalbit as part of Operation Nukkuja

GA October Tuesday:	State your name for the record.
Agent Marriot:	Agent Brendon Marriot.
GA OT:	What is your relation to Operation Nukkuja?
AM:	I am current Lead Agent in charge of P-Class 1983, aka Wilthaven.
GA OT:	And do you know why you are in front of me at this moment?
AM:	(Sighs) The failure of Sub-Operation Kumalbit
GA OT:	For the record, that is the illegal Sub-Operation Kumalbit.

	You have nothing to say to that correction?
AM:	No.
GA OT:	Now let us start at the beginning. You were denied permission multiple times by BPD Director C3, yet still acted. Why was this?
AM:	(Pause) I believed I was acting in the best interests of the Bureau, sir.
GA OT:	Explain.
AM:	I believed there was great danger in… sorry, I believed Herb was in danger.
GA OT:	For the record, 'Herb' is a P1983 Individual discovered within this Dimension. Please, continue.
AM:	As I say, I believed the P-Class Individual was in danger, and felt an extraction was the best action at that time.
GA OT:	Despite orders to the contrary from BPD Directors?

	Agent has refused to give an answer.
	I will ask again: What made you believe you had better judgement than the BPD Directors?
AM:	(Pause) Gut instinct.
GA OT:	Gut instinct?
AM:	I genuinely believed that if we didn't act then, we would lose a valuable asset.
GA OT:	I will remind you, Agent, that this "asset" you talk of was a human being.
AM:	I know that.
GA OT:	And you went with an instinct that was also not passed through a Grounding Agent such as myself for risk assessment?
	Agent has refused to give an answer.
	In the opinion of the BPD Directors, due to the Individual's situation, and the intel you provided regarding his carer and relationship with the local

	Police Department, they believed that to perform such a drastic action would result in casualties. This was after consultation with us, where Grounding Agent July Monday provided a 94% chance of danger. What made you disagree with this?
AM:	I thought I could perform a non-violent extraction. As you say, we had a 6% chance.
GA OT:	Have you ever performed an extraction, Agent Marriot?
AM:	No.
GA OT:	Have you ever seen an extraction, before this one?
AM:	No.
GA OT:	Then what made you believe in that 6%?
AM:	In my defence, I didn't know the percentile was…
GA OT:	Because you didn't consult us.

AM:	(Sighs) I didn't think that Agent Lane would be so gung-ho.
GA OT:	The late Agent Lane and his Recon Team were assigned by your orders. Did you not consider their protocols before doing this?
AM:	I didn't think…
GA OT:	No, you did not, Agent. You didn't think to review the situation. You didn't think to consult Grounding Agents. You didn't think an extraction would be a risk. You didn't do your research. If you had, you would know that Recon Teams are only activated in areas or situations of moderate danger. By bringing D7 in, you immediately placed a danger on this whole scenario, not just to your fellow Agents, but also the BPD Directors.
AM:	I admit, I was naïve.
GA OT:	You were reckless. Now please, what happened after you were repeatedly denied permission?
AM.	I spoke with Agent Coombs & Agent Lane, and… (Pause)

GA OT:	Go on.
AM:	And informed them that we'd been given the go-ahead.
GA OT:	To clarify, you deliberately misinformed a fellow BPD Agent?
AM:	Yes, but…
GA OT:	And attributed this misinformation to the BPD Directors?
AM:	Yes, but…
GA OT:	I want to take time to point out how serious this is, Agent. Do you understand that?
AM:	The thing is…
GA OT:	Yes or no, Agent.
AM:	(Pause) Yes.
GA OT:	Please, continue.
AM:	We prepared for Sub-Operation Kumalbit – at the highest level of professionalism, I should add - by

	deciding to strike at the residence where James Cotton & Herb were living. As far as we could tell, there was no sign of danger on approach nor had there been any suggestion beforehand.
GA OT:	Continue.
AM:	(Pause) Do I have to?
GA OT:	Yes, Agent, you do.
AM:	(Long pause) Agent Lane led the front line, while Agent Coombs led the rear. I spectated from a vehicle 3 miles away, monitoring cameras that Recon Team D7 had set up outside the residence and upon their person. After breaching the residence, Agent Coombs and his men were taken out by a homemade incendiary device.
GA OT:	My notes here say it was napalm.
AM:	I believe so.
GA OT:	Were your team prepared for such level of reaction?
AM:	(Pause) No.

GA OT:	Why not?
AM:	(Sighs, pause) Because I didn't think there would be a danger of this magnitude.
GA OT:	A danger that was enhanced by use of materials that you provided in exchange for information, correct?
	Agent has refused to answer.
	Tell me, did you know that they would combine the toxins you had acquired from BPD Storage in an incendiary device?
	Agent remains quiet.
	Agent Marriot, have you seen the autopsy reports? Have you read about the violations that occurred to the bodies of those caught in that explosion?
AM:	Come on..
GA OT:	I agree, this is irrelevant questioning at this time. Therefore, what happened next?

AM:	The explosion distracted Agent Lane, who was then shot by an unknown assailant. This began a firefight between the remaining D7 members and an unknown number of armed assailants within the residence.
GA OT:	Would it be safe to say these included James Cotton & Herb?
AM:	It would.
GA OT:	And why is that?
AM:	As the firefight went on, Agent Lane recovered enough to do a sweep of the residence's basement. There, according to the footage, he discovered an armed James Cotton, an armed Herb, and…
GA OT:	Go on, Agent.
AM:	(Long pause) A substantial amount of incendiary materials.
GA OT:	Which were?
AM:	Which were connected to Herb.

GA OT:	For the record, can you state what Mr Cotton said about seeing Agent Lane.
AM:	(Laughs) He said something along the lines of "If Hq'tar wants him, Hq'tar can come get him."
GA OT:	And then what?
AM:	He blew the fucking house down.
GA OT:	I'll allow the language this time, Agent Marriot, but one more instance of that and it will be added in consideration of your sentence.
AM:	Understood.
GA OT:	For the record, there were no survivors, aside from yourself, is that correct?
AM:	(Pause) Correct.
GA OT:	Which means that 2 Primary Agents, 6 Recon Team Agents, 4 civilians and one P-Class Subject were killed, is that correct?
AM:	Yes.

GA OT:	How would you describe that, Agent Marriot?
AM:	(Pause) A failure.
GA OT:	At the very least. And all because you acted on your own instinct, did not follow the correct procedures, and ultimately disobeyed direct orders from BPD Directors?
AM:	Yes.
GA OT:	Do you have anything else to say?
	Agent is shaking his head.
	Interview over. Sentence to be adjudged by BPD Directors.
AM:	October?
GA OT:	Yes?
AM:	What are my odds?
GA OT:	(Pause) Very low.

INTERVIEW ENDS

NEWSPAPER ARTICLE (12/02/97)

The following is the only public notification of the Sub-Operation Kumalbit Disaster. Thanks to the quick thinking of on-site Agents, no further distribution occurred and this story appeared in The New Tremaine Chronicle, which only had a low circulation, preventing a potential intel outbreak.

EXPLOSION LEVELS SUSPECTED DRUG DEN

Chaos reigned in New Tremaine this week when a huge explosion tore through a home on East 17th Street. The abode, which police sources say belonged to James Cotton, had previously been suspected of being home to a burgeoning drug lab, with a mixture of cocaine, meth, and other assorted narcotics being produced on a growing scale.

Officers from the New Tremaine Police Department arrived on the scene, and were told by witnesses that a paramilitary force had stormed the building before the explosion. While no knowledge of any sort of agency is known, witnesses speaking to The New Tremaine Chronicle told us that they did not resemble any group they are aware of.

"If they were military, I would have known," one resident told reporters. "I served in the war a few years back, and I don't remember seeing anybody who dressed like them. But I tell you what, they were too well armed and too well coordinated to be your average gangbangers."

Once the scene was under control, and a suspected biohazard was confirmed to be benign, police confirmed 8 fatalities found in the rubble. However, due to the severity of the explosion, they advised there could be more.

Speaking on behalf of the New Tremaine Police Department, Officer Roderick Curtis told us: "We were aware that James Cotton and his associates were dealing in some high-level substances, but were building a case before moving forward. Whoever these folks were who rammed themselves in, they obviously had no idea what they were dealing with."

Continuing, Officer Curtis confirmed that the explosion had sent figurative shockwaves throughout the community, with one officer in their department tending their resignation.

"We're a small town, pretty close-knit. When you discover stuff like this, it hits home, and it hits hard. We've lost a good officer because of this, as well as some good people. James Cotton wasn't the best egg, but with the right rehabilitation, he could have been. Now, we'll never know."

The officer who resigned, known locally as Officer Numan, denied the request to comment.

Our thoughts are with the families who lost relatives in this tragedy.

CONCLUSION

Due to the reckless actions of Agent Marriot, and the needless loss of life involved as well as the loss of a P-Class Individual, the file on P1983 is closed until re-assignment (which will take place on 01/01/2000 at the earliest).

Agent Turner, aka Officer Numan, has been re-assigned to Green Level desk duty pending psychiatric evaluation.

As previously confirmed, Agent Marriot has been assigned to Black Level Field Duty. At time of writing, this has resulted in being assigned to P11745.

— BPD Director Zeta

DIRECTOR'S NOTE:

From this point, P1983 ("Wilthaven") was assigned to Agent Alexis Petrovic. Agent Petrovic was chosen due to her professionalism, experience in dealing with P-Class Dimensions that have gone dormant, and an enthusiasm combined with a level head.

No Changeover report was deemed necessary due to the time elapsed and nature on which previous reports ceased.

- BPD Director Alpha

LOST DOG

Found attached to a telephone pole in Bruges, Belgium on 26th July 1999. It was brought to the attention of BPD Agents stationed in Belgium due to the difference in colloquial language, and the number offered being alien to any other known phone number. When questioned, some locals had no idea when the poster first appeared, but stated an overall time frame of 2 weeks. Further questioning revealed they did not report anything as they felt it was "some sort of prank".

Analysis by our fledgling Digital Team has revealed no source for the number, and no source stamp from the image used. Any further mention of the names mentioned within is to be reported to the P1983 team led by myself.

Due to previous issues related to P1983, this material is only now being filed within this report (dateline 02/01/2000).

Material transcribed below along with non-corrupted imagery.

- Agent Petrovic, BPD

HAVE YOU SEEN THIS DOG?

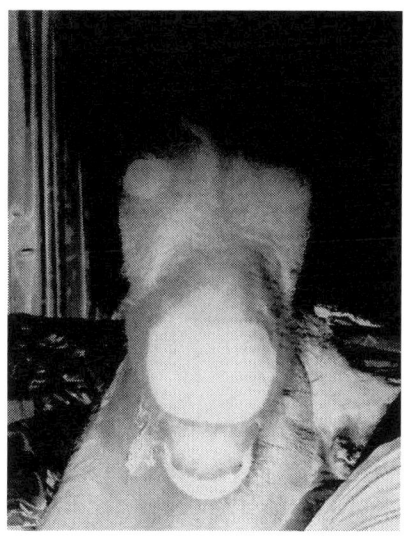

Answers to Lucky, Lou-Lou, Achtir the Destroyer of Dimensions, Defiler of Time, Ravager of Senses, or Loopy Lou!

If found, please contact Josie at:

063948 265 84 376 424 H

THANK YOU

REPORT: OPERATION DUNKELHEIT

OBJECTIVE: OBTAIN A CACHE OF MATERIALS RELATED TO P1983

BACKGROUND

It was brought to the attention of the BPD that a collection of various materials related to P1983 (Wilthaven) was secured in an old storage facility in the town of Sheffield, England. This information was passed to us by antiques collector Jeffrey Parsons, a civilian working with the BPD in the capacity of supplying items deemed "unusual" and thus potentially related to P-Class Dimensions.

Parsons had previously provided BPD Agents with partial diary entries that were associated with P1983. Upon further investigation, it was deemed that more materials revolving around P1983 might be available.

The following partial interview (edited for brevity at the permission of BPD Directors) recounts how this information came to our attention.

— Agent Petrovic, BPD

PARSONS INTERVIEW 08/03/01

Agent Petrovic:	So what can you tell us about the person you acquired these materials from?
Jeffrey Parsons:	Just your average dealer, really. Middle-aged, quiet, ordinary in every single way.
AP:	No defining features?
JP:	I wish I could tell you.
AP:	How about a name?
JP:	Let me think… (Pause) Hobkins? Dennis Hobkins? Or Hopkins?
AP:	We can work with that. Did he mention how he came to acquire these materials?
JP:	I asked, of course, given that the diaries he sold to me were incomplete. He informed me that he had a small selection of items that he had collected over the years.
AP:	Such as?

JP: (Pause) Leaflets, newspaper articles, various scrapbooks full of random items. Oh yes, he did mention he had some tapes as well.

AP: Tapes?

JP: Yes, but when I enquired further, the price he asked was much too high.

AP: I understand. We can assist with any financial difficulties if it results in acquisition of materials. Did he give any more details about where he kept these?

JP: I didn't think to ask.

AP: Again, understandable. Is there anything else you can tell us? Anything that seemed abnormal or strange?

JP: Like I say, he was painfully average in every way. The only abnormal thing I can think of are the diaries I gave you.

INTERVIEW ENDS

From there, BPD Officials researched the name given to us by Parsons, that of a Dennis Hopkins. While a common name, his identity was linked to several pawn shops located in the South Yorkshire region. While the materials acquired were minimal – mostly items traded at other jumbles and boot sales – what caught the attention of officials was his unusual behaviour in dealing with the pawnshop owners. One described him as 'skittish', and 'not sure what he was doing'. This behaviour, as well as his link to P1983 materials, led us to conclude a positive identification.

A BPD Surveillance Team were sent to Sheffield to track down Hopkins, but unfortunately due to a combination of erratic movement and low-level stamping, they were unable to locate the subject.

However, a link was uncovered of a recent residence - a hotel establishment that housed Hopkins for a period of 2 weeks. The following is a partial transcription (edited for brevity at the permission of BPD Directors) of the interview with the hotel manager, Sean Harris.

- Agent Petrovic, BPD

HARRIS INTERVIEW 12/03/01

Agent Petrovic:	So Mr Hopkins stayed for 2 weeks?

Sean Harris:	That's correct.
AP:	And did you notice anything unusual?
SH:	Like what?
AP:	Behaviour? Speech? General interactions?
SH:	Well he always paid in cash, usually right before he was about to be thrown out for overstaying his welcome. We'd give him fair warning, and he'd go out for a couple of hours, and then come back with the necessary funds.
AP:	I see. Anything else?
SH:	He was often confused. We found him staring at the local attraction flyers for a good hour one day.
AP:	Did he say anything during this time?
SH:	Nope, just stared and read through a number of them, like they were alien to him.
AP.	What makes you say that?

SH: Just the way he read them. I've never seen someone read one of those so intently, you know? I mean, most people are interested, but not many people look at it like it's in another language or something.

AP: Interesting. Was there anything about his room that made you curious? Any items left behind or conditions that you thought unusual?

SH: (Laughs) I've seen a lot of unusual conditions, if you know what I mean. This one time…

AP: Please just answer the question, Mr Harris.

SH: Oh, sorry. Um, not really.

AP: Are you sure?

SH: Yeah. He was a very light packer, as far as I could tell. Only had the clothes on his back.

AP: He had nothing else?

SH: No.

AP:	Again, are you sure? The slightest detail could be important.
SH:	Really? Well… OK there was a leaflet for the local storage facility at the Parkway, but aside from that…
AP:	Storage facility?
SH:	Yeah, you know the ones, where you just dump a load of stuff there because you don't have the room. I mean, I suppose he could have stored his belongings there but…
AP:	That's perfect, thank you Mr Harris.

INTERVIEW ENDS

With this fresh information, it was decided to visit the storage facility to discover if there were any leads on Hopkins, or on his apparent cache of materials. When arriving, BPD Agents asked about Hopkins and his use of the facility, but were turned away by the facility manager. Therefore, even after the assistance of local authorities, it was decided to perform a Smash Operation on the facility to further the investigation.

The BPD Technical Division were brought in to hack into the storage facilities files, and discover which storage belonged to Hopkins. To no surprise, the facilities files were not easily protected, and we discovered the following information.

The receipt has been transcribed in full as presented to us.

- Agent Petrovic, BPD

STORAGE RECEIPT

STORAGE 79:	Mr Dennis Hobpkins
PERIOD:	1 Month
ITEMS:	12 Medium-Size boxes
PAYMENT:	Pending
NOTES:	Mr Hopkins has agreed for us to hold the items as collateral while he acquires the funds to pay for the storage use. Mr Hopkins also offered a gold pendant as collateral in order to further facilitate this transaction. In all honesty, the guy seems like a kook, so we'll play it by ear for now.

A BPD Investigative Team led by Agent Strachan was sent to access the facility, and Operation Dunkelheit was performed on 15/03/01 at 2AM. BPD Technical Division cut all security to the facility, and Strachan's team were able to go in, access the storage facility, and leave with the contents without need for engagement.

In regards to the materials found, there were only 8 of the 12 boxes listed in the original file, with 1 of the boxes opened and half-empty. No personal materials belonging to Hopkins were found, and any further investigation in Hopkins has resulted in a dead end. It is assumed Hopkins learnt of BPD involvement, and has since gone off-radar.

The materials found were invaluable to BPD Officials, and those heading up investigation into P1983. They consisted of:

- *3 boxes of scrapbooks containing various news articles*
- *2 boxes of flyers & leaflets of assorted sizes and volume*
- *1 box of multimedia materials such as videotapes, cassette tapes, and floppy disks*
- *1 box of books, currently being catalogued*
- *1 box of various trinkets and jewellery, currently being investigated by the BPD Resources Division*

Items of interest will be added to the P1983 file as and when they are made available.

- Agent Petrovic, BPD

CONCLUSION

Operation Dunkelheit is considered a 2* success. While the amount of materials found were less than hoped, they are in excellent condition and give us a wealth of data on P1983 (Wilthaven) that help fill any gaps previous material has given us on the curious conditions within the P-Class itself.

The only other disappointment is the disappearance of Dennis Hopkins. BPD Surveillance Teams have scoured CCTV footage to track Hopkins last movements, but found that, other than a final sighting on 21/03/01, he has not been located. The following is a transcription of Hopkins's last seen movements on CCTV tape.

- Agent Petrovic, BPD

SECURITY CAMERA FOOTAGE

STORAGE FACILITY SECURITY CAMERA 3 –
21/03/01 4:00AM

Hopkins enters the facility and approaches his storage unit. He sees the unit has been emptied, and looks around in a panic. Hopkins runs out of the facility.

STORAGE FACILITY SECURITY CAMERA 2 – 21/03/01 4:02AM

Hopkins appears, stops, and looks around. He seems to slump in place, and walks toward a small alcove found between the storage units. This is the last sighting of Hopkins on all cameras.

```
    A search of the alcove found no remains, nor
anything to suggest Hopkins was there. He is being
treated as an Unknown Subject from now on.
    All materials found during Operation
Dunkelheit are being processed and added to the
P1983 file on a rolling basis, dependent of
authorisation from the relevant BPD Divisions.

                    -     Agent Petrovic, BPD
```

THE WILTHAVEN WAY

Found as part of the cache during Operation Dunkelheit, this flyer was kept in remarkably good condition due to preservation coverings that were applied. A handwritten note on the back of the booklet tells us that this document was from 1923, with a stamp noting that it was from the 'Wilthaven Public Library'.

Despite some degradation on some of the pages, most of the text material remained intact and is published in full herein.

- Agent Petrovic, BPD

Greetings! And welcome to the wonderful town of Wilthaven. It's a Hell of a town, as we folk say, and we hope you'll agree during your stay here. But before you take a wander through the town centre, and peek at our various market stalls or consume our many delicacies, you must first know one thing.

The Wilthaven Way

You see, being a gentleman - or indeed a lady - in Wilthaven isn't simply a matter of doffing your cap to your fellow passerby, nor making sure to use the right pleasantries when interacting with the townsfolk. No, being a resident in Wilthaven takes pluck, vigour, and a certain derring-do that most folk don't even think to have.

So, without further delay, we will outlay the many steps to acquire the Wilthaven Way in this pamphlet and hope, by the end, you will feel both learned and comfortable enough to be a proper Wilthaven resident.

1. *Know your place*

Wilthaven considers itself a progressive town, and therefore any rudeness or misbehaviour toward any other resident will result in some stern words coming toward you from the local authorities. Therefore, it is imperative to know your standing within the community, and learn to rise up the ranks both naturally and as pleasantly as possible. Any instances of ruffian-like behaviour will be dealt with quickly and sternly, with the worst offenders finding themselves outside after curfew, and you don't want that!

By questioning or showing defiance toward any local before you, you will set a precedent that your behaviour isn't to be tolerated, and this may result in your own demise. Please be aware that this is not a threat on behalf of the people, more a stark warning of the ailments that plague Wilthaven on a regular basis. Take heed, be humble, and ingratiate yourself into the community before attempting any acts that could be seen as impulsive or, worst, arrogant.

2. *Be welcoming*

One of the main things that places Wilthaven above all other towns in Cromshire is the welcoming atmosphere it presents. Every man and woman's home is their neighbour's, and vice versa. Never be against offering a night's dwelling to a friend or member of the community should they need it after curfew, as you could not just be offering someone a comfortable bed to sleep, but also be saving their life.

Each home is expected to have a guest room, and supplies that can last a period of no less than one (1) week, should a catastrophic event occur. As of writing, it has been a near decade since such a tragedy, but such timeframes can easily fool the unprepared. Better to be a ready paranoiac, than a naïve corpse.

This welcoming attitude will also find you in good stead should you find yourself far from home come sundown. By approaching a fellow Wilthaven resident, and explaining your situation, you too will be welcomed with open arms and a warm brandy to see the night through.

BE AWARE: At times, an afflicted individual will attempt entry into your property. These abominations tend to only make themselves known after sundown, so a refusal of entry is advised in this instance. Even the most frantic sort may be an abomination, so remember yourself to instantly find sanctuary once the town bell rings.

3. An inquisitive mind is a doomed one

The first thing you will note about Wilthaven is its peculiar atmosphere. Those interested in the reasons behind these happenings can research at the local library, for the breadth of information is too much to go through here! Suffice to say, Wilthaven has a rich history, and one you should definitely know.

However, such a thirst for information should be sated by books and not by actions. The person who ventures out to discover what is making the nocturnal noises, or who has taken their neighbour, will soon find themselves in a dire situation indeed. Proper authorities exist in Wilthaven to make sure these disturbances are fully investigated and resolved, and so any new member of the community would do well to look after their own family, rather than play the hero.

4. Have a firm gait

Now ladies, we understand that this sounds more like advice for the gentleman in your life, but such information may help you not only have more confidence in your step, but also recognise any wolves in your midst, as they say.

When walking, do so with a straight back and strong, steady stride. One should not shuffle nor meander when moving about Wilthaven, lest one be mistaken for an abomination. Step with strength in your heart, and joy in your demeanour, and the people of Wilthaven will respond in kind. Wilthaven is no place for the maudlin or afflicted – outside of the abominations – and so you should not act like one. After all, this is a happy town, so why not enjoy your stay?

5. *Join in!*

The last lesson in adopting the Wilthaven Way is a remarkably simple one: Simply join in! Don't be one of those folk who hide behind their curtains, and make quiet, curt conversation with venders and neighbours. Embrace your fellow Wilthaven resident, and enjoy the pleasure of their company. Who knows, you may not have it for long!

Town events are expected to be attended by all, not just for community spirit but to share ideas, the fruits of your labour, and hope. By connecting together as one community, we become stronger than the plague that taints the town. Those that hide away usually find themselves alone when they no longer wish to be, and this can result in dire consequences. If an invite is extended, do take it, and don't be afraid to throw the odd gathering or two. Wilthaven is a town for all, so don't be the individual who soon finds themselves alone at the wrong time!

And that should pretty much have you covered! Obviously, being a Wilthaven resident is more than a good walk and a welcoming abode, but these five (5) lessons should start you on the right track.

In fact, the only other item to address is that of the local greeting. You'll find that, instead of a simple goodbye, most residents will bless a departing party or conversationalist with 'Hail Hq'tar'. IT IS IMPERATIVE that you adopt this ideology also, lest you fall victim to lesson number three (3)!

By adopting these approaches, you will soon find yourself not only settled in Wilthaven, but not wanting to ever leave. After all, with a healthy mix of community spirit, plucky courage, and a warm bed wherever you turn, why would you? That, my friends, is:

The Wilthaven Way

Hail Hq'tar!

NEWSPAPER ARTICLE - 03/03/1975

Found as part of Operation Dunkelheit, this material shines a light on some very interesting developments from within Wilthaven itself. With the knowledge we already have regarding the Mayorship of Wilthaven, this newspaper article - found laminated and sealed within a box folder - is considered a high priority material in P1983 as not only does it give a social insight into the power structure within the town, but also the consequences if that structure is threatened in any way.

Key names within the document have been added to a reference file, with any corresponding materials to be noted in future.

Material has been transcribed in full, with no omissions.

- Agent Petrovic, BPD

MARCH MADNESS AT MAYOR MASSACRE

There were dark times at Wilthaven Town Hall today, not just due to the sudden passing of Mayor Robert Crest, but also the anarchy that spawned due to this

Robert Crest, who was tragically taken from us last Tuesday, was meant to be succeeded as per tradition by his young son, Grant Crest. However, there was a late challenge from local resident Winston Bowery. Mr Bowery, 42, believed that the town of Wilthaven had been under the thrall of the Crest's for too long, and led a campaign under the motto: "Let's Cut the Crest's Off the Wilthaven Loaf!"

Well, unfortunately, it seemed like the Crest's were an integral part of Wilthaven's structure, as the upon the results of the election, all Hell literally broke loose.

Bowery's campaign, helped along by his daughter Marjorie, began as a huge success; many Wilthaven residents were taken by Bowery's ease upon the microphone, noble promises to remove all grips of fear that had tormented the town since the beginning of the Crest's rule, and his proficiency with a guitar. Leading joyous sing-a-longs, spirited debates, and even a candlelight vigil after curfew that amazingly yielded 0 casualties, Bowery's cult of personality was proving to be very popular, especially compared to Grant Crest's own campaign.

Crest, 19, was the first to admit that he was ill prepared for the role of governing, but was spurred on by his mother and wife of Robert

Crest, Louisa. Running the campaign on behalf of her son, Louisa Crest simply leaned on the need for a Crest to lead, citing her great-great-great-grandfather-in-laws motto – and indeed the Crest family motto – "There Must Always Be A Crest".

Unfortunately, this was not deemed a strong enough platform, and in one particularly fiery debate, Marjorie Bowery decimated Louisa's singular campaign with the sort of chicanery befitting of a seasoned politician, or Lady Macbeth.

Once it came to the public vote, Bowery (Pictured above) arrived at the Town Hall full of confidence, while Grant Crest seemed distracted and, in the words of some residents, "too cocky by half". The results were read out by Head Councillor Milton Sand, and it was unanimous: Bowery was to be the new Mayor, by a margin of more than 23%.

It was then that things took a turn for the worst. Despite the curfew not being due for another 5 hours, the sky turned a shade of black never before seen, and seemed to split, revealing a crimson rain that hit with such venom, several elderly residents were knocked unconscious.

Reports vary – with this particular reporter suffering from a concussion in the early stages of the matter – but several witnesses say they saw many albino-like creatures burst onto the scene. Lisa Quirke told us that some of them "literally appeared out of nowhere, like they emerged from rips in space."

During the chaos, Winston Bowery tried to provoke calm in the face of ensuing panic, only to be struck dumb as a giant arm emerged from the ground, picked him up, and dragged him to an unknown location. His daughter, Marjorie, grief-stricken by her Father's abduction, tried in vain to dig the spot where he had gone, and was duly overwhelmed by the albino beasts.

In all, 78 residents – including the Bowery's – were slaughtered in the chaos, with all reported to be supporters of Bowery's campaign. The Crest family themselves were revealed to be unharmed – and unfazed – by the whole incident, with resident Henry Aaron saying he saw the mother & son "stand there without a care in the world, just watching as people died."

In the aftermath, Louisa Crest spoke to Head Councillor Sand, and it was universally agreed by all present to announce Grant Crest as the new Mayor of Wilthaven. Many lauded this new appointment, and Mayor Crest himself was noted as being "nonplussed" about the whole thing.

Once local cleaners sorted the mess, most residents filed back to their homes and looked forward to another wonderful reign under a Crest. Any survivors who voted for Bowery denied doing so, and claimed they'd never heard of him.

Reports that Winston Bowery has been seen in the Eternal Plains are still yet to be substantiated.

SAFETY DANCE

The following material was found as part of Operation Dunkelheit, stored between a number of files listing material still being reviewed by our Linguistics Division. Handwritten on basic lined paper and duly photocopied, the relevant department still has not been able to link the handwriting to any known individual within our database.

Our Historical Division has worked with the Culture Division in order to ascertain whether this 'Safety Dance' has any ritual link to any other events, sacrifices, or gatherings we have encountered before – both within P1983 and beyond. At time of writing, no link has been found.

Material is presented digitally below, transcribed in full from original material.

- Agent Petrovic, BPD

45th Annual Safety Dance!

Rook's Farm are honoured to present this years Safety Dance, a Wilthaven Tradition dating back to the days of our very own inaugural mayor, Charles Crest.

The Tri-Annual event will feature many exciting stands and competitions for all Wilthaven residents to take part in, including (but not limited to):

Miss Wilthaven, Fried Breads, Gutted Goat, Floral Displays, Whetstone Sharpening, Skeletal Identification for Kids, Fruits of the Forest, Make Your Own Doll, Dunk an Avatar, Best Costume, Bear Staring, Men With Hats, Linked Sausage, Flayed Countrymen, Devil's Eggs, Queen for the Day, Evening Isolation, Ham, Hoopla…

And, of course:

The Safety Dance itself!

Remember the fine traditions of the Safety Dance, everyone. Wear your best finery, arm yourself with firm devices & cudgels, and most of all, have fun!

See you there.

Wendell Wretch – Safety Dance Commissioner, 1994

THE DIARY OF CHESTER LAYMON

Found as part of Operation Dunkelheit, the following material consists of pages found scanned on a USB stick filed within an envelope marked PROOF #6. PROOF #1-#5 could not be found.

The pages was the only files on the memory device, and saved as a series of JPEG files that provided only minimal issues to our Technical Division. Due to issues with digital materials before, it has been ascertained that these materials were scanned within P0. The original materials are yet to be found.

Rather than recreate the files here, the contents have been transcribed and presented below where possible.

- Agent Petrovic, BPD

THE DIARY OF CHESTER LAYMON

ON SIGHTING, CURIOSITIES, AND OTHERS

ENTRY #1

Yes, dear reader, it is I, Chester Laymon - wordsmith extraordinaire and unofficial chronicler of all that is Wilthaven. At least, I wasn't.

Until now.

It is time someone took the proverbial bull by the horns, and jotted down exactly what the deuce is occurring in our quiet little town. For too long people have looked the other way, turned the other cheek, or generally been too dozy or ignorant to make note of the curiosities that exist here. If you were to speak to any member of Joe Public, they'd say we are no different that Quinton Valley down the road – just a typical, everyday sort of town with a few quirks.

Well let me tell you, vanishing people and evil demons are not quirks!

So, yes, it is time someone made a stand and put the truth out there… in words. That someone is me, and I'll be damned if I won't provide you – whomever reads this book – with anything less. This won't be a Howard Williams hack-job; this will be the real thing. With real words. And real truth.

"But Chester," you may ask, "why now? Why on this particular day?"

Like I said before, I will not lie, and I will fully confess that the reason for my prosaic rebellion is due to one thing, and one thing only.

The loss of a perfectly good view from my bedroom window.

Sure, you'd argue that a view is a mere slight on the larger skin of life, but where once was glistening fields and frolicking wildlife, now is a wall of ice, marked only by odd insects that scream at me when I try and catch them.

Quite frankly, it is bang not on.

In normal circumstances, you could complain to your local authority and have such issues resolved forthwith. However, while I do appreciate that one cannot move a whole mountain range, I do expect some degree of sympathy. Not a look out of their own – unobstructed – window with a shake of the head. No, I deserve real answers.

But real answers do not come to Wilthaven. Oh no. Not one man, woman, or whatever are under the thrall of Mayor Crest; the supposed "destined" leader to our fair town. As if destiny is a firm foundation to place a democracy on! No, Wilthaven isn't a democracy, it is a dictatorship.

And Crest isn't even the dictator.

If you believe everything you hear.

At this point, I would have to sign off with a quick "Hail Hq'tar", a sign of respect to our supposed benevolent "God" who terrorizes us and makes sure we all keep in line. Well balls to that, I say. Balls! I'm afraid of no supposed "God", no matter how much Crest demands we bend the knee and thank It. I no longer plan to be under this infernal cosh, and will instead be writing my own take on the madness that has befallen this otherwise quaint little town.

After all, who else is experienced but I? For as you may well know, I have walked into Wilthaven Woods and survived! Therefore, much like our dear Mayor, I can claim affinity to the darkness that swarms across the land.

I look forward to sharing these takes with you.

Sincerely, Chester Laymon.

ENTRY #14

Dear reader, my wits are at an end.

The sudden increase in activity at night is not only putting my nerves on edge, but ruining the ambience of our wonderful town of Wilthaven. Since my move a few weeks back – something Crest is still grumpy about, ha! – I have been subject to a campaign of incessant noise and constant aggravation.

Yes, I will confess that some of these feelings are born out of an insomniac mind, pocked by paranoia. But that doesn't excuse the fact that every night, without fail, I have to listen to a cacophony of noise that would drive even the sanest man insane.

It always begins with those damn "Avatars" - the stupid people who happened to be outside after curfew and, now, are under the command of "Hq'tar". Of course, my suggestion that it is all one big folie a deux, and that some simple sense be knocked into these people, went down like a lead balloon at the town meeting. Then again, the Avatars present were keen for me to join them after dark to attempt said sense-knocking.

But that is neither here nor there, because every night they are knocking on my door – or my windows! – and demanding I come out and inspect some bizarre incident. Whether it is finding my cat (I do not have a cat), someone breaking into my automobile (I do not own an automobile, my trusty bike will do, thank you very much), or even to offer me a light snack (suggesting I need to go on a diet, I tell you…).

Every night I get these damned folk outside my door, making one excuse after another to open up and come out.

And that isn't even the start!

After a good few hours of telling these bloody idiots that I am not interested and to go away, I am then subjected to the incessant howls and screeches of... well... I don't know what. I haven't cared to investigate. But it is almost constant and, dare I say, upsetting to my ears. No matter how much I complain, no matter how much I make a fuss, all I get from Crest and his cronies is to "invest in soundproofing".

Oh, of course. Mayor Crest's patented soundproofing methods. Why, I should have known. Make a tidy profit out of our pain, eh Crest? Continuing your family trait of opportunist charlatans, selling your snake oil to dumb-dumbs and sycophants.

Well, Chester Laymon is not so easily fooled. No matter how much you insist it goes back into the town, these funds always funnel back to the higher points of government, Crest, and I am determined to expose you for the rotter you are.

In the meantime, I shall try and get some sleep with some good old-fashioned blinds, and earplugs.

Sincerely, Chester Laymon.

ENTRY #22

It is with a great deal of aggravation that I write this latest entry, dear reader. For, you see, I am dealing with issues that, while familiar to most of the crazed residents of this town, I myself am not usually prone to.

In reality, the issue itself is so minor to potentially be obscure to the attention of many. But this does not mean it still does not prick like the thorn of the rose.

I digress. Allow me to start from the very beginning.

You may remember that a few entries ago, I spoke quite heartily of enjoying weekly games of chess with Bernice McCall. Bernie – as I called her – was a sweet woman who shared my love of in-depth conversation about local matters, and also had a fierce wit that allowed me some quite enthusiastic verbal jousting. I do not think I am being presumptuous, but I feel a deep bond was forming between the two of us that could have potentially led to romance down the line. Crazy, I know, that ol' Chester Laymon could be smitten. The stoic façade finally breaks, dear reader.

At least it could have done, had foolish things not occurred.

The series of events are hazy to me, I'm afraid. It was the fault of the wine that I had produced from the cellar, and allowed both of us to indulge in. Now, some may blame me for what followed, but Miss McCall had the option to leave when she requested. The sun was going down, and I was certain that another hour was still due. She only lived 5 minutes walk, and so my offer of one more game – and one more glass – was perfectly within reason.

Of course, by the time she left, a great pallor had stricken the Wilthaven sky, and night drew in a little quicker than normal.

Next thing I know, I'm being told off by the local officers. Something about endangering a resident. Quite ridiculous, I tell you.

Fortunately the charges never came to fruition. Like myself, Miss McCall was a lady bachelor with no close family, so no parties came forward to complain. Crest, naturally, wanted my head. But he would not get it, oh no. He would just have to watch while I walked away, head held high, knowing I did everything I could.

Besides, she turned up fit as a fiddle not three nights later.

She was now an "Avatar", but that meant nothing to me. All I saw was my good old friend, and witticism conjurer. All was right with the world, despite Crest's damned grumbles.

But all is not well, dear reader. All is very unwell, in fact. Yes, Miss McCall is eager to resume our activities – and is even showing a more aggressive stance toward some form of courtship. However, her insistence that we take moonlit walks and embrace that fantastical stooge "Hq'tar" has sullied any enjoyment I had out of her company.

Now, I am vexed by what these "Avatars" really are: pale imitations of the person before, obsessed with getting you into their "Hq'tar" nonsense. Well, quite frankly I do not have time for such playtimes, and will discontinue my friendship with Miss McCall.

This is a shame, as friendship is rare for a man of my years. Not to mention one who has a reputation such as mine.

Oh well. Onward we go.

Sincerely, Chester Laymon.

ENTRY #42

Dear reader, these are trying times.

I'm not the young firebrand I once was. Since the events so many years ago, my will has been chipped away at an incredible rate. My lust for life is eroded one day at a time, and I fear that I will die a miserable, lonely soul.

In the meantime, I have this diary to keep me motivated. And motivate me it shall.

The events I described in my last entry have come to pass. That tragic group, left in such a terrible situation not of their own choosing, has now been found. Well, most of them, anyway. What hasn't has been put aside as mere, "collateral damage", to use the official wording, and everything else is being assembled as much as possible to provide closure to the families involved.

I will confess, that given my own experience, I maybe should have said something. I should have told of my recurring nightmares from the years when I was bedbound and lost within my own self. I should have recounted the fractured memories of my own group jaunt within the woods, and what terrors still lurk deep within my waters today.

I did not. I remained silent – much like I imagine Mayor Crest does – and instead bore witness to these tragic events.

This... this is a warning.

The monsters still prowl at night, scratching at windows and calling forth a chorus that disgusts me in my bed. Before, they were a hindrance. Now, they are a real terror. I begged Mayor Crest to grant me something to help ease my fears, but he just looked solemn and gave me the same advice he gives all who visit his office.

"Maintain."

But maintain what? Maintain this shared madness? Subscribe to a so-called God who now punishes us for some perceived slight? Are the tears of parents, lovers, and friends not enough for it? Does it really need to demand flesh? Does it need to construct terrible games in order to feed its sick desires?

Oh, so many questions. So many doubts. I miss the days when my mind was a steel box, shrouded by any negativity. Before it was broken open by vile hands. Maybe it is age that has rusted its hinges, weakening my resolve.

Not all of it, of course. I will maintain, as the Mayor advises, but I will not change who I am. I will not amend my views just to placate some bizarre ritual. Dark thoughts swirl throughout the day in Wilthaven. This is par for the course for the month of Zephiber, but they have increased parallel to the amount of loss we have suffered.

The Avatars stare at my window, sometimes. I used to shout at them to go away. Now I simply draw the curtains.

Life was so much simpler when I was younger.

So simple.

Sincerely, Chester Laymon.

ENTRY #71

Dear reader, I cannot resist the call of home no longer. Instead, I believe.

This is not some flippant comment. This is truth. I am an old man now, so close to death we seem to converse with each other every night. But little did I know that Death was to take a form that I had denied for so long.

It came to me. He came to me, me! A withered body trying to support a firm mind.

He came to me, and he told me.

Everything.

Everything I have tried to deny from that very first day. From the moment I stepped out of Wilthaven Woods, ravished and rotten and with a black stare hiding the chaos under the skin.

The monsters are his children. The Avatars? His followers. His chosen brethren. His elite.

His *true* believers.

Simply saying his name is not enough. Simply following his rules a mere pitiful attempt to placate. He demands more. He demands complete servitude.

And once this is written, he shall have it from me.

My doors are unlocked, my windows open. With the last ounce of strength my body will allow, I will greet the Avatars and walk with them into the starry night.

Into his full embrace, once again.

You may ask what He looks like, and I cannot tell. I cannot spoil the wonder that is He.

Hope that you will have the revelation that I have had, before your life is no more.

Hail Hq'tar!

Hail Hq'tar!

Hail Hq'tar!

Sincerely, the late Chester Laymon.

WILTHAVEN CHURCH

Found as part of Operation Dunkelheit, the following material consists of pages found in a sealed box. The material itself was in a state of great decay, not helped by the fact that many pages were either burnt to a cinder, or suffered so much damage the content was no longer legible. However, it seems whoever was collating these items managed to save the pages that make up this entry.

The material has been transcribed where possible, with any omissions due to elemental damage. Please note, that Page numbers do not represent the material, but the order our Linguistics Division believe it falls in.

- Agent Petrovic, BPD

PAGE 1

Wilthaven Church – A History

By
Georg…

PAGE 2

…urch finally began construction in 1845, where under the supervision of Sebastian Grimes, a foundation was built on grounds belonging to Alistair Phelps. Mr Phelps was a majority landowner in the village, second only to the Edison family, who were linked to the Gough Royal Family. The land, sitting between Oak Meadows and Lilac Walk, would provide easy access for all villagers, and also present a safe-haven from events that had occurred at the time. Of course, knowing wh…

PAGE 4

…nd without a doubt, Timothy Walters was a fine choice for the first Wilthaven Pastor. Born in the village in 1820, Pastor Walters was a growing intellectual who studied hard throughout his youth, and developed a strong belief in the Christian faith that would guide him toward his path. Wilthaven would be his first – and only – placement as a man of the cloth, which was to his pleasure. Pastor Walters loved Wilthaven and its people, and wanted to bring about a new sense of peace and hope to those that may have previously lost it. He would preach in Village Square, saying words of such positivity that people fell in spiritual love with him. They believed his message of joy and hope, and helped begin a renaissance toward faith in Wilthaven.

But to simply believe Pastor Walters was a mere man of God would be to belittle his other accomplishments. He was a physically fit individual, who was on record as setting several records in walking & running at the annual Wilthaven Harvest Festival. He would often be found in the morning, taking his daily swim across the lake near farmland, and was always eager to indulge the physical pursuits of Wilthaven residents.

Of course, with his position came the questions that would always come. One resident, whose name would soon become synonymous with Wilthaven, often clashed with Pastor Walters. He would challenge him on theology, and the ideas of what God actually was, or represented.

His name, of course, wa…

PAGE 7

…n open standard to listen to what Mayor Crest would have to say. Much complaint was made that by embracing the laws of Hq'tar, it would sully the very nature of having a church at all. And if one was to amend the needs of the Church to fit with the lore that Mayor Crest advised upon, then this would be a heresy that would damn them all anyway.

Mayor Crest, in his eternal wisdom, recognised this issue, and therefore it was with strong voice that he demanded Wilthaven Church remain – as much a symbol of hope and innocence, than a mockery of the dark forces that blighted the emerging town.

Change did indeed come, but in a steady, almost mundane way. No new Pastor came to preach the word of God. Instead, a revolving series of volunteers were arranged to keep the Church in good condition, and see to it that any visitors are kept from harm or stern words. In terms of the structure, Mayor Crest spoke to the many handymen who resided within Wilthaven, and advised them that special funds would be available should the need arise. True, there was much fear from these workers that by looking after the Church, they would tempt the wrath of Hq'tar, but the value of Mayor Crest's funding was too good to turn down.

Mayor Crest admitted in private, to his wife Victoria, that he knew the Church had no real power over the forces taking over Wilthaven, but he hoped that as a symbol, it wo…

PAGE 12

...ody time. It was noted in the local newspaper that Mayor Crest felt great pain by what had happened, and while denouncing it in public and preached a message of strength, internally he was torn apart. Some confide that this is what led to the torch passing to his only son, Gregory, who many believed was ready to take on the burden itself. Indeed, when the carnage finally reached a crescendo, it was Gregory Crest who stepped forward and led officers to siege the Church and recover what they could. His actions, while heroic, did leave scars upon Gregory – both physical and mental. Once he took charge of Wilthaven, he did not share the same compassion his father did, and so the Church remained in the state it had suffered during the damned ritual.

Now that Mayor Crest had changed from Charles to Gregory, and the Church was deemed to be "tainted stock", there was not much more to be said about the building. Wilthaven Church remained stained with the blood of innocent children, and the terrible memories it provoked – with rotten beams and broken stone littering the ground around it. Since the geological change as well, the foundation had taken some beating, with some areas of the Church collapsing into the ground below. Wilthaven Church stood as a broken horse waiting to be put down, until one resident took the initiative and challenged Mayor Crest to restore it.

That resident – Victor Fenton – was known locally as a successful trader who had not only managed to settle a foot in Wilthaven business, but had also began doing so to other nearby towns & villages. It was with his substantial funds that Wilthaven Church was to be given a second change.

As long as Mayor Crest would agree.

It took nearly 3 years, and countless stern words, before Mayor Crest wiped his hands of Wilthaven Church and signed over the deeds to Mr Fenton. From that moment, there was a strange sense of antici…

PAGE 15

It was first reported by Cynthia Marigold - who was known for perusing the various tombstones and crypts that Wilthaven Church had to offer… …inging it to the attention of Mayor Crest and his assistant George Connor. Upon arrival to the Church – along with Chief Constable Samuel Wayne – the trio inspected the pit that used to house the dead of Wilthaven, and a slab of concrete that painted its bottom. This concrete would eventually be discovered to be located primarily in the empty graveyard itself, and at least 10 feet deep.

It was indeed a strange turn of events, and many residents at the time were confused how such an event could have happened. It seemed a physical impossibility that the hundreds of graves and tombs that were housed within the cemetery could disappear so easily, and so cleanly.

Of course, its return would be equally as amazing.

Upon venturing into the pit and looking for any evidence for what could have caused several tonnes of land to vanish, Mayor Crest, Mr Connor, Chief Constable Wayne and Pastor Michaels looked over every inch of the area and came up with no answers. However, when Mayor Crest and Chief Constable Wayne climbed out, the most extraordinary thing occurred.

No physical evidence was taken to prove that the absurd happened, only the hysterics from witnesses who saw it. Once Mayor Crest was out, there was a rumble of thunder across Wilthaven, and residents could look up and see a giant land mass collapse out of the sky, above the pit itself.

Unfortunately, Mr Connor and Pastor Michaels did not leave in time, and thus were crushed by a vertical landslide of dirt, stone, bones and assorted waste. Any attempts to excavate the land to find their bodies was unsuccessful, and the scenario was chalked down by Mayor Crest as another "show of Hq'tar".

Nat…

PAGE 42

…pation for the event was high, as at the time the residents of Wilthaven had suffered a lot of terrible events that left town morale low. However, Wilthaven Church was once again turning into a beacon of light puncturing a grey mist that hung over the town. As the day of the wedding approached, the Church burst more and more into life and colour, and those that remember that day say it was one of the brightest in Wilthaven history.

Under the guidance of Pastor Orville, Mayor Grant Crest and his new wife, Beverley, made their vows to each other. The sun shone that day, illuminating them both in a hearty glow that gave colour via the stained glass windows that flanked the Church walls. Songs were sung praising the Lord, and many prayers were made. However, while some were directed toward the traditional Christian God, there were of course many directed toward Hq'tar. This was the point that Wilthaven Church found that to survive in modern times, it would have to incorporate a bit of overlap with Hq'tar, in order not to suffer any further wrath. Mayor Crest understood the discomfort this gave many, but equated it to loving a Mother & Father equally.

Even today, you can find a marker dating the Grant & Beverley Crest's wedding in the East-facing wall of the Church. As the first Crest to be wedded there, the date now has vast significance, and will be reme…

PAGE 57

... upon finding it, several Wilthaven residents were intrigued by what, exactly, it was. Of course, the most obvious thing was it was a canister, but the question was what it contained, and where it came from.

By now, it was considered the norm for strange things such as this to occur in not only the town, but the Church itself. Many times the Avatars made their presence known outside the Church, but never did they enter. The only occasion recorded where an Avatar was brought into the Church resulted in severe injuries to all parties involved.

Therefore, it was decided that the canister could not have been placed by them, nor the other curiosities that stalked the town at night in Hq'tar's name. While Pastor Orville was perplexed by the vessels arrival, he is recorded as confiding in Mayor Crest a great unease regarding it. Because of this, Pastor Orville was sent to another parish, and the Church was once again temporarily placed under the hold of Wilthaven Council.

Any attempts to remove the canister resulted in strange preventions occurring. One resident – Harold Cousins – found himself deluged by a plague of rats when trying to cross the Church's threshold with the canister. Another – Valerie Engelton – was assaulted by a group of homeless vagrants who had not been seen before and – according to census records – had never been seen since.

Therefore, it was decided by Mayor Crest to keep the canister within the Church itself, and study it to see what it was, and what it contained. It was only the intervention of a traveller by the name of Wong who prevented the unfortunate occurring. Wong – never known by any other name, nor any other name listed since of the census – informed Mayor Crest that the canister contained some sort of ancient evil, and that to open it would unleash Hell upon Wilthaven, and the whole planet.

Of course, given the town's situation under Hq'tar, this wasn't the threat it first appeared. In fact, by keeping the canister shut, horrific events could have indeed unfolded further. Instead, Eric Anders eventually opened the canister, and confirmed that the liquid that was flowing inside was nothing more than a lime-based carbonated drink.

Wong admitted his error, but was still duly welcomed to Wilthaven. As for the canister, s…

PAGE 103

..o the fact it was the 150th Anniversary of the Church, and the events that unfolded, it was decided that whoever Atticus Plinth (pictured below – photo courtesy of Kerry Smith who was documenting the event with her disposable camera) was, he was something quite unlike anyone had seen within the Church, and signalled that perhaps it was no longer the sanctuary that many believed it was.

PAGE 119

Note: Due to circumstances related to the events on the 6th of June 1985, any further additions to this book are to be directed to Mayor Crest's office. Due to the fact that several pages depict events yet to occur, Wilthaven Council should be made aware to help prevent the disasters that occur.

Thank you, and hail Hq'tar.

- Kirstin Fox, assistant to Mayor's Offi…

TV REPORT 2

The following transcription comes from footage received as part of the cache in Operation Dunkelheit. According to records salvaged from that Operation, Subject A in footage - "Sophie Collins" - was not seen again afterwards. Subject B has been assigned as a Subject of Interest relating to P1983, as per BPD procedures.

Transcription is in full, with no information omitted for research purposes. Additional records are currently undergoing study by BPD Analytics Division. Unfortunately, any attempt to garner screenshots from the below material have yet to be successful, but the BPD Technical Division continue their efforts.

- Agent Petrovic, (BPD)

FADE IN:	MCU of SOPHIE COLLINS sitting behind a desk with the WPN logo behind her. She is a young woman, approx. early 30s, dressed in a powder blue suit with cropped brown hair and glasses. She is seated in a position that makes her face slightly to her left.
SOPHIE COLLINS:	Good evening. Tonight, we take a look into the phenomenon that has been plaguing

Wilthaven for… well… for a long time now. A phenomenon passed down from our parents, from their parents, and beyond. I talk of course of…

SCREEN GOES TO STATIC FOR 2 SECONDS

SC: Joining me to talk about these phenomena and more, is Professor Lazlow Nitko.

CUT TO: MCU of PROFESSOR LAZLOW NITKO, equally within his early-to-mid-30s, with short blonde hair and dressed in casual clothing. He is smiling as he faces slightly to his right.

(BPD NOTE: For the purposes of this transcription, be aware that any time Collins or Professor Nitko are speaking, the camera has cut to them.)

SC: Professor Nitko, good evening.

LAZLOW NITKO: Good evening, Sophie.

SC: Now, Professor, you're fully aware of the events that are occurring, and indeed have been occurring, in Wilthaven for a long time, yes?

LN: That is correct.

SC: You even wrote a thesis on them, called Whispers in the Night: Wilthaven & its History.

LN: (Chuckles) That is also correct.

SC: Can you expand on this?

LN: On the thesis?

SC: Yes.

LN: Of course. I simply looked at, what you call, the phenomena that Wilthaven seems to attract; that being the strangeness of its nights, and various other occurrences that one would label, perhaps, peculiar.

SC: Such as?

LN: Well, the electrical shortages, for one. Um… the sightings in the nearby forested areas…

SC: The disappearances.

LN: (Smiles) Of course, the disappearances.

SC: And what did you find in those particular instances?

LN: In the disappearances?

SC:	Yes.
LN:	Not much. (Chuckles)
SC:	You think they're amusing?
LN:	I think finding nothing on missing people is amusing wordplay, yes.

STATIC FOR 3 SECONDS

LN:	… not an investigator.
SC:	OK… but in your findings in your thesis?
LN:	Well, I see an almost… shared psychosis, if you will, across the town itself. Mass hysteria, much like one has seen in places like Chistingham in the 50s and Beauriat in the last decade.

(BPD NOTE: According to the BPD Geographical Division, these places do not exist, lest have recorded instances of Mass Hysteria)

SC:	So you believe this is just, as you say, Mass Hysteria.
LN	Of course.
SC:	Despite the evidence to the contrary?

LN:	Which evidence do you mean?
SC:	Well…

STATIC FOR 18 SECONDS

SC:	…versations with Ellie. Tell me about that.
LN:	Well, in working on Whispers in the Night, I came across the interesting character of Ellie Bay, a very troubled individual. We had a series of interviews – with the consent of her parents – to look into the psychological issues that plagued her.
SC:	Psychological issues that were related to previous incidents referenced in your thesis?
LN:	If you're referring to the 'animal-like noises' and 'disappearances' then, yes, those issues.
SC:	And what did you find?
LN:	Well I'm sure you've read the book.
SC:	(Smiling) For the purposes of those that haven't.
LN:	Very well. I found Miss Bay was suffering greatly from a number of psychological delusions, everything from auditory

	hallucinations to extensive bouts of schizophrenia.
SC:	That manifested how?
LN:	The hallucinations or schizophrenia?
SC:	Both.
LN:	(Chuckles) Well, the hallucinations were, as you previously mentioned, connected to the noises that took place at night. As we both know, this is a common complaint in Wilthaven, and in the case of Miss Bay it was in the form of voices that would speak to her from her bedroom window.
SC:	What would they say?
LN:	If I recall correctly, Miss Bay believed she heard people chanting, and beckoning her in some fashion. Sometimes using a tongue she was not familiar with, or that was, shall we say, inappropriate for a girl of her age.
SC:	How old was Ellie?
LN:	I don't recall.
SC:	It says in my notes here that she was 14?

LN: Certainly poss…

STATIC FOR 8 SECONDS

SC: … were monsters?

LN: (Chuckles) Now, Miss Collins, don't put words into my mouth. Miss Bay simply recounted them as 'monsters'. In my analysis, I found them to purely be extensions of a deeply troubled mind.

SC: So you don't think…

STATIC FOR 17 SECONDS

SC IS SAT THERE, LOOKING ABOUT THE STUDIO. THE LIGHTING HAS DIMMED CONSIDERABLY AND SHE LOOKS CONCERNED

SC: Err… apologies there. We seem to have had a slight technical hitch.

LN SITS THERE, SMILING AND LOOKING INTO CAMERA

SC: Let's… let's just move on. Your most recent paper, an article in the Wilthaven Chronicle, delves into another psychological aspect that you believe is a symptom of this, 'Mass Hysteria'.

LN NODS

SC: I talk of course of the time when you spoke about how some residents suffer from Multiple Personality Disorder.

LN NODS AGAIN. HE LOOKS DISTRACTED

SC LOOKS AROUND THE STUDIO SUDDENLY

SC: W… Would you care to expand on that

STATIC FOR 5 SECONDS

LN: That about sums it up.

SC: You don't wish to…

SC REACTS TO SOMETHING OFF CAMERA

LN CONTINUES TO EXCHANGE LOOKS BETWEEN THE CAMERA AND AT SC

STATIC FOR 6 SECONDS

SC: …tential paranormal phenomena?

LN: Your words, not mine.

SC: A curse that has haunted this town for hundreds of years.

LN: (Laughs loudly, shaking his head) Again, a symptom of a Mass Hysteria that…

SC: Professor Nitko, I don't believe you're taking this seriously.

LN SITS THERE SMILING

STATIC FOR 4 SECONDS

SC PRESSES HER FINGER TO HER EAR TO LISTEN, REMAINS DOING SO FOR 3 SECONDS

SC: Um… it seems like I've lost contact with the Production Team for the moment.

LN IS SMILING AND LOOKING OFF CAMERA

SCREEN GOES TO STATIC FOR 18 SECONDS

SC: OK we've managed to get someone on the line. You're through to the show, what's your question.

CALLER: Well, Sophie, my question has not much to do with what's happening in Wilthaven, rather Professor Nitko himself.

LN IS NOW LOOKING INTO THE CAMERA

SC: OK, which is?

C: Well, you've talked about his papers and his work on Wilthaven, and, well, I like to read up on this sort of stuff so I tried looking for it.

SC: OK, and how did you find Professor Nitko's work?

C: Well that's the thing, Sophie, I didn't.

SC: I'm sorry.

LN STARES INTO THE CAMERA

C: I didn't find anything. No Whispers, no Conversations with Ellie, not even the article you mentioned. What date was it?

SC SHUFFLES HER PAPERS

SC: Um… well I don't have a date here…

C: Either way, Sophie, there ain't no mention of Professor Nitko anywhere. In fact, I couldn't find him in any paper, article, journal or…

STATIC FOR 8 SECONDS

SC: … you like to comment on that, Professor?

LN: Comment on what?

SC JUMPS AND LOOKS OFF CAMERA.

SC: Err… our c… caller's claims that you… (coughs) Don't exist.

LN SMILES, LOOKS OFF CAMERA

SC: Professor?

LN: You should sign off now, Sophie.

STATIC OVERLAY OVER SCREEN FOR REMAINDER OF FOOTAGE

SC: Professor Nitko, what's going on here?

LN: Sign off, Sophie.

SC PRESSES AGAINST HER EAR, LOOKS OUT PAST THE CAMERA

SC: Hello?

LN: Seriously, you'll want to sign off.

SC STANDS UP, LOOKING AROUND

SC: Hello? Frank? Clive?

LN LOOKS PAST THE CAMERA, SMILING

FAINT NOISES ARE AUDIBLE OFF CAMERA

(BPD Note: The BPD Technical Division could not ascertain the source of these noises, only noting that they were "animal-like" in nature.)

SC: Anyone?

LN: They don't want to see what's about to happen.

SC LOOKS AT LN. LN SMILES INTO THE CAMERA AND WINKS

NOISES BECOME LOUDER

SC LOOKS OFF CAMERA AND WIDENS HER EYES, HER MOUTH OPENING

STATIC FOR 18 SECONDS

FOOTAGE ENDS

POLICE REPORT - 14/09/1998

Discovered as part of the cache of materials found during Operation Dunkelheit, the following Police Reports have been highlighted due to their relation to other materials found and their relative interest toward P1983.

Due to the issues that occurred with the archived materials we discovered under Agent Marriot (~~DECEASED~~ MISSING), these two main Reports have been transcribed and digitised as a matter of priority, while other minor materials are currently under the strict supervision of our Digital Division.

Material has been transcribed with no omissions. Unfortunately, any additional material referred to herein has not yet been found.

- Agent Petrovic, BPD

WILTHAVEN POLICE

INCIDENT REPORT #201105051

REPORT ENTERED: 14-09-1998

REPORTING OFFICER: PC MATTHEW HUGHES

APPROVING OFFICER: CHIEF CONSTABLE JANE CARTER

INCIDENT TYPE: PROPERTY DAMAGE

LOCATION: ARKANA ROAD

PERSONS INVOLVED: STANLEY FARADAY

OFFENDERS: GARETH HAYNES, STELLA CHERRY, CRAIG AARON

NARRATIVE: ON 13/9/98 AT 14:86PM, OFFICERS PC MATTHEW HUGHES AND PC MIKA STANE WERE CALLED TO A PROPERTY BELONGING TO STANLEY FARADAY ON ARKANA ROAD. MR FARADAY COMPLAINED THAT A NUMBER OF VANDALISM INCIDENTS HAD TAKEN PLACE OVER HIS BUILDING – NAMED HOLLOWAY HOUSE – INCLUDING SMASHED WINDOWS, BROKEN MASONRY, BURN MARKS APPEARING ON INTERNAL WALLS, AND SEVERAL HOLES APPEARING IN THE REAR GARDEN. MR FARADAY ADVISED OFFICERS THAT THESE INCIDENTS HAD INCREASED IN VOLUME IN THE LAST 24 HOURS, AND WISHED FOR PC HUGHES & PC STANE TO INVESTIGATE FURTHER. BEFORE THE OFFICERS COULD ENTER THE PROPERTY, A SIDE WALL TO THE BUILDING COLLAPSED AND 3 INDIVIDUALS APPEARED FROM WITHIN THE BUILDING IN A DISHEVELLED STATE. THESE

INDIVIDUALS WERE IDENTIFIED AS: GARETH HAYNES, STELLA CHERRY, AND CRAIG AARON.

ALL 3, WITH THE ADDITION OF THOMAS WYATT, SANDRA YEOMAN AND ROBERT JOHNSON, WERE REPORTED MISSING ON 04/02/1993 (SEE REPORT #926082017) AND PRESUMED DECEASED. WHEN MR HAYNES, MISS CHERRY, AND MR AARON SAW PC HUGHES & PC STANE, THEY RUSHED TO THEM AND SEEMED IN A STATE OF INTENSE HYSTERIA. MR FARADAY INSTANTLY ADVISED THAT HE WAS WILLING TO PRESS CHARGES, AND THE 3 PERPETRATORS WERE TAKEN INTO CUSTODY.

UPON INTERVIEWS WITH PERPETRATORS (SEE ATTACHED DOCUMENTS), IT WAS CONFIRMED THAT MR WYATT, MISS YEOMAN, AND MR JOHNSON WERE INDEED DECEASED. HOWEVER, WHEN AN INSPECTION WAS SUGGESTED BY PC STANE, MR HAYNES INSISTED THAT THEY DO NOT ENTER THE PROPERTY, ADVISING THAT IT WAS IMPOSSIBLE TO LEAVE. IN MISS CHERRY'S INTERVIEW, SHE ADVISED THAT THE DAMAGE TO THE PROPERTY WAS DUE TO THEIR ATTEMPTS OVER THE PAST 5 YEARS TO ESCAPE.

MR FARADAY HAS ADVISED HE STILL WISHES TO PRESS CHARGES AGAINST

THE 3 PERPETRATORS AND THE FAMILIES OF THE 3 DECEASED MEMBERS OF THEIR PARTY.
CASE HAS BEEN PASSED TO MAYOR CREST FOR A FINAL DECISION ON THE MATTER.

POLICE REPORT – 23/08/2000

See above note for further details.
Material has been transcribed without omissions. Unfortunately, any additional materials referred to herein have yet to be found.

- Agent Petrovic, BPD

WILTHAVEN POLICE

INCIDENT REPORT #301727089

REPORT ENTERED: 23/08/2000

REPORTING OFFICER: PC WES KEEN

APPROVING OFFICER: CHIEF CONSTABLE JANE CARTER

INCIDENT TYPE: TRESPASSING

LOCATION: WILTHAVEN RADIO STATION, COURTYARD

PERSONS INVOLVED: PAUL HAVEN

OFFENDERS: OLLIE COLE

NARRATIVE: AT 18:59PM ON 22/08/2000, OFFICER PC WES KEEN WAS CALLED UPON TO

INVESTIGATE A BREAK-IN AT THE OFFICES OF WILTHAVEN RADIO STATION BY RESIDENT DISC JOCKEY, PAUL HAVEN. MR HAVEN ADVISED THAT HE HAD ARRIVED TO PERFORM HIS NIGHT-SHIFT SHOW AND FOUND THAT THE LOCK ON THE DOOR HAD BEEN BROKEN INTO. UPON INVESTIGATING THE INTERIOR OF THE BUILDING, PC KEEN CAME ACROSS OLLIE COLE – REPORTED MISSING ON 03/10/1999. COLE DID NOT RESPOND TO QUESTIONING ON LOCATION, BUT DID RESPOND TO MR HAVEN WHEN ASKED IF COULD HELP. MR COLE ADVISED HE WAS HERE DUE TO A "SECURITY RISK", AND WISHED TO PROVIDE ASSISTANCE TO MR HAVEN.

DESPITE THE INSISTENCE THAT PC KEEN TAKE MR COLE IN FOR QUESTIONING – ESPECIALLY IN LIGHT OF HIS DISAPPEARANCE AND STATUS AS AN AVATAR – MR HAVEN REFUSED TO PRESS CHARGES AND INSTEAD CALLED FOR A LOCAL LOCKSMITH – LATER REVEALED TO BE LISA MERRYWEATHER – TO COME FIX THE DOOR BEFORE CURFEW. IN ADDITION, MR HAVEN WAS HAPPY TO KEEP MR COLE INSIDE THE STATION WITH HIM, AND PC KEEN REPORTED THAT BOTH PARTIES AGREED TO PERFORM AN INTERVIEW LATER THAT NIGHT.

PC KEEN RETURNED TO THEIR HOME BEFORE CURFEW AND RANG IN A REPORT TO BE FILED BY THEMESLVES THE NEXT DAY TO THE WILTHAVEN POLICE NIGHT SHIFT.

MAYOR CREST HAS BEEN NOTIFIED, AS WELL AS AVATAR CHRONICLER GERARD BAIRD.

RADIO REPORT 2

Found as part of the cache of Operation Dunkelheit, this recording was found on cassette tape along with POLICE REPORT - 23/08/2000. Labelled 'AVATAR INTERVIEW', the recording has been analysed by our Audio Department and fully transcribed.

All connections to Subjects mentioned in previous material are to be filed and referenced accordingly.

- Agent Petrovic, (BPD)

"Good evening, and welcome to another night with me, Pete Haven. I hope you're having an OK one so far. Remember, folks – lock your doors, close your windows, and keep those curtains drawn. No need to be tempted tonight.

Talking of temptation, tonight I have a rather special guest in the studio with me. You may remember listed on our Missing Persons one Ollie Cole, who was last seen near the Plains on 3rd October, 1999. Well, Ollie is back, and decided to come pay me a little visit. Say hello to the listeners, Ollie.

(Silence for 4 seconds)

Don't be shy, now. They won't bite. Heh.

(Silence for 2 seconds)

Hello, listeners?

There we go. Feel better for talking?

(Silence for 3 seconds)

Dead air isn't great for me, Ollie. Gotta keep that talk flowing.

Indeed. How about we continue this discussion in my vehicle outside?

Ha. Nice try, Ollie, but we're not leaving the studio tonight.

I believe it would be prudent to go to my vehicle.

Well, Ollie, the sun's down and I don't fancy my chances.

Do not worry, Peter Haven, I will make sure you come to no harm.

I bet you will… well, for now, let me ask you a few questions, sound good?

And then we shall depart for my vehicle, correct?

You got a deal.

Excellent. Then please ask your questions.

Let's start with the obvious, Ollie. Where you been the last 10 months?

(Silence for 4 seconds)

Like I said, Ollie, you've got to keep talking on Radio. People can't see you.

I can see them.

Of course you can, Ollie. Now, where were you?

I appear to have gotten lost among the nearby fields. This was quite troublesome for me, but I am glad to be home now. Perhaps you'd like to come to my lodgings and discuss this more.

Would this mean going to your car?

You wish to go to my car? Well then, we can leave now…

Ollie, sit down. I haven't finished.

(Sound of shuffling heard faintly)

So, you were lost on the Plains, correct?

This is correct, Peter Haven.

For 10 months?

That is correct.

How did you survive?

(Silence for 4 seconds)

OK, let me put it this way. What did you do in those 10 months?

(Silence for 4 seconds)

Ollie, you ain't much for answering questions, are you?

> I apologise, Peter Haven. How about we open the door and get some fresh air. Maybe I will be more receptive then.

How about we keep it closed. Don't know what is out there this time of night.

> I do, Peter Haven.

I know you do, Ollie. I know you do. So let me ask you this instead… tell me about Hq'tar.

> Hq'tar is the great and powerful one. The one to save us from ourselves. The one who will bring order amongst the chaos. He is the one who wishes to embrace us in the bosom of his wonder, and never let us come to harm. Without Hq'tar, life is merely death. Hq'tar gives us everlasting peace and life. Therefore, we should love him, give ourselves to him. Perhaps you would like to do so now?

(Haven laughs)

I still have questions, Ollie. Remember, you said you'd answer them and then I'd come with you?

> I believe you have asked enough questions, Peter Haven.

When were you taken by Hq'tar? Or was it one of his minions?

        I gave myself to Hq'tar. He loves me as I love him.

Was it one of those freaky long-legged albinos?

Hq'tar's children are merely that, Peter Haven, children. They cause no pain to you or I.

Maybe not you, but I'd argue the former.

        We should discuss this outside.

So you can take me to love Hq'tar too?

        You wish to give yourself to Hq'tar? How delightful, Peter Haven. Together we shall meet with him and enter his celestial embrace. Hail Hq'tar.

What if I don't?

        Hail Hq'tar!

Answer me, Ollie. What if I don't want to be embraced by Hq'tar?

        Hail Hq'tar! Hail Hq'tar!

You're a stuck record, Ollie. You want to leave?

Hail… yes. Let us open the door. Let us go meet with my brothers and sisters. Let us go to Hq'tar and be one with his love.

(Silence for 2 seconds)

That's not gonna happen, Ollie. First a few more questions…

(Glass smashing is heard in the distant)

One of your friends?

> You deny Hq'tar. This is displeasing, Peter Haven.

Yeah, well, I aim to displease.

(More sounds of glass smashing. Another unknown noise is heard)

Ollie, let's talk more about Hq'tar…

> Hail Hq'tar.

You say that. Why should we?

(The sound of metal bending is heard faintly)

Your friends are persistent, I'll give them that.

> Hail Hq'tar!

Folks, so you know, Ollie here is… drooling, something, from his mouth and nose. You sure ain't pretty right now, Ollie.

> Hail Hq'tar!

(Loud clashing against metal is heard)

You also ain't going anywhere. That's reinforced steel your buddies are trying to break. Tough enough to keep Wilthaven safe for the last few decades.

(A loud click is heard)

And as for you, well, we got a lot more questions after this lovely little song by Elsie Carlisle. Pretty Days. I'm sure you'll enjoy it, Ollie.

Hail Hq'tar.

You're damn right."

(The sound of metal creaking slows, as an intro for a slow Jazz song starts to play)

TAPE ENDS

WILTHAVEN WALKS

Found as part of Operation Dunkelheit, this leaflet was in pristine condition with only a plastic pocket folder as protection. Every other document in the same box-file was hit by severe water damage and, thus, are deemed irretrievable.

The BPD Geographical Division have attempted to use this material to ascertain a topography of Wilthaven itself using previous materials, but after 198 hours non-stop work, and 4302 attempts to create a map, they have decided that Wilthaven is subject to an alien geometry and cannot be subject to cartographical attempts¶

Material text is reproduced below, with maps provided replicated by the BPD Graphics Division. If you wish to view the originals, please consult either Agent Spencer of the Graphics Division or myself.

- Agent Petrovic, BPD

(DIRECTOR'S NOTE:

Due to reports of symptoms occurring similar to those experienced with file materials The Children of Little Thwopping, all maps have been removed. If you really need to see them, go see the Graphics Division.

- BPD Director Xi)

WILTHAVEN WALKS

A collection of the finest jaunts our town has to offer

Contents

- Wilthaven Town Centre
- Wilthaven Woods
- Butcher Farms
- Gough Mountain
- The Everlasting Plains
- Baker's Cornfields

COMING SOON (We're still awaiting walkers from these jaunts!)

- Quazta Jungle
- Samuel's Tomb
- Quint's Hill
- The Naxon Paradox
- Iron Lake

- Walk 1: Wilthaven Town Centre
- Approx. time: 32 minutes

What better way to start your journey around Wilthaven than from within the town centre - a place full of life and wonder that will introduce you to the wide variety of friendly faces Wilthaven houses, and a good look at what sights there are to see.

1. To begin, you want to start your journey at Wilthaven Town Hall, facing West. There, you will see several roads that lead all sorts of tantalising directions. Do not be distracted by the ones that lead North, South, and East, for those only recommended to seasoned travellers.
2. Head West down Marcos Street, where you will have the opportunity to take in the various shopping outlets Wilthaven has to offer, as well as the plaque celebrating our inaugural Mayor – Charles Crest – and his dwellings.
3. Once you reach the end of Marcos Street, take a U-turn and you'll find yourself down the dizzying, zig-zag staircase of Rotter's Alley. A fun little cut-through that most residents know and use often, you'll note how the architecture around seems to move more as your descend the alley. Take care not to gaze too long in the windows you pass, as some residents like their privacy!
4. After what seems like 40 small sets of steps, you will come across a small gate to your right. Enter this, and you'll find yourself looking at Wilthaven Church in all its splendour. Guarded by the two statues of gaunt figures, take time to appreciate the dark clouds that circle the weathervane, and feel free to read all about the rich history of the denizens of its graveyard.

5. Now this is where you'll take the next step on your journey. Entering the crypt of Cersei Coddle, you'll make a brisk diversion past the old, open tombs, and find an opening that will take you North-West. While this may seem to take a long time – much longer than simply leaving the crypt itself – a confident walker will realise that time is an illusion, and the end of the passage is reachable within mere minutes.
6. Once you've escaped the crypts endless passage, you'll find yourself coming out next to Wilthaven Police Station. Close to the Train Station, this will be where you can ask the local officers of what dwellings are best, where to go for the finest hospitality, and how much tickets are.
7. From there, march forward 85 steps and, lo and behold, you'll find yourself outside Wilthaven Town Hall, ready to tackle another jaunt around Wilthaven!

- Walk 2: Wilthaven Woods
- Approx. time: 1 hour, 6 minutes

The more daring hiker will be enthralled at the prospect of taking in the purest nature of Wilthaven via a brief excursion through Wilthaven Woods. The Woods themselves – famous for being a regular attraction for all residents and their lost ones – cross several thousand acres, and some say no two journeys through are the same!

1. Ideally, you want to start at the Eastern entrance, near Covenant Grove. Here, you will be entranced by the clear, welcoming pathways flanked by giant oaks that seem to smile down upon you. Take time to breath in the fresh air, watch the wildlife frolic above your heads, and take one last look at the town itself.
2. After a mile or walking, you'll find a sign bearing the legend LOST HOPE. While this may seem intimidating, it is actually a helpful notice in your hike. Venture to a 38 degree angle – no more, no less - from the sign, past the withering pine, and you'll find a stone path that weaves toward the East. This will open up a veritable feast of sights, as you'll encounter vistas not thought possible at that stage of your entry to the Woods.
3. At the vista that shows you a range of giant mountains, take a left and make careful attempts to walk down the hillside range. The path may seem too thin to walk, but a courageous heart will bear the fruits of wonderful caverns protected by only the lightest bush.
4. Once you find yourself on solid ground, bear right and walk toward a cluster of trees near the Northeast. Here, you will find yourself on a road overgrown with moss. This road – christened Harlot's Avenue by local historians – will take the

majority of your overall hike, and allow you to really soak in the trees and creatures that lurk beyond. Just be careful not to fall prey to any of the feminine calls that echo through there!

5. If you've safely navigated down the Avenue, you'll find the road forks into 4 paths. For the love of whatever Gods there are, take the ~~3rd~~ ~~2nd~~ 3rd path from the left, and carry on for 480 yards. You may think that the sun has set early and, indeed, the arch of foliage makes it seem that way. But by continuing down the trampled stone that guides you, you'll soon find it was all an illusion, and you're at a rather warm clearing.

6. While it is tempting to stay within the clearing for a small picnic, make haste toward the Southern part of the clearing. At first, you'll believe that no such path exists, but by brushing aside the thorns, you'll be entranced by a sudden drop that will take you back toward the edges of Wilthaven Woods.

7. Once you've survived your landing, be wary of lingering too long. It is a wonderful view, and the swirling mists between the trees are literally intoxicating, but you'll want to pick up the pace and make a speedy retreat toward the blinding light to the West. Here, after an unknown period of time, you'll find yourself falling from a tight bramble, and back into the welcoming arms of Wilthaven Town Centre!

- Walk 3: Butcher Farms
- Approx. time: 56 minutes

It may seem strange to indulge in a walk through farmland, but when it is as rich as lush as the fields making up Butcher Farms, it is almost a sin not to walk its public footpaths! Not only will you find yourself amazed at the crops that grow and wildlife that walk, but also you'll engage with witty locals who are more than happy to lend an ear or a hand. Just don't fill yourself up on their pies!

1. Begin your adventure across the rural lands of Butcher Farms by entering via the gate on North Hooper Way. Here, you will be greeted by acres of green grass – all year round – that gives way to a horizon that never seems to end. Take some time enjoying this view, before making your way forward and ready to navigate the wonders on hand.
2. After 10 minutes, you should see a bright yellow field to your immediate left, with only a solo barn marking it. Head toward this field, taking a shortcut through the lithe growths that mark the green grass, and enter via a small pathway that curves to the right. Once inside, make your way toward the barn, making sure to breath in the fresh smells of the unidentifiable crops that surround you.
3. Once you arrive at the barn, resist the urge to take a peek inside – **trust us** – and head North. You'll find the yellow crops die away a little, but don't be disheartened, as you'll soon spot a hillock in the immediate vicinity. Climb up this hillock, ignoring any sounds you may hear, and take in the view all around you.
4. Upon the hillock, you will see an active farm just West of your location. Make your way down the hill and through the tall

grass of the adjacent field, and you'll find yourself upon the land of the Sawyer family. Why not make friends with the Sawyers, and watched the woodwork skills of their youngest, Thomas. Maybe even grab a souvenir while you're there!

5. After saying goodbye to the Sawyer's, quickly make your way down a dirt road that cuts through the bushy fields off to the right. Down this road, you may catch sight of the rabbits that inhabit this area. While it is tempting to pet them and take them home to show the family, they are wild and at 6-feet high fully grown, are capable of tearing a person apart. Still, the little critters do love having their picture taken, so grab a few snaps while you can.

6. After a few steps, you'll find a clearing in front of you, just off to the left. This clearing – known to locals as Arnopp's Grace – is just the start of a long stretch of natural land that is tilled all year round. The flora that grows from the dirt, and the aroma that emanates from its beauty, are enough to make you want to start your own home away from home. But remember: the Butcher's aren't selling yet!

7. If you've resisted the urge to take a seat and remain there forever, a quick jog West will find you on a golden row of reds and greens. These fruits – which we advise against consuming – direct toward the main part of Butcher Farms, and the main home of Stanley & Barbara. Known to greet all travellers with a smile and plate of pastry cuts, they'll safely guide you to Wilthaven Town Centre, where you can reminisce about your adventures within the fields.

- Walk 4: Gough Mountains
- Approx. time: 2 hours 35 minutes

For those that love a challenge, the Gough Mountains on the Northeast side of Wilthaven will tickle your feet-based tastebuds. A leisurely start evolves into something much more tackling, but the rewards are off the scale. Just remember to pack the right clothing, or you could end up like those who veer off the suggested path!

1. Start your journey skywards at the suggested point of Grundy's Hut, found just off Vendredi Road in Wilthaven. Here, you will no doubt come across many other excited explorers who will no doubt expunge their wandering philosophy to you. Do not listen to them, and instead take your first steps up the carved staircase to the right of the Hut.
2. After ascending the steps, you will reach a point where the path diverges into 2 paths: left and right. Now, the safest path can vary depending on the climate, so take note of which way the DANGER sign points toward. Whichever way it directs you, take the opposite path. Please note - if the sign points to the mountain, wait for a light gust to help its decision. If it points toward you, climb down immediately and seek a police officer.
3. After choosing the correct path, you will note that your ascent has become quite high, and that temperatures have decreased and winds increased in velocity. This is just an illusion, so take care in following the weaving path as it crawls up the mountain. Why not take time admiring the view from Stein's Ledge, or taking a peek in the various caverns that dot the mountain itself.

4. At this point, you'll note the path gives way to a more erratic landscape. With no clear path, it would be easy to get lost, but proceed in a straight line from the end of the path and you should be fine. Do not listen to any other potential climbers at this stage, as they are merely sirens designed to get you to join the climbers frozen long ago up there. If the sirens do not respond to simple ignoring, then do not feel the need to assault them, for this will result in a fatality. Simply shout, "No!" and all will be well.
5. With snows no doubt forming a fine mist at this stage of your walk, you could be tempted to return down the path trodden. This would be a mistake, and instead we recommend carrying on your trajectory. You may feel at times that you are walking in a circle, but trust your instincts and ignore the litter of moaning corpses that plead for help, and you'll eventually get through the snowstorm.
6. Now this is the point all climbers/hikers/explorers wait for: the peak of Gough's Mountain. The time your climb has taken may not fit with the height in which you seem to sit upon, but this is just an illusion designed to scare you. Sit back for the designated 3-minute relaxation, and then firmly stand and take the path the old man points toward. Unlike most you have encountered on this journey, he can be trusted.
7. Upon taking the path alluded to by the old man's gnarled finger, you will find quite a firm set of steps that takes you back down the other side of the mountain – or so you'd think. Of course, eventually, you will recognise familiar sights, including many recognisable travellers attempting the climb themselves. Do not interact with them, as this could cause temporal disturbances. Instead, continue down the mountain, and enjoy a nice cup of hot tea at Madam Wellington's Spiced Beverages. Don't worry,

they're toasty hot all year round and designed to treat even the severest case of frostbite!

- Walk 5: The Everlasting Plains
- Approx. Time: Forever

The most intimidating walk on our little list is probably the most exciting. The Everlasting Plains was created by Hq'Tar at an unknown point in Wilthaven's history, and has been a source of much adventure ever since. While some never leave the large white expanse, those that have talk endlessly about their experiences – some of which are good! It is difficult to recommend what to take on such a journey, so just go crazy and dive straight in.

Good luck.

1. While The Everlasting Plains are infinite and endless, the best place to enter is near Leper's Farm, just Southwest of Wilthaven Town Hall. Here, you will get the best idea about how far the plains stretch (forever), and can plan your journey forthwith. What we would recommend, first of all, is to step onto the white sands and start walking forward for a mile.
2. Once you have entered the Plains, and see nothing but endless white around you, turn right.
3. Turn right.
4. Turn right.
5. Turn right.
6. Turn right.
7. Turn right.
8. Turn right.
9.
10. Turn right.
11. Turn right.
12. Turn right.

13. Turn right.
14. Turn right.
15. Turn right.
16. Turn right.
17. Turn right.
18. Turn right.
19. Turn right.
20. Turn right.
21. Turn right.
22. Turn right.
23. Turn right.
24. Turn right.
25. Turn right.
26. TurnHright.
27. Turn right.
28. Turn right.
29. Turn right.
30. Turn right.
31. Turn right.
32. Turn right.
33. Turn right.
34. Turn right.
35. Turn right.
36. Turn right.
37. Turn right.
38. Turn right.
39. Cry.
40. Turn right.
41. Turn right.
42. TurnEright.
43. Turn right.

44. Turn right.
45. Turn right.
46. Turn right.
47. Turn right.
48. Turn right.
49. Turn right.
50. Turn right.
51. Turn right.
52. Turn right.
53. Turn right.
54. Turn right.
55. Turn left.
56. Turn right.
57. Turn right.
58. Turn right.
59. TurnLright.
60. Turn right.
61. Turn right.
62. Turn right.
63. Turn right.
64. Turn right.
65. Turn right.
66. Turn right.
67. Turn right.
68. Turn right.
69. Turn right.
70. Turn right.
71. Turn right.
72. Turn right.
73. Turn right.
74. Turn right.

75. Turn right.
76. Turn right.
77. Turn right.
78. TurnPright.
79. Turn right.
80. Turn right.
81. Turn right?
82. Turn right.
83. Turn right.
84. Turn right.
85. Turn right.
86. Turn right.
87. Turn right.
88. Turn right.
89. Turn right.
90. Turn right.
91. Turn right.
92. Turn right.
93. Turn right.
94. Turn right.
95. Turn right.
96. Abandon hope.
97. Turn right.
98. Turn right.
99. Turn right.
100. Turn right.
101. Turn right.
102. Turn right.
103. Turn right.
104. Turn right.
105. TurnMright.

106. Right turn.
107. Turn right.
108. Turn right.
109. Turn right.
110. Turn right.
111. Turn right.
112. Turn right.
113. DO NOT MOVE.
114. Turn right.
115. Turn right.
116. Turn right.
117. Turn right.
118. Turn right.
119. Turn right.
120. Turn right.
121. Turn right.
122. Turn right.
123. Turn right.
124. Turn right.
125. Turn right.
126. Turn right.
127. TurnEright.
128. Turn right.
129. Turn right.
130. Turn right.
131. Turn right.
132. Embrace death.
133. Turn right.
134. Turn right.
135. Turn right.
136. Turn right.

137. Turn right.
138. Turn right.
139. Turn right.
140. Trun riht.
141. Turn right.
142. Turn right.
143. Turn right.
144. Turn right.
145. Turn right.
146. Turn right.
147. Turn right.
148. Turn right.
149. Hail Hq'tar.
150. Turn right.
151. Turn right.
152. Turn right.
153. Turn right.
154. Turn right.
155. Turn right.
156. Turn right.
157. Turn right.
158. Turn right.
159. Turn right.
160. Turn right.
161. Turn right.
162. At this point, you should have either gone totally mad from isolation or reached one of the many exit points of the Plains. If it is the latter, take time to relax, get to know your surroundings again, and check your camera for all the wondrous pictures you would have taken!

- Walk 6: Baker's Field
- Approx. Time: 50 minutes

After the previous walks, you're probably after something a bit more clement! Well, look no further than Baker's Field, an old piece of untouched nature that is home to the annual Harvest Festival, and is a favoured spot by our very own Mayor Crest. Take a picnic, sit down, and look back on all the things you've been subjected to in Wilthaven!

1. Start at the entrance near the Nettle's Spice public house, and top up on the famous Wilthaven Ale while you are there. Once the important stuff is out the way, enter the gate and follow the path as it eases you to the West.
2. You will begin noting the expanse of green that welcomes you to the fields, but do not fear the infinite – these areas are marked by helpful signs placed by Wilthaven residents to remind walkers that all is well here. Why not grab a picture of yourself with one of the many Wicker Men that line the paths. Just don't look inside!
3. You will reach a point where a lone oak stands in the middle of a field. Approach the tree and look around you to see all manner of places to go. Do you visit the tilled fields to the North? The haven of rabbits to the West? Well, in this guide, we encourage you to take the best option: the continuation of corn that glides softly to the East. **Never go South**.
4. Once within the cornfields, you'll feel a sense of ease and calm that you may not have indulged within Wilthaven prior. It is tempting to lie down and look at the clouds gather, but carry on until you breach the corn and are greeted by signs of

civilization again. Ignore the whispers, and make your way toward the hillock to the West.

5. Owain's Hillock is a lovely location to stop, drop, and have yourself a little gaze at Wilthaven all around you. Take in the sight of the church from afar. Look upon the realms you have already trod upon and survived. Pick some daisies to take back to your one true love. Just fall in ~~lust~~ love with nature again, and enjoy a sense of calm.

6. Once you feel refreshed, walk to the right of the hillock, and head down a stone path that winds toward the East. Here, take sight of the length of Baker's Fields and the various beauties that live within. If you're lucky, you may catch sight of a deer frolicking. If you're unlucky, that deer may attack you. Why not grab some of the local grains from baskets left by residents to feed the animals and gain their trust?

7. Finally, the stone path will lead you to a gate, which will allow you entry to a stone arch untainted by modern hands. Enjoy the tapestry and carvings within the arch, but do not take any pictures of them. Enjoy them for what they are, and do not taint any other memories by chronicling them. Once out of the arch, you will find yourself back at Nettle's Spice just in time for their famous Epidermal Flan. Enjoy!

HQ'TAR REPORT #6

(21/12/2009)

Fed back to BPD HQ in El Paso, Texas, the following transcript was recorded by Agent Chavez during an off-duty visit to a bar named Ol' Scratch in El Cenizo. While drinking with friends, Agent Chavez began speaking to a fellow patron who mentioned some trigger words in relation to P1983, and using quick thinking, Chavez began to record the conversation using a personal recording device upon his person.

While the identity of the patron has not been concluded, Agent Chavez managed to grab a picture that is provided at the end of this transcript. For his diligent work, even in a period of downtime, Chavez has been given the Rose Star, and a substantial leave bonus to spend time with his family. Of course, given standard BPD policy, this leave bonus has also been offered to be traded for premium rations on a 10-year basis. Agent Chavez has still yet to come back to us with his decision.

- Agent Petrovic, BPD

AGENT CHAVEZ: So you mentioned some place called...

PATRON: Wilthaven. Yeah. Proper beer there, son. None of this piss-water you find in these parts. No offence.

(Grumbling heard in distance)

AC: I hear ya. So where is this "Wilthaven".

P: Ah, just down in the shires, y'know? Get on the train from the Capital, toodle along a bit, and there you are.

AC: In England?

P: The King's very own country.

AC: King?

P: Yeah. King Wallace the Third. Come on, mate; I know you're a yank but you must know your monarchies?

AC: I'm a bit rusty.

P: Yep, this'll do that to you! (Laughs)

AC: So what brings you to El Cenizo?

P: Is that what this place is called? I've no idea, to be honest. Just popped out to get the paper and, well, here I am!

AC: Wait. You popped out to get a paper? In England? And ended up in Texas?

P: I know. Queer as you like. Just turned a corner and then, pop, ended up on some street I'd never seen before.

AC: And... that doesn't... bother you?

P: (Laughs) Mate, I've seen worse things than to be randomly transported to a bar in the Americas.

AC: Such as?

P: Oh, you don't want to know, son. You do not want to know.

AC: Try me.

P: (Pause) Is there a beer in it?

AC: Let's make it tequila.

P: Ooh. Saucy.

(Background chatter as the sound of drinks ordered, and received, are made.)

AC: So what are these "worse things" you were talking about?

P: Well. You name it, I've probably seen it. Babies ripped from their mother's wombs. Men flayed alive in a fire as cold as ice. And ducks.

AC: Ducks?

P: Ducks.

AC: What about "ducks"?

P: Upside down.

AC: Upside down ducks.

P: Yeah.

AC: And that's bad because…

P: Ducks aren't supposed to be upside down.

AC: (Pause) I don't see how that's comparable to forced childbirth…

P: You ain't seen these ducks, mate.

AC:	Right… so it doesn't bother you that you're now thousands of miles from home?
P:	I'll be honest, it's a nice break. Rarely get the chance to go on holiday. Last time I did, it was my honeymoon with my first wife. It was the most wonderful, and most heartbreaking, time of my life.
AC:	How so?
P:	She got eaten by a tree.
AC:	I'm sorry?
P:	Clean out your ears, boy! She got eaten. By. A. Tree.
AC:	(Pause) Eaten by a tree?
P:	That's the one.
AC:	How…
P:	How do you think? One minute you're walking along a forest glade, carefree and in love, the next thing you know a branch has scooped up your missus, and shoved her into its trunk.
AC:	Just like that.

P: Just like that.

AC: I'll be honest, this is all a bit…

P: Weird? Well, that's why I say come to Wilthaven, my friend! Have some proper local ale, some proper local food, and try not to be killed or worse by Hq'tar.

AC: Hq'tar?

P: Oh yeah. Big deal in Wilthaven, don't you know. Can't move for Hq'tar. Everywhere you go it's Hq'tar this, and Hq'tar that. If I were a braver man, I'd say the whole thing gets on my tits.

AC: You just did.

P: Well then, I'm either braver than I thought, or that's the booze talking! Cheers!

AC: Cheers. So, anything else you can tell me about this "Wilthaven"?

P: Oh plenty, son. Plenty! Just let me empty the ol' saddle-bag at the little boys room, and I'll tell you tales that'll make your willy shrink.

(Sound of chair squeaking against floor, and footsteps going off into distance, merging with background noise.)

RECORDING ENDS

(Agent Chavez reported that after Subject left for the lavatory, 5 minutes passed before the Agent went to investigate. Upon entering the men's room, he was shocked to find an explosion of viscera covering the whole room. A BPD Clean Up Crew were notified, and the incident was cleared without further issue.

Please find below the aforementioned picture obtained by Agent Chavez of the Patron

- Agent Petrovic, BPD)

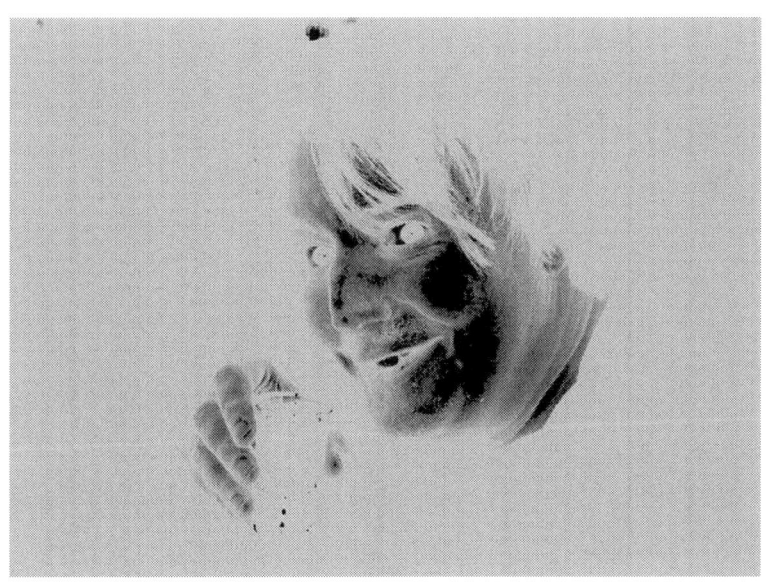

BUSINESS PROPOSALS

Found as part of Operation Dunkelheit, this typed list - complete with hand-written note -s was on a piece of lined paper carefully laminated and placed within a box file listed MAYOR MEETINGS. The numerous other files are being looked over by our Digital Division, and scanned for notable content and chronological placement.

The handwriting has been studied, and has yet to be related to any known individual related to P1983 (Wilthaven). As per procedure, names within the material have been added to reference notes for P1983.

Document is presented transcribed as found, with no known omissions.

- Agent Petrovic, BPD

List of Business Proposals – Amendments by Mayor Crest

RESIDENT: Bob Gray

PROPOSAL: A children's entertainment service using Mr Gray's unique clown costume and proficiency with balloons.

Who on Earth is Bob Gray? I can't find him on the Wilthaven Census, and have no known knowledge of ever meeting the fellow. Until we know more about him and his intentions, this is a hard DENIED.

RESIDENT: Karl Towers

PROPOSAL: Midnight tours around Wilthaven, showcasing the best that the nightlife has to offer, and more.

Is he insane? Are you insane for even suggesting this to me? Suffice to say, Mr Towers is a known Avatar. For this alone, this is DENIED, and whoever accept this is to be screened for Avatar activity.

RESIDENT: Laura West

PROPOSAL: Tentacle Massages. These in-depth and unique massages provide a sensory experience for those with a wide range of ailments, and come courtesy of recent addition to Miss West's team, Elaine Hagerty.

It is known that Miss Hagerty is a recent Avatar, even without noting her... additions. Still, I have tried the massage itself and found it not only to be completely safe, but very relaxing. APPROVED.

RESIDENT: Christopher Williams

PROPOSAL: Scuba Diving in Wilthaven Lake. This would allow residents to experience the lake like never before, and also allow the scientific community a unique look at the Lake itself. All safety measures looked into can be found in Document 375.

I won't lie, Document 375 is incredibly detailed, but we still must note the dangers that the Lake presents. If it was any other body of water, this would quickly be pushed through, but even with the safety measures proposed and the boon it would provide the scientific community, it is a reluctant DENIED.

RESIDENT: Mr Japes

PROPOSAL: Re-opening the Void Wall at Japes' Fun Park. The educational benefits speak for itself, and any madness-inducing side effects have been toned down.

Toned down? DENIED. In future, anything from Mr Japes is instantly DENIED.

RESIDENT: Carol Stephens

PROPOSAL: An annual festival during the month of Zephiber. Due to the eternal isolation it brings, a festival could brighten the spirits of residents, and also allow them to show off their finest cookery and creative skills. Not only will this be fun but also a distraction during this terrible month.

This is an excellent idea that I cannot imagine we have not considered before. Everyone in Wilthaven likes a festival, and Zephiber is a moral-killer every year. APPROVED.

CREST FAMILY TREE

In what can only be described as a curious find, the following chart was found scratched in a cave within Sector W-4 in Antarctica by BPD Exploration Team Indigo Minor on 21/10/2015. Junior researcher Agent Yi made the discovery while tracking an unusual seismic signal in the area, and reported back to Head Researcher Agent Kurnov immediately. For her discovery, Agent Yi has been awarded the Director's Commendation.

What added to the discovery was that the engraving was created by no known tools, and had trace elements of blood within some of the grooves. Analysis is still pending on the DNA, but the BPD Genetics Division are confident of a match.

Given the content of this discovery – a flowchart tracking the family tree of the well known Crest family, who are Key Subjects relating to P1983 (Wilthaven), it was brought to my attention and added to file.

Full engraving has been transcribed in full below.

- Agent Petrovic, BPD

1859-1886 Charles & Victoria Crest
|
1886-1910 Gregory & Katherine Crest
|
1910-1950 Harry & Rachel Crest
|
1950-1970 John & Laura Crest
|
1970-1975 Robert & Louisa Crest
|
1975-1993 Grant & Beverley Crest
|
1993-? Leonard & Cheryl Crest

(BPD Note: The following statements were scratched around the central chart listed above)

1 SON NO DAUGHTER
NEVER BREAK THE LINE
NEVER BREAK
NO DAUGHTER ONLY SON
HQ'TAR LIVES

REPORT: OPERATION POROPITI NGARO

OBJECTIVE: ~~TRACK LOCATION OF WILTHAVEN~~
MAINTAIN CONTACT WITH AGENT WILDER

BACKGROUND

On the 14th April, 2015, an unscheduled train arrived at Platform 6 of London Marylebone Station with markings that connected it to P1983 (Wilthaven). With the assistance of BPD Agents working within National Rail, the driver was temporarily detained while Agents studied the train and decided on a course of action. While discussions with the driver were ultimately fruitless, it was decided upon by BPD Directors to use this opportunity to fit a GPS Tracking Device within one of the carriages and observe its movements as part of Operation Poropiti Ngaro. While applying the Tracking Device, the Operation changed irreversibly.

Agent Wilder, an operative with the BPD for 3 years, was tasked with placing the Tracking Device within the carriage. However, during this procedure, the train driver broke free of containment, and managed to board and activate the train. While most BPD Agents managed to disembark before the doors locked, Agent Wilder was not so fortunate, and was on the train as it left Marylebone Station.

A BPD Surveillance Team were tasked with monitoring the GPS signal from the Tracking Device, but lost all electronic communications as the train entered a tunnel. From there, the Operation was deemed a failure, and Agent Wilder was designated MIA.

However, on 9th May, a similar train appeared at Kawasaki Station in Kawasaki, Kanagawa, Japan. Before BPD Agents could act, the train left, but BPD Surveillance Teams clarified that the GPS signal placed by Agent Wilder was active. Further sightings were made in Brussels, Belgium, Saskatoon, Canada, and Johannesburg, South Africa. Eventually, the train was derailed upon appearing on a disused rail-line outside of Baxter in Victoria, Australia on the 2nd December 2016. BPD Agents arrived on the scene to find the driver – different from the original figure interviewed previously – deceased. The GPD Tracking Device was found, along with a USB Device taped tightly onto it.

Upon examination of the USB Device, several DOC files were found that were written by Agent Wilder, confirming that she was alive and well. Digital analysis showed the documents to be written recently, and data-stamped with ID similar to BPD files.

The following are the documents Agent Wilder wrote, in full, providing countless amounts of information and data regarding P1983 (Wilthaven). This information has proved to be exceptionally useful to the BPD, and Operation Poropiti Ngaro has been amended to reflect the new status of the

```
mission: to retrieve Agent Wilder, and establish a
connection between P0 and P1983.
```

```
                                   - Agent Petrovic, BPD
```

```
DIRECTOR'S NOTE:
     BPD Directors have noted Agent Wilder's
actions and overall professionalism, and should a
successful link be established between P1 and P1983,
a promotion is being strongly considered. All Agents
would learn a lot by studying these reports, and the
manner they have been written and provided to us
here at the BPD.
                                   - BPD Director Upsilon
```

REPORT 1

I believe it goes without saying that my current circumstances are unique, to say the least. Not only was I trapped upon an anomalous vehicle associated with a P-Class dimension, but I now find myself typing this document within said dimension. Therefore, to my colleagues hopefully reading this document, know this:

I am currently in P1983, aka Wilthaven.

The circumstances I have already mentioned above, so I shall cut to when the anomalous properties in my journey began. After entering the tunnel, instead of coming out via the South Hampstead region, I instead found myself gazing upon a more rural landscape. It was at this point that I realised I was no longer in P0, and so took the time between this discovery and my arrival in P1983 to take stock, and remain calm. My training in BPD Field Duties helped me with the psychological toll such an event had on me, and I was soon calm enough to gather intel, and work on a cover story for my sudden presence.

I should also note at this stage that I was the only person on the train. While this is not strange in that when we encountered the train, it was already empty, I do consider the fact that it remained unoccupied, even after passing through – what I assume is – a dimensional gateway, to be anomalous in itself. I have heard from Senior Agents on the case, such as Agent Petrovic, that such encounters in P0 are by design, and so I can only consider that this event is one that was equally pre-determined.

Theories aside, the journey itself went without any hostile situations. At no stage was I asked for a ticket, nor did any other passengers board at any other stations. The stations themselves were equal anomalies – bearing names that have no correspondence with P0. Those that I can recall at this time are:

EXHIBITION STATION
JARRETT STATION
BEECHEN STATION
CHEPPING STATION

After approximately 50 minutes, the driver announced arrival to Wilthaven, where the service would terminate. Entering P1983 - which for brevity I shall call by its 'official' name of Wilthaven - by train did not give me any notice of its already known strange properties. From what I could see when I disembarked, the town was a normal, English territory, with an assortment of residential and commercial districts in sight. The only potential anomaly was a slight mist that clouded the sky that had unusual properties compared to normal cloud coverage, relating to its hue and composition. With the full weight of the opportunity I had been presented with, I exited the station – thankfully without the obstacle of a ticket gate or master – and entered Wilthaven.

There's a dark ambience around the town. Almost in a Stepford vein, that the region itself is not overtly ominous, but the feeling one gets from walking around is… unsettling. It's

…

I can't do this.

REPORT 1.5

Agent Brezchev was right. All you need to write a good report is a few shots of vodka. Typical Russian.

I mean, we all knew what we were getting into. I knew what I was getting into walking onto that damn train. At least we aren't Red or Black Level. Those bastards have it the worst, either dying or…

Well, you don't want to know. When it comes to working for the Bureau, dying is your best option sometimes.

I remember when I started Field Work, started working for the Bureau. I was 19, studying hard at Uni. Breaking all sorts of records for excellence. Next thing I know, I'm given my degree early, one last meal with the family, and in an official looking car with official looking people, to go to an official looking building.

There's your history of Agent Wilder of the BPD. A young girl who ended up trapped on a damn train in a universe – or P-Class if you want to be official – known for being terrorized by an Eldritch.

I tried to come back. I really did. Told by the guy behind the counter at the train station that "no more services were running at this time". When I asked why, he just laughed. I wouldn't get the joke until later.

Anyway, the cover story. An old BPD classic: the confused tourist. Hello, Wilthaven, what have you got? Near the station was an old pub known as The Belle's View. Your typical old village drinking establishment, complete with sign straight out of the 50s – all buxom wench behind the bar with tits the size of Gibraltar. I went in to try and get some sort of bearings; ascertain where I was, what I was going to do, and how I was going to do it.

I stumbled at the first hurdle.

Let me just say that the people of Wilthaven are exactly what you'd expect. They're jovial, kind, and almost oblivious to the general atmosphere of doom that slithers in the sky above them. Aside from a few odd looks from those who'd had far too many, the landlord of the View welcomed me in, and was happy to serve me a big measure of the aforementioned Brezchev Solution.

The problem came when it was time to pay.

One thing you don't get in your BPD Field Kit is alternatives to money. You have money, of course, but it's all emblazoned with the figures we know and love in P0. Your royalty, your presidents, all the usual faces. Which is great, if you're in a P-Class where they are known.

I wasn't.

The landlord looked at the note about half-dozen times before suddenly clocking something unsaid, and smiling politely. He said something about a phone call, left me to my drink, and went into another room. The other patrons around me seemed friendly enough – asking who I was, where I was from, and how I got to Wilthaven. I gave the stock answers we'd all been trained on: I'm a tourist, from a few towns over, looking to visit Wilthaven.

The last bit was of great amusement to my new friends.

The Landlord came back, gave me that same reassuring smile, and advised me that someone was on the way to sort things out. Meanwhile, I should just relax, enjoy my drink, and take in the pleasures of the View.

I had a lot of that by the time Herring arrived.

I'll type more up in the morning. My head is killing me, and I need some sleep. Not that that'll be easy. You know how in some of the documents the folk of Wilthaven tell of strange noises during the night?

Well, as soon as the sun went down, they started. And to whoever reads this, they are worse than described.

REPORT 2

Herring is – or at least, alludes to be – the local law around Wilthaven. He was the man the town went to when they had problems, and he usually managed to sort them. Not that he was the main authority in the village; that went to the familiar Mayor Crest, and his team of officials. The actual Chief Constable was Jane Carter, who we know from previous reports available in P1983. However, as good as she was, Herring was the main man. He looked into the disappearances, studied the deaths, and was in tune with the weird and wonderful. Anything slightly crazy – and there was a lot of it in Wilthaven as we know – Herring was on it.

For good reason.

He was the one who actually helped me after that first night. As I said in my previous report, it was fucking horrible. I probably slept an hour, if that. The rest of Wilthaven seemed to doze happily, probably due to being used to the incessant noise, but for a newbie like me?

It was Hell.

I know detail is the name of our game at The Bureau, but fuck that. All you need to know is that there are sounds that are not on the spectrum of what we know, what we've heard. Noises at levels that seep into your brain, and voices that… are wrong. Just plain wrong. They say words, which seem to form actual sentences, but it just isn't right. It can't be, because if this was normal, then you'd do whatever you could to never hear another sound again.

And that's not even touching upon the damned Avatars. You've read about them in reports and materials – the missing who come back, and who are determined to make you join them. One kept knocking on my door, asking me to come with them, that they had something special to see. Each time they were led away, and a whispered apology was passed under the door. But they'd come back, again and again. Each time asking me to follow them.

It started creepy. Then it just got annoying.

Maybe I am getting used to this place.

Once again, though, I can't fault the hospitality of Wilthaven. The landlord of The Belle's View – who I learned was a Mr James Cottrell – provided me with a lavish breakfast and comfortable clothing that he had sourced from a supply kept in a nearby, unattended room.

I didn't ask who they used to belong to. It was just nice to clean up, get comfortable, and get fed.

And as tempting as an actual drink was, I stuck to water.

Less than an hour later, Herring arrived. He was fully suited in police-wear, and exchanged pleasantries with Mr Cottrell. It was the usual Village Talk about upcoming events, and confirmation of gossip around town. But it was really all leading up to the main event.

Me.

Herring came over, and thanked Mr Cottrell for looking after me, and that he'd take it from here. Cottrell left, and I was left alone with Herring.

Or rather, Agent Harmon of the IUW.

The IUW is the Institute of Unknown Worlds, a parallel to The Bureau itself. They operate very much like we do, and are *very* aware of Wilthaven and its anomalous properties. Not only that, they are very aware of people like me – transients from other dimensions who have ended up in their P-class. Normally, they are integrated into society until a solution can be ascertained to place them back in their own world.

But for Herring, I wasn't any normal transient. I was a member of The Bureau, and he knew that straight away. Apparently, my cover story, strange clothing and belongings, as well as my cash collection were all signifiers of this, and so now, in a weird way, I was no longer alone.

Herring provided me with money relevant to this world, and gave me the low-down of his status and that of the IUW. He had been stationed as an Undercover within Wilthaven, working with several other Agents in gathering as much information as possible, and as to whether there was a way to combat the Eldritch known as Hq'tar.

And let me tell you this, folks – Hq'tar isn't as benevolent as we think.

But that's all I know so far. Although, if you think about it, a God-like being who can change landscapes and turn people into their own personal puppets probably isn't a prankster God.

Given his knowledge of Wilthaven – as well as his affiliation with an organisation very similar to our own – I was hoping Herring was going to provide me with a way out of here. But if that was the case, I wouldn't be sending you this report, would I?

Despite my questions regarding the matter of an exit strategy, Herring tried to defer the conversation. He encouraged me to look around the town, get to know the residents, and use this as an opportunity to research Wilthaven as a whole. I confess, in my panic I had lost sight of the main intention of this whole saga, not that being in Wilthaven was part of the plan.

But like Herring said, recon would be a good idea, and so I set about speaking to the people here. I'll write up my findings once I have enough to go on, but for now, know that I am taking my experience as a chance to learn, rather than a chance to fear. After all, we've seen Agents ripped apart by physical anomalies in space, warped by strange atmospheres, and even corrupted by things beyond our imagination.

A little sightseeing is light work compared to that. Even if it is sightseeing in a town ruled by an Eldritch.

REPORT 3

Wilthaven is an interesting town; that goes without saying.

It is also very much a typical town. There are shops selling groceries and goods, people clock in and clock out of their jobs, and children play and go to school. If you didn't know of Hq'tar, you'd think it was any other place.

Then residents greet you with the phrase "Hail Hq'tar", and the reality hits you.

The greeting seems to be some way to appease their nefarious ruler; a subservience born out of survival. There's no word on what would happen if you didn't, nor any warning, written or otherwise, explaining why you should. Instead, it is tossed around as casually as "hello" and "goodbye", and after a while you find yourself saying it almost as casually.

On Herring's advice, I've integrated myself into the community. Speaking to your regular townsfolk is an exercise in the minutiae of everyday life. People give their histories, their regular experiences in Wilthaven, and their thoughts on others. Key figures are highlighted, such as the aforementioned – and well known to The Bureau – Mayor Crest, the aforementioned Chief Constable, local author Quinn Tharman, and Kirsten Verren, head of the Wilthaven Society, and I have a notepad full of these figures who I want to get an audience with as soon as possible.

However, the thing that is mentioned most, in a way that makes me think my time here is about to get even worse, is the mention of Zephiber.

I've seen it mentioned a lot in the case files, but with knowledge of what it actually is a complete mystery. As far as I can determine, it is a special date for those in Wilthaven, much like Christmas or Easter, but without the same level of frivolity. Don't get me wrong, there is some sort of macabre celebration that revolves around it, but it is said to me with a hint of warning. I'm asked why I would come at such a time, almost warned, but then welcomed to join in the celebrations. I'm due to meet up with Herring again tomorrow, and will probe further then.

In the meantime... life is normal. Well, bar the bizarre landscapes that dominate the horizons. If you stand in the town centre, you'll see snowy mountains to the East, vast plains stretching beyond the North, and deep forestry to the South. Then again, even those directions are debatable. I've stood in the same spot and seen different things appear at different angles. Where once were mountains, now sits a cyan skyscape. Where there was rich wildlife, now a barren desert. It takes some getting used to, but if it doesn't bother the residents, it will not bother me.

I've relocated from The Belle's View to the vast Grady Hotel, where my stay has been comped by Herring and the IUW – under a different name, of course. The Grady Hotel is a monumental achievement in architecture, although not free from the weirdness of Wilthaven as a whole. There are curious things that I have witnessed while settling here, such as corridors leading nowhere, and rooms being locked or out of service. The owner – Phillip Stone – is aware of these anomalies, but insists they are harmless. I'm yet to see evidence otherwise.

Here, the advent of Zephiber is more pronounced. The grand ballroom is being decorated for the occasion, and a number of residents are checking in to celebrate. From those I've spoken to, even the Mayor may join this year. Apparently, he likes to spend time away from his residence to spend time with the locals during this celebration. That's either very nice, or very suspicious.

The bar is well stocked, though, so I'm not asking too many questions. If I'm on holiday, I'm going to enjoy myself when not investigating. Tonight's menu included a nice bottle of claret, and the best damn roast chicken I've had in a while. At least, I think it was chicken.

In Wilthaven you can never be too sure about anything.

REPORT 4

Damn Herring.

Damn him, damn the IUW, and damn Wilthaven as a damn whole. Oh, and most of all, damn Zephiber. Fucking Zephiber. A celebration? An event not unlike Christmas? Fucking HA.

Try a month of complete darkness, where the nightmares that trot around during the night-time hours have free reign of the town, and you're stuck inside with only a bottle of booze and the incessant… niceness, of the fucking people here.

I'll write more when I'm less angry, and less drunk. Fuck. I wish I'd stayed at uni.

REPORT 4.5

Right, Zephiber.

It's around 4AM in the morning, or at least I think so. All I've got to work on are the variety of clocks that litter the Grady Hotel. Some with sweeping hands that tick along, some digital with head-aching inducing LEDs that glow in the void of night. They sit everywhere almost as a reminder, a countdown to the end of this nightmare. For better, or for worse.

Let me start at the beginning. I met up with Herring, and we discussed me getting out of Wilthaven, and this P-class as a whole. He advised the IUW are working on trans-dimensional hardware to help ease exploration of P-classes. More intriguingly, he said the major project of the IUW has been to create a map of dimensions - a giant landscape showing the connectors and subtle differences between each universe, from the very minor, to the absolute major. When I watch him talk about it, I am awe-struck at the scope of this project. It makes The Bureau look like part-timers.

It also shines some light on how Herring found me, or was at least aware of me. Apparently, being from "my" dimension means a slight difference on a sub-atomic level. Some structuring of my DNA coding is highlighted by the IUW's algorithms, and this subtle difference was enough to highlight me. Apparently, I represent a certain co-ordinate to P0 – which I should note, is not what they call it, but for brevity I'll keep it like that for this report - and with that, a figurative & literal helping hand to their trans-dimensional map.

(Curiously, when I asked about Grounding Agents, Herring seemed unaware of them. Strange, but to be honest it wasn't the most pressing of matters.)

Herring advised this hardware may be able to get me back home, but made no promises. No problem with me; promises were rare in The Bureau anyway. They represented the vague, whereas we know that we deal in the facts of reality, no matter how strange. Occam's Razor if designed by Dali. However the knowledge that there was an exit strategy was enough for me.

That was the good news. After that, Herring hit me with the bad.

Zephiber.

I like to think he had his reasons for not telling me beforehand. Maybe it was some mental manipulation by the powers that exist in this town. Maybe he thought there was nothing he could do anyway. Then again, I think the more likely fact is that he saw this as an opportunity for a fellow operative from another dimension to experience the strangest, and most disturbing event Wilthaven has to offer.

Zephiber is essentially a month off the calendar. A time that exists between April & May, although technically it doesn't exist. Outside of Wilthaven, time ticks along as usual – April 30th turns into May 1st at the stroke of midnight.

Not in good ol' Wilthaven though. As soon as it gets dark on April 30th – today – it stays dark.

For 3 goddamn weeks.

As Herring told me this, I wanted to get out even more. I asked – Hell, ordered him – to take me outside the town limits. To get me to safety.

But it was too late. Wilthaven was closed to the outside world as of that morning. No one came in, and more importantly, no one got out.

I was the only one who was seeing this as nothing short of pant-shittingly scary. I panicked rather vocally to the news, and sped through quite a few emotions in a short space of time. Once calm again – an experience becoming more and more difficult as my stay went on – I asked Herring for more info.

During this 3 week period – although it could be longer or shorter, depending on the whim of Hq'tar – there is no day, only night. The sun never rises, and dawn never breaks. The town is plunged into an eternal evening, and all security measures are put into place for the various buildings where people dwell. The only people who can roam the streets freely are the Avatars, with some select dwellings assigned for them to stay. Apparently, it is more hassle to have them inside with them during this time, as they become even more incessant about going out.

I tell you what, I'm bloody glad of that. I nearly broke the jaw of some guy the other day that tried dragging me out "to see the moonlight". Wanker.

Herring advised me that it was good I was stationed in the Grady Hotel, as it was known to be one of the most secure buildings in Wilthaven during Zephiber, outside the Mayor's residence. That's why the bulk of the celebrations took place here, although a final scout of the town showed a few large homes and businesses holding their own Zephiber celebration. Each resident beamed and spoke highly of their own plans, just like it was a New Years party. But they weren't celebrating the dawn of a new year, they were celebrating the fact that there won't be a dawn for a very long time.

They're lovely in Wilthaven, but they're bonkers as well.

And yeah, I know that's not official terminology. Bite me. If you can find me.

Anyway, Zephiber in the Grady Hotel was my best option, and probably why Herring and the IUW set me up there. To them, I was a prime bit of intel, as well as a person. Someone to be protected at all costs. It was why Herring was here, both in his capacity as Wilthaven's premier defender of the weird, and top Undercover Agent of IUW.

The night came quickly and suddenly, but aside from the Avatars, no one was on the street. The residents all expected this instant night, without the comfort of dusk. There was also no deceit or trickery from the Eldritch who caused this phenomena; the time was constant, even if the length wasn't. It was like Hq'tar knew he could plunge Wilthaven into darkness at any point, but instead allowed them time to prepare.

Not that everybody was. As we settled in for the night, there was the odd gossip of a few who had ended up outside when night fell. The chilling thing was that there was no sympathy, just tuts and rolls of the eyes. The common denominator between those that stayed out was that they were either young or reckless – those without the experience of dealing with the weirdness of Wilthaven, or those craving more of it.

Along with Herring, we attended the opening night of the Grady Hotel's Zephiber Celebration. The grand hall looked gorgeous, decked in tons of celebrating bunting and décor. Staff passed around complimentary food & drink, and music played loudly and joyously.

I was pleased with the former as well, because as quick as night fell, so began the screams of the monsters outside.

Later, I watched more than a little tipsy as Mayor Crest took to a stage and addressed the crowd, numbering in the high hundreds. He thanked them all for attending, wished them well, and said he was looking forward to bonding with us over the next few weeks. There were other details I'm sure, but I was too busy angrily steeling myself with free bubbly.

My plan today… tonight… whatever… is to speak to Mayor Crest. Get the scoop and drill him for any info I can. Hell, if he wants to bond, then I'm more than open to do so.

Oh, and as for Herring, he can take a beating, that's for sure. Although I wonder if it's the first time he's been subjected to one after breaking such news.

REPORT 5

Now that days seem to lack any sense of time, it feels redundant making these reports daily. Especially as once you're away from a clock, the constant howls of the night make time variable.

I honestly don't know when I sleep, or when I wake. The Zephiber celebrations at the Grady Hotel are designed to keep you in some form of cycle, but as an outsider, I'm not really getting as involved as I should.

I know, I know. That goes against the whole mantra of an Agent of The Bureau. But fuck it, I'm on holiday, right? If I choose to spend some time getting drunk and depressed in my room, why shouldn't I? Yeah, Herring is trying to coax me out, but he's as irritating as the Avatars that throw stones at my bedroom window.

Maybe I'm depressed. Mental health evaluations are done for every Bureau Agent, but none of those were subject to a night that never ended, and was scored by the incessant howls of some ungodly creature. And it. Is. Constant. These… abominations, all they do is screech and moan into the night. As I said, the sound is unholy, and despite the efforts of Wilthaven in re-enforcing their windows – even, I'm told, to the point of sound-proofing – it doesn't work. Nothing works.

I haven't spoken to the Mayor yet. Not sure what I could gleam from it. Everyone around here steers around any question you ask. You query the weird landscapes, and they tell you how wonderful the walks around Baker's Field are. You mention the Avatars, and they speak of their past and to just ignore them now. And those… things, at night?

A polite smile, and a change of subject. Almost as if they don't exist, or it isn't worth believing they do.

And every damn time, they greet and goodbye with Hail fucking Hq'tar.

I am not suicidal, though. I feel that needs to be said. Yes, I'm trapped in a hotel with hundreds of happy-go-lucky yokels who live in a horror movie, and the whole thing is soundtracked by Hell's personal orchestra, but I'm not suicidal. To entertain such a notion isn't becoming of a Bureau Agent, after all.

Maybe I need some sleep. Or another drink. That's all I'm doing – drinking and sleeping. A damned routine for a damned soul.

I wish I was home. Not P0, not The Bureau. Home. Back in Portsmouth, with my parents.

I miss them.

REPORT 6

It took 4 days of mental isolation before I broke through, thank whatever Gods there are.

Certainly not Hq'tar, that's for sure.

It almost felt like an initiation, a rite of passage, to get me into the "Wilthaven Way", as it were. A descent into mental Hell until I could get up, dust myself down, and get on with the mission at hand.

To investigate Wilthaven from a front row seat.

To Herring's credit, he did excellent work in managing me through this ordeal. He informed me afterwards that he had seen many Agents crushed by the mental toll of Wilthaven. He even commended me on adapting during the trying time of Zephiber, and queried if a weaker mind would collapse under the strain of it all. Apparently, I'm made of sterner stuff, although I could have told him that anyway…

Once retrieved from my plush, hotel room prison, I joined in the "morning" celebrations. A grand buffet of breakfast foods were available, and townsfolk sat around and chatted of various minor topics. Through every conversation I heard, none seemed to touch on the strange events they were experiencing, nor the howls from outside. This was their life, for better or worse, and they were living it the best way they could. Through the chats I participated in, I learnt that nearly everyone in the town had suffered a great loss to the whims of Hq'tar. Family, friends, even beloved pets had either vanished or been harmed in some way, and everyone had their own horror story. But through each lament, came a strange thing.

Hope.

Really, you have to respect that.

Herring knew I wanted an audience with Mayor Crest, and vowed to get it for me. I was also hoping to gain an audience with other key figures, only to learn they were based in other dwellings. The only other person of note in attendance was Quinn Tharman, the author in residence for Wilthaven. I made a mental note to talk to him in the future.

Naturally, the Mayor was staying in the Executive Suite of the hotel, but had actually opened up the excess rooms there to various families. He took one of the smaller rooms, and seemed happy to see his loyal residents relax around him – couples bonding, and children playing. For him, this was what a town should be.

I was aware of the Crest family history, reading the short book by Charles Crest from P1983's materials. Crest himself was impressed by my knowledge, and in the usual way for Bureau Agents, that knowledge helped open him up to me.

To deny much knowledge of the state of Wilthaven would be stupid. He explained how he left that to the average townsfolk, as he didn't want them entering states of agitation that had erupted over the years. He spoke of how his father – Grant – had gone through some tough times as modern mentalities shunned the happenings as mere superstition, and mentioned a great number of incidents that I need to record and write down in future. Seriously, speaking to the man is like unlocking a treasure chest of information for Wilthaven. Herring admitted afterwards that he had all this on file as well, and was more than willing to share across dimensions. With this knowledge, the file for P1983 would be as thick as the Bureau cell walls.

One thing that stood out about the man, in addition to his blunt honesty about the town's situation, was his demeanour. While he did exude a certain joviality, he also was fully aware of the seriousness of their situation. As Mayor – he explained – it was his job to maintain this awareness. To simply smile and ignore would be to belittle his responsibilities, ones that extended far beyond his little township. He is all too aware of his history, and the threat of Hq'tar beyond the realms of Wilthaven. He is in the belief that by simply treating the town as his warped playground, he will be placated enough not to expand from beyond.

I don't know how to break the theory of materials appearing in our dimension being clues from the Eldritch, so I remain silent and keep listening.

Throughout our conversation, Mayor Crest continues to come across as nothing short of a gentleman. He is a devoted family man – although still waiting for that firstborn prophesied by their ancestry – and open to anyone who courts his attention. I don't know why, but you'd expect authority figures such as himself to be villains in the play of the paranormal. Instead, he is genial, caring, and willing to help in any way.

As a "tourist", he even worries how being caught during Zephiber will affect my viewpoint toward Wilthaven and himself. Not that the town is known for its tourism anyway – the joke now making more sense than when I first arrived – but there's a quiet pride in this man that worries about such things.

He should not worry. It is clear that this is not a town with a dark secret; it is one under siege, one that has lasted generations. It has crafted its own unique persona in spite of that, and even when confronted with the husks of loved ones long gone, monsters that break the weakest of minds, and a landscape fraught with danger, they keep plodding along. Wilthaven lives, in spite of the threat of death that lingers.

This, I would say, is why Zephiber isn't seen as a dark time of eternal night, it is seen as a chance to celebrate. To adopt the Blitz Spirit, you could say.

It helps. More than you could possibly imagine.

REPORT 7

Herring died last week.

I couldn't bring myself to write about it. I couldn't write about anything. We are trained to report in the face of even the most severe danger or atrocity, but this place… this whole fucking town.

It's doomed.

Such a word is laughed about in The Bureau, I know that. It was a word used in a bygone age when it actually meant something, and wasn't parody. You'd add "Of Doom" at the end of something to make it scarier or evil. Man, we laughed about that in the rec room.

But you don't know what doom is until you see it.

It was all going so well. The people of Wilthaven were not just surviving, they were living. Yeah, it was night 24 hours a day, 7 days a week, but that didn't bother them. They played games, sang songs, danced with their loved ones and debated their less-so-loved. Children enjoyed themselves. People became closer. It was good for such a bad situation.

Then someone opened the damn door.

You know what? I'm not going to skirt around the issue. It's not the way of The Bureau. It was a kid, a fucking kid, who opened the door. Casual as you like, as if they were letting in a loved one.

Which, I suppose, they were.

As soon as that happened, people panicked, but it was too late. The lights went out – both main and backup – and before you could even adjust to the gloom there was screaming and… other sounds. I can't describe them, but I will hear them until I die. Scraping? That'll do. Damned scraping.

And something else.

Fuck.

For a load of homely townsfolk, they were alarmingly prepared for an unpreparable situation. Yeah, people shat themselves, but others took charge and did their best to limit the amount of dead or damned there would be.

Herring wasn't one of them.

In the confusion, I went along with a small crowd who rushed to one of the conference rooms of the hotel. I watched as torchlight cut through the dark, and saw as Herring waved around some sort of sharp object.

Whatever it cut, wasn't happy.

That was the last thing I saw.

Which is a lie.

It isn't the last thing I saw. The last thing I saw was one of those… things. The creatures that crawl through Wilthaven at night. Not the

Avatars, who mutely wandered around gathering new sacrifices for that fucking "God". Not even the usual ghouls or ghosts that you'd expect. These things were something else. Rotten, inhuman. Yeah, looking over the rich history of The Bureau you see some things, and maybe I have seen worse. Maybe there have been monsters in other places that would shake you. But this was worse because it wasn't a picture in a book. It was right in front of me and, for a moment, it was looking at me.

It looked, and I laugh as I type this, like a baby. But engorged and wrong. Eyes black. Head lumpy and white.

And it screamed.

It's taken me a week to get any sleep. It'll take me longer to forget.

I want to go home.

REPORT 8

And like that, Zephiber ends.

It seemed all that was needed was a good old-fashioned massacre to get the sun to come back up. As families recovered and found out what loved ones were gone – possibly forever – everyone else watched from windows as Wilthaven lived once again. The roads glistened with a light dew in the morning light, and nothing was out of place.

It was like nothing had happened at all.

Mayor Crest went about his business, organising the local law enforcement and other authorities to try and get things to some sort of normality. In the East of the town, a new hillock has risen like a tumour. It didn't seem to be mounted on any sort of plain, but just hovered on the horizon. A new geographical gift for the town to investigate.

Since my last report, I've tried relaxing in my room. I offered to help, but was just met with polite smiles and kind words. Even in the face of such horror, these people still live like nothing was out of the ordinary. Maybe, though, it is because this is their ordinary; this is their real life, their everyday. Get up, eat breakfast, go to work and hope not to be turned into a puppet of the damned.

It's certainly one way to look at it, I suppose.

Before we left, I had the chance to speak to Quinn Tharman about the town. I'd love to say it was insightful, but the man was more than a little aloof. Like he was distracted by something else. Either way, the few minutes we did speak were of little value. He'd lived in the town since birth, used the events that occurred around them to craft his tales, and how much he hated Howard Williams for Little Thwopping. Apparently, that was Tharman's idea.

He did marvel at the new hill, though, saying to me how charming it looked. He told me he hoped the people in Wilthaven liked it, and told me to enjoy the rest of my stay.

Seeing as I'd just seen several people die – or worse – I can't imagine not.

But I'm lost now. I've experienced Wilthaven first-hand, but my contact who was to keep me wise – Herring – is dead. I saw his body being carted away, and actually breathed a sigh of relief that he wouldn't come back later to beckon me into becoming one of Hq'tar's friends.

Which, I suppose, is one of the few blessings people take here. If their loved ones are dead, they smile, because they are not going to see them again.

Because if they did, they'd never want to be near them anymore.

REPORT 9

This'll be my last report.

Why? Because I'm now under the protection of the IUW.

Early this morning, I was greeted outside the residence where I had temporarily taken up by a man and a woman. They looked like Bureau types, and acted like them as well. The man was Singh, and the woman was Elodie, and they knew about Herring and, more importantly, about me.

And with that, I was recruited.

The simple matter of fact was that I was technically already an IUW Agent, just in another dimension. My BPD identification and belongings were in sync with what the IUW already knew about our world – what we would call P0. Their interdimensional map was progressing well, and my presence helped craft a more precise link between our two worlds. Not enough to get me home yet, but enough to mean that you may actually get these reports.

More importantly, they got me out of Wilthaven.

It was weird leaving. There was no significant sign that I was crossing a supernatural divide, no sudden strange feeling. We drove down a small country road, passed a sign thanking us for visiting, and were cruising past fields leading to the next village.

And for the record, I looked back as we left. There were no mountains, no tropical jungles, no new hillocks.

There was just a town, settled in the middle of the countryside, like it should.

For a moment, my head hurt. Then I just sat back and enjoyed the journey.

To describe the IUW would be to betray its secrecy, so I shall just say that it resembles the BPD HQ in many ways. Think our own Madrid HQ, but with better paintwork. I was introduced to the Directors, and given full IUW ID and clearance, after a few psych tests, of course. I was given a tour and, let me tell you, in many ways they are light years ahead of us.

Their library is extensive and has technology we can only dream of. You'd think digital libraries would be small and unobtrusive, but walking into the room and seeing everything in front of you was… it was staggering. The sheer scope would amaze even the most veteran BPD Agents, and the reason they even had this scale of technological glory was thanks to visiting worlds we have never heard of. I wish I could tell you everything, but even if I lived another seven decades, I would run out of time.

But they key thing is Project Knit.

A team in the hundreds sit at desks in a hangar sized room, with a small globe in the middle. This globe doesn't have countries as we know it, it has dimensions; little pockets of reality spread across infinite miles. Fire it up, and it expands to the sky above you. Co-ordinates number in the thousands, and I nearly cried when Agent Elodie showed me P0.

It's as close to home as I'm going to get for now, and it was beautiful. It wasn't much more than snippets of information and little visuals – think a crap version of Google Maps – but for them, it was a start.

And now they have their own Agent to help work on connecting us. And Director, if you're reading this, if we connect it changes everything. That isn't hyperbole, that's an understatement.

As for Wilthaven, the file they have is encyclopaedic, but does come with a warning. Due to the fickle nature of Hq'tar, there is no definitive information about the place. One day there could be a Town Hall, the next it is a field. For example, reading the IUW file, Quinn Tharman doesn't exist, despite the fact that I met him and everyone in Wilthaven heralded him as their greatest scribe. Some of the events we already have on file were also archived due to a lack of current relevance. But, as Agent Singh advised me, this is ever-changing. What could have ceased to exist today, may turn up again tomorrow. You just don't know.

Or I should say, you don't know for sure. The algorithms on Wilthaven are… again, it would take me decades to explain. You have to see them for yourself.

And you will. There is already a link between our world and this one. I'm told this is a huge step already, and it is just the slow, patient work to cement that link that is required now. The web of Project Knit is growing, Director, and it is amazing.

One final conclusion though: treat Hq'tar seriously. Do not think it is not malevolent. It is. It doesn't play or stagger where other Eldritch would destroy. It is crafty and it is cunning. The IUW have advised me that the droplets of material we have received is not without reason. Our theory that Hq'tar is trying to break through to our world is very real, and we should be very concerned about this. Look out for any changes in personality, any curious developments in other materials or behaviours. And most of all, watch out for anyone who pledges fealty to it. If this happens, they need to be given Black Level Work ***immediately***.

I hope to see you all very soon. Send my love to my parents, and tell Agent Hussey that I lost the game. I wish I could see his face.

Be safe.

HQ'TAR REPORT #7

(19/08/2017)

There is no doubt there is still lots to learn about Wilthaven. To say otherwise would be a betrayal of everything the BPD stands for. It is not just the effort of discovery that we venture forth with, it is also protection.

Operation Poropiti Ngaro showed us that we are not alone with our concern over the happenings in Wilthaven. Through co-operation with the IUW - and, by extension, our Agent in the field Agent Wilder - we are getting a firm idea of how to control the situation in P1983 and, ultimately, control Hq'tar.

The issue, however, comes down to one simple question: Is Hq'tar a threatening abomination? Or are they simply another in a long line of muted monstrosities that play on the fear-drenched minds of humanity? For too long, the BPD and our fellow agencies across dimensions have dealt with what we believed were great risks to life - and indeed, existence - itself, only to find these threats were nothing more than animals that needed to be trained. The Threat Risk to our lives is invariably 1/8, with the Risk to reality being 1/20. So far, in our dealings and readings with Wilthaven, I am loath to place P1983 in either category.

Is this to say Hq'tar - and in addition, Wilthaven - are not dangerous? No. The BPD has never underestimated the Threat Risk of Eldritch in its 132-Year existence. It is minimal, at most, toward our way of life, and certainly containable in a series of safeguards that I will be putting forward to the relevant Directors. Already, I have been assured that we have received comms from P87 (SCP) on how best to contain such an abomination, and are working on the schematics they have transferred to us.

    This has not been an easy journey. There have been unfortunate bumps in the road (see: Operation Nukkuja) and, despite our best efforts, there have been some losses. However, the wealth of materials, as well as a Trans-Dimensional Network of information, mean that as a Risk, P1983 can be downgraded to White Level. This of course would mean the end of my work on the file, and indeed the end of the file itself, but I am confident that the name of Wilthaven and Hq'tar is at a peaceful end. Now, we can safely rest content that P1983 is a safe, and friendly associate of the BPD.

    And, of course, it would be gauche not to end this report with a thank you to the main party in helping us achieve this peaceful resolution.

    Hail Hq'tar!

- Agent Petrovic, BPD

The author would like to thank the following for their co-operation with this title:

Rob Andrews

Chris Bignell

Dane Cobain

Liz Holland

Sam Hussey

Lady Jacobs

Marc Paterson

Matt Street

Abraham Wallace

Cheryl Wheatley

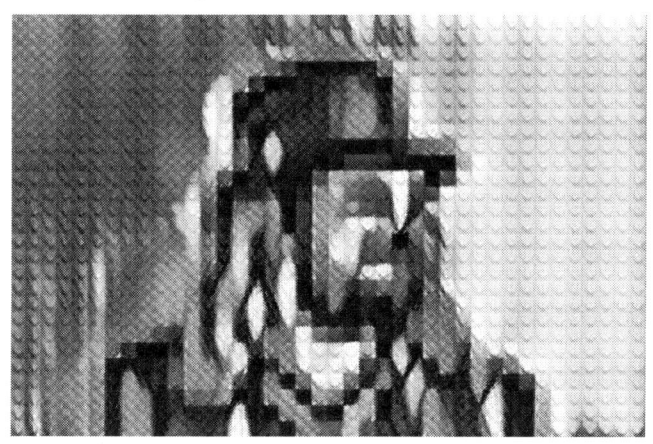

Oli Jacobs is a man who exists, nothing else is relevant. As always, he hopes you enjoyed.

Check out his writing at:

https://olijacobsauthor.wordpress.com/

Follow him on Twitter at:

https://twitter.com/OliJacobsAuthor

Watch him on Twitch at:

https://www.twitch.tv/olijba

Printed in Great Britain
by Amazon